**'Miss Emma Lyn~~~~~~~
serving-wench.'**

'Well, she's certainly a dashed pretty female.'

Benedict raised his eyes from their contemplation of the liquid in his glass. 'Didn't you notice the way she spoke? Her voice was educated—that of a lady.'

'Yes, now you come to mention it,' Harry remarked. 'Deuced odd.'

'Yes, most intriguing,' Benedict agreed. 'I think it might behove me to further my acquaintance with Miss Emma Lynn.'

Harry didn't attempt to hide his astonishment. 'What, you, break one of your golden rules by tampering with a serving-wench?'

'Oh, no. I have no intention of—er—tampering, at all.' The thoughtful expression remained as Benedict continued to study the contents of his glass. 'All the same, I think the landlady would be well advised to maintain her strict vigil where Miss Emma Lynn is concerned.'

Anne Ashley was born and educated in Leicester. She lived for a time in Scotland, but now lives in the West Country with two cats, her two sons, and a husband who has a wonderful and very necessary sense of humour. When not pounding away at her keyboard, she likes to relax in her garden, which she has opened to the public on more than one occasion in aid of the village church funds.

Recent titles by the same author:

THE RELUCTANT MARCHIONESS

and in *The Steepwood Scandal* mini-series:

A NOBLE MAN
LORD EXMOUTH'S INTENTIONS

TAVERN
WENCH

Anne Ashley

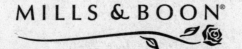
MILLS & BOON®

First published in Great Britain 2002
Harlequin Mills & Boon Limited,
Eton House, 18-24 Paradise Road, Richmond, Surrey TW9 1SR

© Anne Ashley 2002

ISBN 0 263 83490 5

Set in Times Roman 10½ on 12¼ pt.
04-0103-75406

Printed and bound in Spain
by Litografia Rosés S.A., Barcelona

TAVERN
WENCH

Chapter One

'Confound it, I'm bored!'

Armed with the latest edition of the *Morning Post*, Fingle slipped quietly into the library in time to catch this astonishing admission, and thought for a moment that he couldn't possibly have heard aright. His master bored...? Surely not!

The butler stared across the wholly masculine sanctum at the spot where the Honourable Benedict Grantley, his fine physique wrapped in a dazzlingly patterned silk robe, lazed in one of the comfortable winged-chairs. With his feet, encased in a pair of fashionable Turkish slippers, resting on a footstool, he appeared wonderfully relaxed, utterly contented.

'Feel free to remain by the door for as long as you wish, my good man,' his master's deep and faintly amused voice invited. 'I assure you I'm in no particular hurry to apprise myself of the latest town gossip.'

Smiling to himself, Fingle came forward, not for the first time appreciating that keen perception. Truly, there were occasions when he almost suspected that Mr Grantley did indeed possess a second pair of eyes, located somewhere in the back of his head, for little ever seemed to escape his notice.

'I do beg your pardon, sir,' he apologised, placing the journal on the table by one silk-clad elbow. 'It was just that I thought I heard you utter something as I entered the library, and wasn't perfectly sure that I could have heard correctly.'

'You will undoubtedly be relieved to discover that your hearing is not impaired. Ashamed though I am to admit to it, I am finding life quite surprisingly tedious. And the truth of the matter is that I have no one to blame for my present *ennui* but myself.'

Swinging his long legs to the floor, Benedict rose to his feet and went to stand by the hearth, where he made immediate use of the mantel-shelf by resting one arm along its length. 'You never knew my father, did you, Fingle?'

'No, sir. I was denied that pleasure. I believe he passed away the year before I was fortunate enough to attain a position in your household.'

'No doubt, though, you have discovered much about him.'

Fingle did not attempt to deny it, for he considered that any servant worth his salt should make a point of discovering as much as he could about the person for whom he worked. Consequently he was secretly proud of the fact that there was very little that he did not know about his kindly master.

Mr Grantley's father, the late Earl of Morlynch, was reputed to have been somewhat erratic by nature; a rakehelly fellow who had brought the family to the brink of ruin on numerous occasions with his excessive gambling. Fortunately, none of his offspring had ever betrayed a weakness for the gaming tables, and his youngest child in particular, although resembling him most strongly in looks, was least like him in character, if common report were to be believed.

'I was determined from a very young age never to follow in my capricious sire's footsteps.' This second unexpected admission interrupted Fingle's thoughts, and he raised his eyes in time to catch a rueful expression flitting over his master's striking features. 'Are you aware that certain members of my family swear that you know precisely where I am to be found at any time of the night or day?'

Although he considered this a slight exaggeration, Fingle, here again, did not attempt to refute it, for the truth of the matter was that it wasn't in the least difficult to keep track of his master's movements.

Orderly in mind, and reasonably sober in habits, Mr Grantley rarely altered his routine. When residing in town, he rose at precisely the same hour every morning, and retired at precisely the same time each night. He visited his club on the same days each week, and favoured his mistress with regular visits, on every occasion remaining for precisely the same amount of time. When he accepted an invitation to a party, he would arrive punctually at ten, and would leave no later than two in the morning. Although this practice might occasionally upset certain society hostesses, not one, as far as Fingle was aware, had ever been overheard to complain, for it was generally held to be no mean feat to persuade one of the most eligible bachelors in London to be amongst one's guests.

'Be assured, sir, that I would only ever divulge your

whereabouts to members of your immediate family and your close friends.'

'It was not intended as a criticism, Fingle,' Benedict assured him. 'And it is a relief to know that, should an emergency arise, you would be aware of precisely where I was to be found.' He could not prevent a sigh escaping. 'None the less, that does not alter the fact that, after a dozen or so years of living a well-ordered lifestyle, I am heartily bored with my lot. What I need, of course, to relieve the tedium is the opportunity to indulge in my little hobby.'

A mystery to solve isn't likely to bring contentment back into your life, Fingle silently countered, as he crossed the room to straighten the curtains. But a wife might possibly do just that.

Never would he have believed it possible that the day would dawn when he would find himself in complete accord with his master's rather overbearing sister. But, yes, Lady Agnes Fencham was right—it was high time Mr Grantley married.

Fingle was very well aware that his master's continued bachelor state was purely and simply a matter of choice. Having attained the age of four-and-thirty, Mr Grantley had enjoyed many Seasons in the capital, and yet not one of the beauties who had crossed his path over the years had come, as far as Fingle was aware, remotely close to tempting him to take the matrimonial plunge, which in itself was testament to his master's strength of character.

For years Mr Grantley had been pursued by countless matchmaking mamas, eager to call him son-in-law. He possessed all the fine qualities any young lady could possibly wish for in a future husband. He was every inch the well-bred gentleman, both affable and charming. His address was excellent, and although he might scorn the use of quizzing glasses, and despise the taking of snuff, he was considered one of the most fashionable members of his class. Furthermore, Mother Nature had seen fit to bestow upon him a well-muscled physique, and a countenance which, although some might not consider it precisely handsome, was blessed with a pair of the most vivid violet-blue eyes, made more striking by dusky lashes and brows, and a shining crop of slightly waving, black hair as yet untouched by any hint of silver.

The fact that he wasn't averse to feminine company made his continued single state more puzzling still, except to those who knew him well. Mr Grantley was a stickler for punctuality and, sadly, there were not too many members of the gentler sex who gave the least consideration to good time-keeping, Fingle mused. And the few who did were, in general, more mature in years, or were dreaded bluestockings, a species that Mr Grantley did not hold in the highest esteem.

His musings this time were interrupted by the sound of the door-knocker being applied with quite unnecessary vigour. The whole of the polite world knew that Mr Grantley never made calls, nor wished to receive any for that matter, before two o'clock.

'Be assured, sir, I shall send whoever it is on his way.'

Having every faith in his butler to do just that, Benedict resumed his seat, and was about to reach for the newspaper, when he clearly detected the murmur of voices filtering through from the hall; evidence enough that the enterprising caller had somehow managed to cross the threshold.

Not for long did Fingle remain in danger of toppling from that supreme position he held amongst the very best of major-domos, for a moment later the library door was thrown wide, and a very familiar, fresh-faced young gentleman, with a decidedly devil-may-care attitude about him, came striding cheerfully into the room.

'What's this? Still not dressed, Uncle! You're turning into a right slug-a-bed! You'll be old before your time.'

Needless to say, this piece of rank impertinence didn't precisely compensate for the interruption of his sacrosanct period of solitude, a fact which Benedict was not reticent in making perfectly plain. 'What the devil do you mean by coming here at this time of day, you obnoxious whelp?' he demanded to know before something swiftly occurred to him. 'And what the deuce are you doing in town in the middle of May, come to that?' He frowned suspiciously up at his nephew. 'Been up to some lark, and been sent down, I do not doubt.'

An expression somewhere between sheer devilment and comical dismay flickered over the Honourable Harry Fencham's boyishly handsome features. 'Nothing but a bit of harmless tomfoolery,' he assured his favourite relative. 'All will be forgiven and forgotten in a week or so. I'll be allowed back in the autumn.'

Without waiting to be asked, Harry went across to the decanters and helped himself to a glass of his uncle's fine wine, before seating himself in the chair opposite the man whom he had always considered to be the very best of good fellows. 'Anyway, you ought to feel grateful that I did take the trouble to pay you a visit. Came here especially to warn you that Mama intends to inflict her company upon you some time during the day, and that she'll have donned her match-making mantle.'

There was just a suspicion of a twitch at the corner of Benedict's well-formed, masculine mouth. 'Loath though I am to interfere in matters that are really none of my concern, I'll do my very best to advise your beloved mama that she really ought to wait a year or two, until you've acquired a little town polish, before attempting to persuade you to take the matrimonial plunge.'

Harry almost choked. 'Not me! It's you she's intent on seeing leg-shackled. I think she's invited almost every eligible female in London to her ball next week.' He shrugged. 'Mind, I've already told her she's wasting her time.... Who'd want to be tied for life to a walking timepiece?'

Blue eyes narrowed. 'I can recall on one or two occasions taking a birch rod to you, Nephew. It would appear that I didn't indulge in the exercise nearly often enough.'

A chortle of wicked masculine laughter echoed round the book-lined room. 'I remember very well that occasion when I stayed with you at Fairview, and sought to prove my equestrian skills by attempting to ride that prize hunter you had at the time. Lord, didn't you make me smart!' Harry confessed, quite without rancour. 'And speaking of Fairview... I don't suppose you'd care to have a break from town life, and take a bolt into the country for a week or two? I shouldn't object in the least to bearing you company.'

'Oh, wouldn't you, you impudent young pup!' Benedict responded, concealing quite beautifully the fact that the prospect of spending a brief period at his country home with his nephew didn't displease him. 'Well, I just might consider it. In the meantime…' he rose from the chair in one swift and graceful movement '…I shall change my attire so that I am not at a total disadvantage when I am forced to face your formidable mama.'

A hint of respect flickered in young eyes. 'You're the only one who does stand up to her. Which reminds me…' Tossing back his wine, Harry followed his uncle into the hall. 'I'd better not be here when she calls, otherwise she'll know I came to warn you. If I don't run across you before, I'll see you at the ball on Friday, and you can let me know then what you've decided about returning to Hampshire.'

Although not prepared to commit himself one way or the other quite yet, Benedict was rather taken with the idea of breaking his routine, and not remaining in town until the Season had come to an end. He had always had a special fondness for his young nephew, possibly because he was the only male amongst the tribe of females both his sister and his brother Giles, together with their respective partners, had managed to produce during the past twenty-odd years, and the likelihood of doing a spot of shooting, fishing, and riding in young Harry's congenial company was becoming increasingly more tempting than remaining in town.

* * *

An hour later, appearing as usual the epitome of sartorial elegance, Benedict returned to his library, ready to receive the steady stream of visitors who invaded his fashionable town house most afternoons. He had only just seated himself behind the large mahogany desk, intending to deal with some correspondence while awaiting the arrival of his first caller, when he clearly heard the door-knocker for the second time that day. Having been forewarned, he expected to see his sister—one of the few females of his acquaintance who had any respect for time—sweep majestically into the room, and was faintly surprised to see his faithful henchman enter.

'Begging your pardon, sir, but there is a lady wishing to see you.'

Benedict swiftly noticed the faintly puzzled expression. It was a well-known fact that Fingle, after just one glance, could pinpoint a person's station in life in ninety-nine cases out of a hundred with uncanny accuracy. Evidently this was one of those rare occasions when his superb intuition was letting him down.

'What—er—sort of female, Fingle?'

'Oh, definitely not that sort, sir,' the butler responded, not slow to follow his astute master's train of thought. 'Very respectable, I should say, even though she is quite unattended. Gave her name as one Mrs Lavinia Hammond.' He saw the slight frown. 'She said in all probability you wouldn't remember her, sir. From what she tells me, she is a friend of Lady Fencham's, and knew you very well when you were a boy. Her father was a certain Colonel Penrose, by all accounts.'

Memory stirred. 'Ah, yes! Lavinia Penrose. Yes, show her in, Fingle.'

Although the name was certainly known to him, Benedict would never have recognised the neatly dressed, middle-aged lady who entered a few seconds later had he passed her in the street. Seemingly, she sensed this at once, for she was not slow to remark, as she came forward to clasp his outstretched hand in both of hers, 'It is so very good of you to see me, sir, considering I must appear now a total stranger. You were only a boy when I married and moved away from Kent, but I would have known you anywhere. You have a great look of your father about you.'

'I clearly recollect your rescuing me from more than one scrape in my formative years, when I had earned your strict father's severest displeasure.' Another memory stirred, as he studied the neatness of her mourning attire. 'My sister did, I remember, inform me of your sad loss, Mrs Hammond. May I offer my sincerest condolences.'

There was more than a faint hint of sadness in the dark eyes which gazed up at him. 'Thank you, sir. And I suppose my husband's unexpected demise is in part responsible for my coming here to see you today.' She appeared suddenly more troubled than sad. 'Although, if I am honest, I cannot say why I'm imposing on you in this foolish way, except…except I could think of no one else who might be able to help me come to terms…help me to understand certain recent events.'

'You are not imposing in the least,' he assured her, ever the polite gentleman. 'Please do sit down. May I offer you a glass of ratafia, or Madeira, perhaps?'

Although readily accepting the offer of a chair, she

declined any refreshment. 'I mustn't take up too much of your time, sir. Besides which, I must return to my hotel within the hour to be ready to make the homeward journey. I was very kindly offered a seat in the carriage of some very good friends of mine who, luckily, were making the trip to London. They wish to be back in Andover in time for supper, and I must not keep them waiting.'

Benedict made himself comfortable in the chair opposite. He had not seen his unexpected visitor in over twenty years. She and her father had been his family's nearest neighbours, and from girlhood she had always been a very close friend of his sister's. When his sister had married Lord Fencham, Lavinia Penrose had paid far fewer visits to the Grantley family's ancestral home. She too had been married later that same year and had moved away from Kent. Apart from the fact that she had married a country practitioner, and had made her home somewhere in the West Country, he knew next to nothing about the life she had led since leaving Kent. Somewhere in the recesses of his mind, however, he retained a memory of a sensible female. So, unless she had changed to a great extent, he could only assume that it was something of the gravest concern which had brought her here.

'In that case, ma'am, how may I be of service to you?' Benedict prompted, when she began to twist the strings of her reticule somewhat nervously round her fingers.

'You are probably not aware of it, sir, but I reside in a village in the heart of rural Wiltshire, not too far distant from Salisbury,' she began after a moment's quiet deliberation. 'Possibly the most influential family in the area is one by the name of Ashworth. Lord Ashworth, as you may or may not recall, died just a few months before my husband. There was nothing mysterious in that. Lord Ashworth had suffered poor health for some time, and as he had produced no legal heir, everyone quite naturally assumed the title would pass on to his cousin Cedric.'

Benedict frowned. 'I seem to remember that there was some dispute over that.'

'Yes, sir, there is indeed,' his visitor confirmed. 'Lord Ashworth had a younger brother. I'm afraid I know little about him, as he had left England many years before I went to live in Ashworth Magna.' She shrugged. 'One can only suppose that his family, never having heard from him again, must have assumed that he had died during his travels abroad.'

'Evidently he did not.'

'No, sir, he did not, at least not for several years,' Mrs Hammond divulged. 'Seemingly he decided to visit America and, soon afterwards, met and married a young woman from an influential Boston family. I am reliably informed that he did, in fact, return to this country with his wife who, I understand, gave birth to a son whilst here. Sadly both George Ashworth and his wife died, and the boy was sent back to America to be raised by his maternal grandfather. Apparently a search has been undertaken to locate his whereabouts. If, indeed, he is still alive, he is the rightful heir.'

'And if he is found to be hale and hearty, it will be a bitter blow to Cedric.' Benedict remarked, not without experiencing a feeling of wicked satisfaction. He did not hold Mr Cedric Ashworth in particularly high esteem, and liked his pompous son, Percy, even less.

'You are perhaps acquainted with him, sir?'

'Slightly, yes.' He regarded her in silence for a moment. 'I do not immediately perceive how I can possibly help in this matter. Locating the whereabouts of the rightful heir is the responsibility of the Ashworth family's legal advisors.'

'Of course it is, sir. And I would never dream of asking you to interfere in such a matter,' Mrs Hammond hurriedly assured him, before her eyes once again were shadowed by sadness. 'No, what I was hoping to persuade you to do on my behalf is to discover whether there is more to my husband's death than—than at first there appeared to be. He—he was believed to have been set upon by footpads, whilst he was out one evening paying a visit to a friend, and was bludgeoned to death.'

'I know, and I'm very sorry. My sister did tell me,' he responded gently. Although he had never met the late Dr Hammond personally, Benedict had heard his sister Agnes say much to the good doctor's credit over the years, and was very well aware that Agnes's regard was not easily won. 'What makes you suppose that he wasn't merely the unfortunate victim of some violent attack?'

'Because of a conversation I had just three weeks ago with a certain Miss Evadne Spears, a woman who used to be employed in the Ashworth household—first as a governess, then more recently as a sort of companion to the late Baron's daughter, and his sister who also resides at the Hall.'

'Were you well acquainted with this woman?' he asked when his visitor fell silent.

'Not really, no. Naturally, I would see her in church

on Sundays, and from time to time when I was invited
to dine at Ashworth Hall, but that was all. So, as you
can imagine, I was rather surprised when quite by
chance our paths crossed in Salisbury one morning,
whilst she was awaiting the arrival of the stage to London. Apparently she intended paying a short visit to
her sister who had been unwell. She seemed in a most
troubled state, and was a little incoherent for much of
the time, mumbling something about paying a visit to
Bow Street whilst she was in the capital, and informing them of her suspicions.'

'And what precisely was preying on her mind?'
Benedict prompted when his visitor once again fell
silent.

'Well, sir, she seemed to imagine that the young
heir's life was in danger. She also kept muttering
something about evil in the Ashworth household, and
the death of a young maidservant a few months before
being no accident. Then, just before she left, she gave
me the distinct impression that she thought there was
more to my husband's death than one might have supposed.'

'And did you believe her?'

'Not immediately, no. As I've already mentioned,
she seemed in a highly nervous state, as though she
feared for her own life.' She raised her eyes to his.
'And with good reason, sir, as things have turned out.
I've recently discovered that during her stay here, she
was run down by a carriage, and killed outright. I did
consider calling at Bow Street myself to discover if,
in fact, she had paid a visit there, but then I began to
think that I might not be taken seriously.'

Being very much the gentleman, Benedict refrained

from suggesting that, in all probability, this would have turned out to be the case. Instead, he asked why Miss Spears simply didn't inform the local authorities of any suspicions she might have been harbouring.

'I'm not certain, but I would imagine it was because the local magistrate, Sir Lionel Brent, is a close friend of the Ashworth family.' Mrs Hammond watched those shapely black brows draw together. 'Are you perhaps acquainted with Sir Lionel, sir?'

'Yes, I am. He's a member of my club. A worthy gentleman, I would have said.'

'Indeed he is, sir. He was a friend of my late husband's and has been immensely kind to me in recent months. None the less, Evadne Spears was right about one thing—there was certainly something suspicious surrounding the death of that young maid up at the Hall. After our chance meeting in Salisbury, I returned home and went into my late husband's study, where I spent some time reading through his personal diaries. In the most recent one I discovered an entry which states clearly enough that he was not happy about certain aspects of that young servant girl's demise.'

When Benedict failed to comment, Mrs Hammond rose to her feet. 'I'm sorry, sir. I shouldn't be wasting your time with this... It was just that I remembered Agnes mentioning once that you had had some success in solving one or two cases in recent years which had confounded the authorities.'

Benedict's attractive mouth curled into a crooked half-smile, as he too rose. 'Well, my dear sister was certainly correct about that. And you haven't been wasting my time, Mrs Hammond. I have found what

you've told me most interesting, and will be delighted
to look into the matter on your behalf.'

He noticed the faintly sceptical glint in her dark
eyes, as though she suspected him of mere gallantry.
'Believe me, your visit has come at a most opportune
time,' he assured her. 'I was beginning to feel decidedly bored with town life, and a spell in the country
is precisely what is required to restore my flagging
spirits. Unfortunately, I cannot leave London until the
end of next week,' he continued, after moving across
to his desk to consult his own diary. 'My sister is
holding a ball on Friday, and my life would not be
worth living if I should dare to miss that.'

His visitor frankly laughed. 'Indeed it would not,
sir. And neither would mine, if ever Agnes discovered
that I was responsible for you missing the event. My
time is limited, and I shall be unable to pay her a visit
on this occasion, so perhaps you would pass on my
warmest regards.'

'Yes, of course. I know time is pressing,' he announced, arresting her progress across to the door, 'but
there is just one small service you could perform on
my behalf before next week. I am not at all familiar
with your part of the world, even though my country
home is situated in a bordering county. However, it is
just a little too far distant for me to stay there. I assume
there are plenty of hostelries in Salisbury?'

'Several very good ones, sir,' she confirmed, before
a thoughtful frown creased her brow. 'But you could
do no better than put up at our local village inn. It has
gained something of a reputation in recent years. It is
situated quite close to the main route to Exeter, and
many travellers now prefer to stay there rather than

put up at the busy posting-houses. The rooms are clean and the food is excellent. Emma will certainly take very good care of you, except...' The frown returned. 'You could always stay with me. I do have spare rooms.'

'I would never dream of putting you to the trouble,' he answered, escorting her to the front door himself. 'I am likely to be bringing my nephew along. Furthermore, it might be wise if we kept my reason for visiting the locale to ourselves for the time being. No, accommodation at the village inn will suit my purposes very much better, I assure you.'

No sooner had he seen his visitor on her way in a hired carriage, and had returned to the comfort of his sanctum, than the brass knocker sounded again. A moment later the library door swung open and a middle-aged lady, dressed with impeccable taste and in the height of fashion, swept quite unannounced into the room, with all the self-confidence of a female who knew precisely her own worth.

'Why, Agnes, my dear!' he exclaimed, with every evidence of delighted surprise. 'This is a most unexpected pleasure.'

'Don't lie, Benedict!' she returned in her usual forthright manner. 'If I know anything, that incorrigible son of mine has already paid you a visit to forewarn you.'

A hint of admiration flickered in Benedict's striking violet-blue eyes. 'No one could ever accuse you of foolishly not knowing your own offspring, Aggie.'

Anyone observing Lady Fencham, as she seated herself in the chair recently vacated by her lifelong friend, would never have supposed for a moment that she had found this mild praise inordinately gratifying, for her expression since entering the room had not changed. There was a hard, determined set to her lips, and her frown, as she watched her sibling move in that natural, graceful way of his over to the decanters, was manifestly one of staunch disapproval, for her young brother was one of the few people over whom she had never been able to exert the least influence.

She had watched him grow from an endearing, mischievous boy into a gentleman of undeniable intelligence, and undoubted strength of character. Increasingly he had become more set in his ways. Most people considered him solid and dependable, a gentleman who knew his own mind. She, on the other hand, was inclined to think that he had become tiresomely stubborn and selfish, simply because he had no one to consider but himself. Sadly, unless something was done very soon he would join the ranks of those confirmed bachelors—quite beyond the pale!

She was fair-minded enough to admit that it was not entirely his own fault that he had turned out so selfishly intractable. Their mother, after giving birth to several stillborn children, had been delighted when she had managed to produce a second healthy son, and had simply doted on her youngest offspring. Benedict's winning ways had endeared him to the vast majority of their relations, most especially the females in the family, several of whom had been only too delighted to make him their sole beneficiary. Consequently his wealth, coupled with an undeniably attractive countenance, had placed him amongst the most coveted prizes in the Marriage Mart for the past ten years. Yet he continued to withstand all the many lures cast out to him each Season, determined, it appeared, to preserve his single state. A highly unsatisfactory situation which Lady Fencham was resolved to change at all costs!

Accepting the glass of ratafia he held out to her, she watched him lower his powerful frame into the seat opposite. The slight smile hovering about his attractive mouth was sufficient to convince her that he was under no illusions about precisely why she had made this visit, so she decided, wisely, not to prevaricate.

'You may possibly recall that in March of this year our brother Giles celebrated his fifty-fourth birthday. I might also remind you that in less than six months you shall attain the age of five-and-thirty.' She watched the wickedly provocative smile grow more pronounced. 'I consider it my duty, therefore, to remind you of your obligations in delaying no longer in relinquishing your single state.'

Those shapely dark brows, which held such a fascination for the vast majority of her sex, rose, but Lady Fencham was one of the few women who could withstand her brother's abundant charm.

'Come, Benedict, you must appreciate yourself that our sister-in-law is unlikely to have any more children. Why, she is five years my senior!'

'Steady, Aggie, steady!' he advised with gentle mockery. 'You have managed thus far not to reveal your own age.'

'Will you be serious, Benedict!' she retorted, determined not to be diverted by her brother's wickedly winning ways. 'Everybody knows that I am ten years your senior. My childbearing days are now over, and so are Serena's, though why she could not have managed to produce one healthy boy amongst five off-spring, I cannot imagine. Even I managed to do that.'

'Yes, very remiss of her,' he remarked agreeably. 'Had she obliged you by doing so, it might have spared you this visit today. However,' he went on before she could give voice to her increasing annoyance at his flippancy, 'as Giles does not appear to be in the least worried, I do not understand why you should be so concerned. After all, Aggie, even if I go to my grave childless, the name is still secure.'

She regarded him in a mixture of outrage and astonishment. 'You do not honestly mean to tell me, Benedict, that you would be content to see the title pass to that idiotic cousin of ours? Why, he's a moonling!'

'Now that, Aggie, is not only most unkind, but also grossly inaccurate,' he countered. 'Lawrence might not be precisely needle-witted, but he certainly isn't a moonling.'

'He's as near one as makes no difference!' she retorted, before she realised that she had allowed her provoking younger brother to get the better of her yet again. 'Oh, you are an abominable person, Benedict!'

'True,' he agreed cordially. 'And that is precisely why I could never bring myself to condemn one of your gentle sex to a lifetime of having to put up with my peccadilloes.'

'That is utter nonsense, and you know it!' she retorted. 'Most members of my sex would be only too happy to become Mrs Benedict Grantley. And it isn't as though you're averse to female company. Apart from those several delicate vessels who have lived under your protection over the years, you number several females among your close friends.'

'True. But not one of 'em has ever tempted me into marriage.'

'But why?' She raised one gloved hand in a despairing gesture. 'That is what I do not understand. What on earth are you looking for in a wife?'

With praiseworthy control, he resisted the urge to torment her further, and gazed for a moment into the contents of his glass. 'I am searching for perhaps a woman who could induce me to change my lifestyle by offering me one with her that I would infinitely prefer. I have yet to meet such a one, Aggie, and it is unlikely I ever shall. But should such a miracle occur, I promise I shall consider very seriously taking the matrimonial plunge.'

Feeling slightly moved by this display of total sincerity, and knowing that to pursue the matter further would avail her nothing, Lady Fencham rose to her feet, smiling a trifle wryly. 'Well, I can only hope that this very special lady is among my guests on Friday, but I do not hold out much hope.'

'You're a sensible woman, Aggie,' he remarked with a rare display of brotherly affection. 'And wise, too, not to have ripped up at that young cub of yours for getting himself into a scrape.'

She shrugged. 'What would be the point of that? He has certainly not been wasting his time whilst he's been up at Oxford. Besides which, he'd be a rare sort of male indeed if he didn't indulge in some harmless foolishness on occasions. Even you, Benedict,' she reminded him with a certain degree of satisfaction, 'were prone to less sensible behaviour at one time. It might prove most interesting if you were ever tempted to err again. But, as you are now an absolute stickler for the proprieties, and never act without due consideration, I do not hold out much hope.'

'Very wise, my dear. Although it might surprise you to know that I am tempted to alter my routine in the near future, take Harry off your hands for a week or two and drag him into the country, if he still wishes to accompany me.'

'I think you know the answer to that already. You've always been a firm favourite of his.'

She chose not to add that it was likewise with her.

Chapter Two

Descending the stairs to the coffee room, the land-lady of the Ashworth Arms clearly detected the deli-cious odour of freshly baked bread. The smell grew steadily stronger as she crossed the tap and went down the passageway to her farmhouse-style kitchen, there to discover the female responsible for producing the mouth-watering aroma.

Her lined, and faintly forbidding, countenance was instantly softened by a tender expression. If any one person could take sole credit for turning the hostelry into an increasingly thriving business, then it was the young woman who was now busily working at the table, preparing the pies which would be consumed with relish that evening.

'Now, Miss Em, don't you go making more than one batch,' she ordered in the same gently scolding tone as she always adopted when addressing the being whom she had brought into the world, and had lovingly nurtured for twelve very happy years. 'I'll not have you wearing yourself out for that rascally bunch who've nothing better to do than sit and swill down tankards of ale all evening. Besides, you might find yourself having to prepare dinner if Mrs Hammond's gentlemen friends should arrive today.'

Rubbing the back of one hand against her cheek, Emma inadvertently transferred some flour to her face. 'Lavinia was a little vague as to when precisely they would be arriving, but she considered it more than likely today or tomorrow.'

The landlady's permanent frown grew more pronounced. 'Did she mention who they were, exactly?'

'The brother and son of her good friend Lady Fencham... You know, Martha,' Emma went on to explain, when those permanent furrows deepened once again, 'she's that very stylish lady of about your own age who stays with Lavinia from time to time. Her last visit was about six months ago, shortly after the good doctor died.'

Memory stirred. 'Ah, yes! I recall her now—always travels with an army of servants, and goes about with her long nose permanently in the air. I hope her relatives aren't so haughty, otherwise they'll receive short shrift here!'

'One must make allowances for those higher born, Martha dear,' Emma responded, hiding a smile at her one-time nursemaid's blunt manner.

'I don't see why,' was the swift rejoinder. 'I don't make allowances for you.'

Strikingly lovely, soft grey eyes began to twinkle wickedly. 'Ah, but you forget, my dear. I'm merely a tavern wench, and expect no special treatment.'

'That you are not!' Martha retorted, the scolding tone very much more pronounced. 'And I'll have no more talk like that! Your dear mama was very respectable, every inch a lady, and your papa was the son of a gentleman. And I'll thank you not to forget it!'

Scooping up the basket of soiled linen, which she had deposited on the floor a few minutes earlier, Martha went through to the laundry, not for the first time suffering pangs of conscience over willingly agreeing to her one-time charge making her home in the tavern. With hindsight, she now realised that what she ought to have done, when Emma had unexpectedly turned up on the doorstep five years ago, was try to make contact with certain of Emma's relations.

Oh, but it was too late to do anything about that now, she reminded herself, depositing the basket none too gently on the board by the sink. At least there was one advantage to the girl's residing in the inn—at least she could continue to protect the sweet child from the unwelcome attentions of predatory males, gentlemen or otherwise!

'Well, in any event, their rooms are ready for them when they do arrive,' she announced, having little difficulty in picking up the threads of the conversation, as she returned to the kitchen to discover the young woman whom she could not possibly have cared for more had she been her very own daughter now seated at the kitchen table, taking a well-earned rest.

'And no doubt you've chosen to place them in the two bedchambers farthest from my own,' Emma responded, the wickedly mischievous smile she had had since girlhood appearing once again. 'I fancy only dowagers and elderly spinsters ever find their way into the rooms next to mine.' Her tone changed to one of gentle, teasing censure, as she added, 'When will you learn, Martha, that I'm no longer a naïve girl, susceptible to the desires of lascivious males? I've lived here for far too long now not to know precisely what takes place between the sexes.'

'Yes, you do know, to my everlasting shame!' Martha joined her at the table, those bitter regrets returning with a vengeance to plague her. 'I should never have allowed you to remain here.'

Easily detecting the note of heartfelt contrition, Emma ceased her teasing. 'What should you have done—packed me off to Bristol to live with my aunt Mildred, where I would undoubtedly have been coerced into marrying that nincompoop son of hers? Had Uncle Arthur still been alive, it would have been a different matter entirely. But you would never have been so cruel as to leave me at the mercy of his cunning widow.'

Reaching across the table, Emma gave one work-roughened hand an affectionate squeeze. 'Besides, I have been extremely happy here. I have been permitted to do work that truly gives me pleasure.'

'Oh, I don't mind the cooking, Miss Em. The good Lord knows you're gifted that way. But I never should have let you venture into the tap of an evening—mixing with all those rascally wastrels, and hearing all their vulgar talk which an innocent like you ought never to hear.'

'Stuff and nonsense, Martha! Papa never attempted to shield me from the unsavoury aspects of life. I've come into contact with poor souls less fortunate than myself for as long as I can remember.'

'Aye, I know well enough you have,' Martha responded, with a look of staunch disapproval. 'But you would never have done so had your dear mama remained alive to protect you. I'm not trying to suggest that your father wasn't a good and worthy gentleman. I remember well enough that he was tireless in his efforts to help the poor and needy. It was just a pity he was less considerate towards his own daughter. He ought to have ensured that you were well provided for, Miss Em.'

She shook her head sadly. 'Well, at least your uncle, God rest his soul, saw to that. It's just a pity you can't touch a penny piece of your inheritance until you're five-and-twenty.'

'Which is less than a year from now,' Emma reminded her, that mischievous smile of old flickering yet again. 'I shall be a lady of consequence then, with five thousand pounds to offer a prospective husband. That is when your troubles will really begin, dear Martha,' she warned, rising to her feet to continue the daily bake of pies. 'You'll have every fortune-hunter for miles around hammering on the door, striving to win my favours. However, in the meantime—'

She broke off as her sharp ears clearly detected the sound of wheels on cobblestones. 'Unless I much mistake the matter, our guests might well have arrived.'

Martha darted over to the open doorway in time to see a very smart carriage pull up in the yard. It wasn't so much the fine equipage that almost had her gaping in astonishment as the tall, dark-haired gentleman who nimbly alighted from it a few moments later.

'Oh my gawd!' she muttered, alarm bells instantly ringing. After casting a furtive and faintly concerned glance over her shoulder, she scurried across to the door leading to the passageway. 'You carry on with the baking, Miss Em. I'll see to the gentlemen.'

She arrived in the coffee room only moments before her husband, armed with two portmanteaux, led the way in through the main entrance. Then her worst fears were confirmed when the tall stranger, preceded by a younger gentleman, entered the inn.

Her first impression had been one of natural grace and unparalleled elegance. Now, as the most striking violet-blue eyes, having adjusted swiftly to the dimmer light in the inn, and having taken swift stock of the surroundings, fixed themselves on her, she was offered her first glimpse of the stunningly attractive features beneath the mane of well-groomed, glossy black waves.

She had never considered herself a fanciful woman. Yet as the sun suddenly disappeared behind that thick blanket of cloud which had been slowly gathering from the west, and the inn's interior suddenly grew very much darker, it was like a portent of doom. This was no ordinary gentleman. This man might well pose a real danger to her innocent lamb.

It took a monumental effort to curtsy and bid welcome, when ''be gone'' was quivering on the tip of her frequently sharp tongue. 'Your rooms are ready, sirs,' she added, glancing briefly at the younger gentleman who caused her no qualms whatsoever. 'If you would follow me, Samuel will see to your baggage.'

After showing the younger gentleman into one of the large, low-ceilinged bedchambers which boasted a pleasant view across the fields at the rear of the rambling, whitewashed building, she threw wide a second door on the opposite side of the passageway. 'I hope you'll be comfortable in here.'

There had been precious little conviction in her

voice which, if the faint twitch at the corners of that disastrously attractive mouth was any indication, had not gone unnoticed by the striking gentleman who continued to cause her no little concern. 'I'll return presently with hot water, and arrange for the rest of your baggage to be brought up to your rooms.'

She turned, about to retrace her steps, when she bethought herself of something else. 'What time will you be requiring dinner?'

'Will seven be convenient?' he responded, after consulting a handsome silver pocket-watch, and Martha was forced to own that he was certainly not lacking in manners.

'That will be fine for us, sir, if you're contented. There's a private parlour off the coffee room, which you are welcome to make use of at any time. I'll be laying the table for any meals you might require during your stay in there.'

After closing the door quietly behind her, she scurried along the passageway and down the stairs, successfully catching up with her husband as he was about to enter the tap.

'Samuel! Samuel! Whatever are we to do?'

The homely, weather-beaten face betrayed surprise. 'What do you mean—what are we going to do? I'm going to help Josh carry in the rest of the baggage, and see to it that the gentleman's groom is made comfortable above the stables, and you are going to fetch our guests hot water.'

'I'm not talking about that!' she responded testily. 'I mean, what are we going to do about...' she nodded in the general direction of the kitchen, before pointing one finger ceilingwards '...and him?'

Samuel did not pretend to misunderstand. 'Oh, for heaven's sake, woman!' he exclaimed in combined exasperation and amusement. 'When are you going to stop mollycoddling the girl? Emma knows what's what. And is more than capable of taking care of herself. Every time a gentleman who's halfway good looking puts up here, you're always in a fidget.'

'And you can take it from me, Samuel Rudge,' she warned, once again scurrying after him, as he headed down the passageway, 'that that there gentleman's a mite different from most.'

The fixed expression of comical dismay on Samuel's plump, homely features, and the severe look of staunch disapproval on his spouse's thin-cheeked countenance, as they entered the kitchen a moment later, was sufficient to indicate to Emma that at least one of the new arrivals was not precisely welcomed by the landlady.

'Personable—er—gentlemen, are they, Samuel, by any chance?' She winked slyly across at him. 'Handsome, no doubt?'

He chuckled. 'You're a downy one, Miss Em. And no mistake!'

'Ha!' was Martha's only response, as she busied herself filling two porcelain pitchers with hot water.

'What a pity Lucy isn't here today,' Emma remarked, mischievously stoking the fires of Martha's displeasure. 'It will mean that I must wait at table.'

'Oh, no, it does not, my girl!' came the swift response from behind her. 'I'll do that, until we get busy in the tap.' Martha tutted. 'Trust Lucy Lampton to take a chill when we've guests putting up at the inn!'

'It's a wonder she don't take a sight more of 'em,

with the amount of time she spends flat on her back in the long grass,' Samuel remarked, thereby earning himself the full fury of his wife's wrath.

'I'll not have talk of that kind in my kitchen, Samuel Rudge! It's bad enough having to listen to the crude remarks spoken in the tap of an evening, without having them uttered in here. How am I supposed to keep Miss Em halfway respectable when she's subjected to such vulgarity?'

'Oh, don't talk so daft, woman!' Samuel returned, half-laughing. 'You think our customers don't know Miss Em's a lady?'

'Which is more than can be said for Lucy!' his wife countered. 'I don't know why you employ her, Sam…really, I don't.'

'Because she's a good worker, that's why, Martha, as well you know. What she does in her own time is her own business. Besides, she keeps the customers happy.'

'Yes, and we all know how!' Martha retorted, before whisking herself away with the pitchers, and leaving the kitchen resounding with deep masculine laughter.

Emma could not help smiling too as she watched Samuel depart by way of the door leading to the yard. Never had she known two people so dissimilar rub along together so well as Samuel and Martha Rudge. Not only were they vastly contrasting in appearance, but they were totally opposite in temperament too. Martha could be quite sharp on occasions, and was not afraid to speak her mind; whereas Samuel was such a placid, easygoing soul, good-natured and amazingly tolerant.

Of course, they had known each other from child-hood, Emma reminded herself, as she removed the bread from the oven and replaced the loaves with the tray of meat pies. Martha had been born in the village, but had left when a young woman in order to seek a position as a domestic in Bristol.

Arthur Greenway, a gentleman of no little impor-tance in that city, having recently married a widow with a young son, had been in need of extra staff and had employed the young Martha. By her own admis-sion Martha had never been fond of her employer's wife. She had, however, swiftly grown very attached to her master's young sister, and had been only too happy to leave with Miss Greenway when she had married the Reverend Mr Joseph Lynn.

Emma clearly remembered how happy she had been as a child. Her mother had been such a gentle, loving creature, and Martha, although frequently cross-grained, had been no less affectionate. Emma also re-called how she had cried when Martha had left them to marry her childhood sweetheart, Samuel Rudge. Later that same year her own dear mother had unex-pectedly passed away, and life at the vicarage had never been quite the same again.

Refusing to become melancholy and dwell on the less happy times in her life, Emma turned her thoughts to what to serve the newly arrived guests for dinner that evening, as she watched Samuel and the young stable-hand, Josh, carrying a substantial leather-bound box past the window. By the amount of luggage Mrs Hammond's acquaintances had brought with them, their stay was not likely to be of short duration. But what on earth could have prompted such fashionable gentlemen to wish to stay in this rather insignificant, if pretty, place?

An hour later the subjects of her thoughts were leaving the inn by way of the front entrance. The thick bank of cloud, which had been threatening to release its moisture since their arrival at the inn, obliged Benedict and his nephew by not doing so until after they had taken an exploratory stroll about the picturesque village, and had arrived back at the Ashworth Arms to discover the table in the very comfortable private parlour already laid in readiness for their evening meal.

The moment he had sampled his first bite of the sweetest game pie he had ever tasted, Benedict was thankful that he had taken Lavinia Hammond's sensible advice and had put up at this local inn, instead of taking rooms at one of the busy posting-houses in Salisbury. The sharp-featured landlady might not be the friendliest he had ever encountered, but the quality of her dinner, beautifully presented, its several mouth-watering dishes cooked to perfection, more than made up for her sad lack of geniality.

'Well, I must say,' Harry remarked, easing his chair back a little from the table in order to unbutton the dazzling waistcoat which had suddenly grown uncomfortably tight, 'that was an excellent dinner. If we put up here for very long, I'm likely to require a whole new wardrobe of clothes, several sizes larger.'

Benedict smiled. 'Yes, the meal was certainly something out of the common way.'

'Pity the landlady's such a sour-faced old besom.

The look she cast you before we left the inn earlier would have withered a lesser man.'

'Ah, so you noticed that too. Very observant of you, Nephew!' Benedict's smile grew more pronounced. 'I strongly suspect that there must be a daughter of the house. Mrs Rudge's attitude will undoubtedly mellow once she realises she has nothing to fear from us.'

'If the daughter looks anything like her she's certainly nothing to fear from me,' Harry assured him.

'No matter what she looks like, I sincerely trust,' Benedict advised, before holding up a warning finger, as his sharp ears detected the sound of footsteps nearing the door.

A moment later the landlady entered to collect the dishes, her expression not softening one iota even when both Harry and Benedict complimented her on the dinner.

'The Ashworth Arms has the reputation for serving excellent food, sirs,' she responded before her nut-cracker mouth snapped shut. Then she unlocked it again to add, 'The person responsible for preparing your meal will be bringing you port in a minute or two.' She sniffed loudly. 'You'll be able to thank her in person, if you've a mind. But you'll oblige me by not keeping her talking. She's had a long day, and needs to rest.'

'Dear me,' Harry muttered, the instant the landlady had departed, 'she don't improve much with knowing, does she? And what makes her suppose that we'd want to hold a conversation with—'

As the door behind him opened again, Benedict saw his nephew's eyes widen in astonishment. Curious, he immediately transferred his attention to the person who had induced his relative to gape like a half-wit, as she obligingly placed the tray containing a bottle of port and two glasses down on the table.

The face beneath the fetching cap was undeniably young and delicately featured, but it was not until she turned her head slightly, and he received the full impact of a swiftly assessing gaze from smoky-grey eyes, flecked with gold, that he could appreciate his nephew's blank astonishment.

'I understand, ma'am, that it is you we have to thank for our superb dinner,' he remarked, momentarily studying the ridiculous length of the dark lashes which framed the stunningly pretty eyes, before reluctantly drawing his own away while he reached for the bottle.

'Yes. I hope everything was satisfactory. Please do not hesitate to inform me if you have any particular likes or dislikes.'

After filling the two glasses, Benedict subjected the sweet face staring down at him to a further swift appraisal, noting the delicate, high cheekbones, the small straight nose and the lips, perfectly moulded and slightly curling above the softly pointed little chin, before returning his attention back to eyes whose gaze was so refreshingly direct, distinctly lacking the flirtatious glints and coquettish invitation he had grown accustomed over the years to receiving.

'Everything is…was perfect,' he confirmed, before lowering his gaze and swiftly noticing the lack of adornment on her left hand, 'Miss—er—'

'Lynn…Emma Lynn,' she obliged him, before enquiring what time they would be wanting breakfast in the morning.

'Would eight be convenient?' Benedict answered, not granting Harry the opportunity to do so.

'That is fine, sir. And will you be requiring your meals served at the same times each day?'

Harry chuckled, thereby swiftly gaining her attention. 'To be sure we shall, ma'am. Not a minute earlier, nor later.' He noticed the delicately arched brows rise in surprise. 'My uncle is a stickler when it comes to time-keeping,' he explained, sublimely ignoring the flashing look of annoyance from the gentleman seated at the opposite end of the table. 'He loathes unpunctuality. His life is run by the clock.'

Fine grey eyes, twinkling with more than just a suspicion of unholy amusement, again focused on ruggedly masculine features still betraying faint irritation. 'Dear me. I should find that most tedious. Each to his own, though, I suppose, Mr...'

Benedict automatically found himself rising to his feet, and reaching for the delicately boned right hand, just as though she had been a young lady presented to him in any fashionable drawing-room. 'Grantley, ma'am—Benedict Grantley. And this incorrigible young whelp, as you may have gathered by now, is my nephew, Harry Fencham,' he added, when Harry, following his example, rose also to make his bow.

'I am pleased to make your acquaintance, gentlemen, and look forward to seeing you both in the morning.'

She made to move over to the door, but Benedict was there before her, and held it open, thereby earning himself a rather sweet smile of gratitude before she swept out into the coffee room.

'Good gad!' Harry muttered, after tossing down his

port and reaching for the bottle again. 'I never thought the day would dawn when I'd be making my bows to a serving-wench.'

Looking distinctly thoughtful, Benedict returned to the table. 'Miss Emma Lynn is certainly no serving-wench.'

'Well, she's certainly a dashed pretty female.'

Benedict raised his eyes from their contemplation of the liquid in his glass. 'What else did you observe about her?'

'She has a fine, trim figure.'

'And?' Benedict waited in vain for a further response. 'Didn't you notice the way she spoke? Her voice was educated—that of a lady.'

'Yes, now you come to mention it,' Harry remarked, after a moment's consideration, 'she did speak in a very refined manner. Deuced odd, now I come to think about it.'

'Yes, most intriguing,' Benedict agreed. 'I think it might behove me to further my acquaintance with Miss Emma Lynn.'

Harry didn't attempt to hide his astonishment. 'What, you, break one of your golden rules by tampering with a serving-wench?'

'Oh, no. I have no intention of—er—tampering at all.' The thoughtful expression remained as Benedict continued to study the contents of his glass. 'All the same, I think the landlady would be well advised to maintain her strict vigil where Miss Emma Lynn is concerned.'

Chapter Three

Neither Martha nor Samuel ever sought their bed of a night until the tap had been restored to order, and everything had been tidied away, by which time Emma was usually sound asleep. Consequently, more often than not, she was the first to rise, and the following morning was no exception.

While she busied herself in the kitchen, making a batch of rolls for breakfast, she couldn't help smiling to herself as she recalled the expression on a certain someone's face when she had emerged from the private parlour the evening before, after having made the acquaintance of the inn's newest arrivals. She doubted very much that the handsome, fresh-faced Mr Fencham was the one causing dear Martha such concern. Oh, no! It was much more likely to be the suave and prepossessing gentleman with the striking violet eyes who was disturbing the calm waters of the landlady's mind. And perhaps there was reason for dear Martha to be concerned, she reflected, for Mr Benedict Grantley was without a shadow of a doubt something out of the common way.

Emma had always prided herself on being an eminently practical sort of person. Although she had been blessed with a good figure and pleasing countenance, she had never attempted to take advantage of the fact that she had little difficulty in successfully attaining a second glance from the vast majority of masculine eyes, and she had certainly never come remotely close to succumbing to any displays of male gallantry. Yet she was forced to concede that when the very gentlemanly Mr Grantley had, seemingly without having to think about the matter, risen from his chair and opened the door for her to pass into the coffee room, she had definitely felt something that she had never experienced before.

She shook her head, as a slightly wistful smile began to play about her mouth. At that moment she could almost have imagined that she was a female of consequence, attending her first lavish ball and receiving the attentions of the gentleman she most wished to escort her on to the dance floor.

Unutterable madness! she told herself. How fortunate that Mother Nature had also seen fit to bless her with a deal of sound common sense! She must never lose sight of what she was—at best a gentleman's daughter—well-mannered, well-educated and definitely chaste. None the less, she was certainly no highborn lady who could choose a husband from the most eligible bachelors in the land. To fall victim to such foolish fancies could only lead to wholesale disaster for someone like her. Perhaps darling Martha was right—it might be wise to steer clear, as much as possible, of the very agreeable Mr Grantley!

Fate, mercurial jade, had, it seemed, decreed quite

otherwise, as Emma discovered for herself when she entered the private parlour a minute or two later in order to lay the table for breakfast, and discovered the immaculately attired subject of her recent thoughts staring out of the window.

The tiny exclamation of surprise was not sufficiently smothered, and she found herself on the receiving end of a rather quizzical gaze. 'I'm sorry, Miss Lynn. Did my unexpected presence startle you?'

He had remembered her name! That strangely pleasing sensation returned to torment her. 'A little,' she admitted, thankful that her voice at least was behaving normally, even if her pulse rate remained annoyingly erratic. She glanced across at the clock. 'I evidently misheard you, sir. I thought you required breakfast at eight o'clock, not seven.'

'Be assured that your hearing is not defective, Miss Lynn. I merely rose earlier than expected.'

His smile seemed effortless, and was all the more attractive because of it, Emma decided, fleetingly wondering why the warmth of that blue-eyed gaze should suddenly make her feel like a gauche schoolgirl. She felt certain she was blushing, and gave herself an inward shake. Why, anyone might suppose that she had never received a smile from a gentleman before!

Striving to maintain at least the outward appearance of self-possession, she busied herself with laying the table. 'How long do you intend to remain here, Mr Grantley?' she asked, conscious that he was studying her every move.

If he considered the enquiry an impertinence, he certainly betrayed no sign of it. 'I have no fixed plans. I intend to visit some of the sights. My nephew is a—

er—gifted artist, and is keen to sketch various places of interest in these parts.'

Emma considered the explanation reasonable enough. 'Well, there's no shortage of those. I hope the weather remains fair for you. At least yesterday's rain has cleared away, and it looks set to be a fine day.' She raised her head to discover him still watching her closely, his gaze not hard, precisely, but certainly penetrating. Not much, she suspected, ever escaped the notice of those intelligent eyes.

'And providing that slug-a-bed nephew of mine rises early enough, we might succeed in enjoying some of it.'

Emma thought she could detect just a hint of disapproval in his manner, before he finally withdrew his gaze from her and turned to stare at the view beyond the window. Was he annoyed that his nephew might well keep him kicking his heels in the inn, or was something else not quite to his liking?

'You reside in a pretty part of the world, Miss Lynn,' he remarked, putting an end to her musings. 'Are you contented here?'

'I enjoy the country, sir. I'm really accustomed to nothing else. I think most people living in Ashworth Magna feel privileged to reside in such a pretty place. Your friend, Lavinia Hammond, was certainly very contented to live here.'

'It would be more accurate to say that she is my sister's friend,' he corrected her, without bothering to turn his head. 'I feel sure you must know precisely where she resides. When I explored the village yesterday evening, I didn't notice any plaque or sign to indicate a doctor's residence.'

'No, Lavinia took it down some weeks ago. There will be a new practitioner arriving any day now, and she didn't wish to give offence to him, or cause confusion by leaving it on show. She resides in the red-brick house set a little way back from the road. You cannot possibly miss it. It's the last house but one along the main road to Salisbury.'

'Ah, yes! I remember. Thank you, Miss Lynn. I shall pay her a call directly after breakfast.'

Faintly surprised to see him quite so early in the day, Lavinia Hammond was none the less delighted when Benedict walked into her comfortable parlour, only moments after the mantel-clock had chimed the hour of nine.

'I never keep town hours when residing in the country, ma'am,' he explained in response to her gentle teasing. 'I have never found it in the least difficult to make the adjustment. Unlike some I could mention.' Expressive dark brows drew together in a slight frown. 'I left that young reprobate of a nephew of mine working his way through a positively disgusting quantity of ham and eggs, and enjoying the exercise so much that it wouldn't surprise me if he demanded a second helping!'

'Oh, so you did bring dear Harry with you!' Lavinia was delighted to discover this, and didn't attempt to hide the fact. 'Deborah will be pleased. She looks upon him as a brother. Not that Harry requires any more sisters. I dare swear he considers he has more than enough with the four he has already, poor boy.'

She gestured her most welcome visitor towards a chair, before seating herself. 'I'm not so foolish as to suppose that you've called merely to pass the time of day. So you must be here to ask questions. Not that there's very much more I can tell you.' As had happened before, when she had called upon him in the capital, she betrayed signs of unease. 'In fact, since paying that visit to your London home, I've begun to wonder whether I didn't simply overreact after that unexpected encounter with Evadne Spears.'

'I have never considered you a fanciful woman, Lavinia,' he assured her, swiftly dispensing with all formality, and smiling in a way which even managed to send her middle-aged heart a-fluttering. 'Please refresh my memory, and tell me, as far as you can recall, exactly what the late Miss Spears did say to you.'

'I came upon her quite by chance in Salisbury, on the morning she was awaiting the arrival of the stage to London,' Lavinia reiterated, after quietly collecting her thoughts. 'She told me that it was her intention to spend two weeks with her sister who had been unwell. She seemed very ill at ease, and, assuming that she must be nervous about making the journey on her own, I managed to persuade her to await the coach's arrival in the inn. Quite unexpectedly she began speaking of the young parlour-maid who had died shortly after being employed up at the Hall, and hinting quite strongly that the girl's death might not have been an accident.'

'And how precisely was the young maid supposed to have met her end?' he enquired, when she relapsed into silence.

'It was generally believed that she must have tripped and fallen down the main staircase at Ashworth Hall. She was certainly discovered lying in the hall at the foot of the stairs.' She frowned. 'I clearly remember that there was something preying on my husband's mind, after he had been to the Hall that day. Although he never attempted to confide his suspicions to me, I did, as I mentioned to you in London, come upon this after my meeting with Miss Spears that morning.'

Lavinia went across to the desk, and drew out a leatherbound diary, which she opened at a page previously marked before handing it to Benedict. It took him a moment to decipher the last entry in the late Dr Hammond's faintly erratic scrawl, but eventually he managed to read: *Not totally satisfied that Sally Pritchard's death was accidental. Injuries not wholly consistent with those one might expect to find from a mere fall. Will consult with Sir Lionel Brent on Friday.*

'And did your husband meet with Sir Lionel?'

'That is the odd thing,' Lavinia disclosed, resuming her chair. 'They not infrequently got together on Friday evenings to enjoy a game of chess. And they had previously arranged to meet on the evening of my husband's death. Sir Lionel assured me, however, that he had sent a note that morning to cancel the arrangement, as he expected to be delayed with extra magisterial duties in Salisbury. After my husband's body was found, Sir Lionel ensured that extensive enquiries were made, but the miscreants were never apprehended.'

Although she had answered his questions clearly, and without betraying the least signs of emotion, Benedict was not so insensitive as to suppose that she was not experiencing a deal of distress. Therefore he changed the subject slightly by asking if she was perfectly certain that there was nothing suspicious about the late Lord Ashworth's demise, which had occurred a matter of a few months before her late husband's tragic death.

'No, nothing,' she hurriedly confirmed. 'His health had not been good for some time, as I believe I mentioned before. His heart was weak. But it was not the late Lord Ashworth's demise which had concerned poor Miss Spears,' she continued, after a further moment's thoughtful silence. 'Though she did seem to suppose, for reasons she chose not to disclose, that his nephew's life might be in danger. It is sheer supposition on my part, but I imagine she must have overheard someone saying something, after the late Lord Ashworth's demise, which upset her greatly. Not that we can ever be certain, of course, now that the poor woman herself is dead.'

'Well, I can set your mind at rest on one point, at least,' he announced. 'The authorities do not have any reason to suppose that her death was anything other than an unfortunate accident.'

She regarded him in some surprise. 'Did you pay a visit to Bow Street, then, sir?'

'I certainly did,' he confirmed, with a smile surprisingly betraying a hint of smug satisfaction. 'I am not unknown there, and so had little difficulty in discovering what I wished to know. If Evadne Spears was uneasy about the death of the young maid, and concerned for the future well being of Ashworth's heir, she certainly didn't voice her worries to anyone at Bow Street. Furthermore, the authorities have no reason to suppose that her own death, as I've already remarked, was anything other than a tragic accident. The jarvey who drove the carriage that ran her down is a law-abiding man, and there were several witnesses who confirmed that he could have done nothing to avoid the tragedy. She simply wasn't attending, and walked straight out in front of his carriage.

'The authorities were kind enough to furnish me with the address of Miss Spears's sister and I took it upon myself to pay her a visit,' he continued, betraying the fact that he had not been idle, after her unexpected visit to his London home. 'She gave me no reason to suppose that her late sister had confided in her. She did, however, impart the fact that she had asked Evadne to live with her in order to help her run her boarding house. Miss Spears, it appears, had eagerly agreed, and on the morning of her death had sent a letter informing her employer that she wouldn't be returning to Ashworth Hall. The sister did disclose that Miss Spears had never been very happy with the Ashworths, finding her charge something of a trial.'

'I do not find that too difficult to believe,' Lavinia responded, after digesting fully what she had learned. 'Clarissa Ashworth is a very beautiful girl, but a trifle spoilt, I'm afraid.'

Appearing more than just faintly shamefaced, she gazed across at him. 'It would seem that I owe you an apology, sir, for wasting your time.'

'On the contrary,' he countered, 'the mystery is far from solved. Just because Miss Spears didn't choose to confide in her sister, or visit Bow Street, does not necessarily mean that she had no intention of ever doing so. Remember, her sister had been ill, and Miss Spears no doubt had been fully occupied in nursing her, and had no desire to plague her sister further with her own problems. No, I fully intend to solve this mystery if I can…providing that you, in return, clarify something that is puzzling me.'

He held her full attention. 'Why is it, Lavinia, that I find a young woman with the most refined manners and of quite apparent genteel birth working in a village inn?'

'Ahh! So you have crossed the path of the divine Miss Lynn, have you?' Half-smiling, she shook her head. 'Well may you ask, Benedict!'

She took a moment to make herself more comfortable in her chair. 'I do not believe I would be betraying darling Emma's trust if I were to tell you that she is indeed the daughter of a gentleman. Her father was a clergyman who attained a living in Dorsetshire. He married Emma's mother quite late in life. He had turned forty. But I do believe it was a genuine love match. Up until her marriage Emma's mother had kept house for her much older brother, who was a partner in a successful firm of lawyers in Bristol. He himself had married a widow, with a young son, only a matter of a year or two before his sister married Joseph Lynn. I also understand that he continued to visit his sister, whom he adored, quite regularly after she had married.

'From what Emma has divulged in the past, I rather fancy that it was fortunate that her uncle did keep in close contact. Although the Reverend Joseph Lynn was a scholarly man, he was not very adroit when it came to financial matters, and would have quite willingly given away his last penny to the poor if Emma's mother had not taken control of the finances, and had received assistance from her brother.

'Sadly Emma suffered the loss of her mother and beloved uncle in quick succession. All financial help then ceased, but her uncle did leave Emma a sum of money in his will. Her uncle was an astute man and, I suppose, fearing that his altruistic but faintly un-worldly brother-in-law would squander Emma's in-heritance, he ensured that she could not touch so much as a penny until she attained the age of five-and-twenty, or she married. Emma, therefore, was forced to make her own way in the world after her father's demise.'

'Understandable enough, but why seek employment in a wayside inn? Surely she could have attained some genteel position as a governess or companion?'

Lavinia, to her surprise detecting a faint note of an-noyance in the deep, cultured voice, shrugged her slen-der shoulders. 'I do not think that would have suited Emma. Besides which, she sought refuge with some-one whom she loved and trusted. The landlady used to be Emma's nursemaid up until she returned here to marry Samuel Rudge.' She cast him a reassuring smile. 'Believe me, Martha guards Emma with all the protective verve of the strictest duenna.'

He did not appear in the least gratified to learn this. 'Maybe so. But that doesn't alter the fact that a girl of that quality ought not to be working in a tavern.'

'Yes, I know what you mean,' she responded, ap-preciating fully now his evident annoyance. 'And I have suggested that she come here to live with me on more than one occasion. I am extremely fond of Emma.' Her frown of disapproval was no less pro-nounced than his own. 'I'm afraid, though, that she has a definite stubborn streak. She is fiercely indepen-dent, and is determined not to accept charity.'

His only response was to give vent to what sounded

suspiciously like a snort of disapproval, before he rose to his feet, scooping up the leatherbound diary in one long-fingered hand as he did so.

'May I take this with me, Lavinia? I'd like to read through it at my leisure.'

'By all means. I do not believe you'll find very much of interest, though. Henry didn't keep a regular diary. He could go for months without jotting anything down. There is, I seem to remember, another one somewhere. I'll look it out and ask Deborah to take it over to you later, when she returns from Salisbury.'

She accompanied him to the front door, extracting a promise that he would dine with her on the following evening, before allowing him to take his gracious leave.

It was while she remained in the front garden, watching the elegant long-striding gait taking him quickly along the road, that it occurred to her as most odd that he should have betrayed such an interest in the welfare of Emma Lynn... Yes, very strange, she mused. Most interesting, none the less!

Miss Deborah Hammond was one of the few people who had no difficulty whatsoever in winning a warm smile from the landlady of the Ashworth Arms. Martha had always been very gratified by the friendship which had quickly blossomed between the well-respected doctor's daughter and her one-time charge. She was always pleased to see the girl and her unexpected arrival later that same day was no exception.

Martha immediately invited her to join Emma and herself at the kitchen table, and for a while they exchanged snippets of village gossip, before Deborah recalled the reason for her visit.

'Is Mr Grantley about, by any chance?'

'He went out, with his nephew, this morning in his carriage.' Martha sniffed rather pointedly. 'He didn't trouble to tell me where he was going, or precisely what time he would return, though he did say he would be requiring dinner.'

Deborah was not slow to detect the note of disapproval, and cast a glance in her friend's direction in time to see Emma attempting to suppress a smile. She knew well enough how Martha fussed about Emma like a broody hen, keen to protect her from life's less wholesome elements. But really, there was absolutely no need, Deborah mused, ineffectually striving to suppress a smile of her own. Dear Emma had a head on her shoulders, and was quite capable of rebuffing the unwanted attentions of any male.

'Harry Fencham's a charming young man, Emma, don't you agree? I've known him all my life.'

'Are you well acquainted with the uncle, too?' Emma couldn't resist asking, thereby earning herself a dour look from a certain quarter.

Deborah freely admitted that she was not, and that she had seen him only once, many years ago, when she had been invited to stay with Lady Fencham. Nevertheless she was quite happy to satisfy her friend's curiosity as far as she could.

'I may have mentioned before that his sister, Lady Agnes Fencham, is my godmother. When people first meet her they think she's unapproachable and very haughty, but really she's a dear. I know she's very fond of her younger brother. Harry says that he's the only member of the family who'll stand up to her. By all accounts she's been trying for years to persuade him to marry.'

'Ha! Pity she didn't succeed!' Martha put in, much to the younger ladies' intense amusement.

'As you may have gathered by now, Deborah, dear Martha doesn't approve of the very personable Mr Grantley. She seems to suppose that I'll succumb to his abundance of charm. She conveniently forgets that he's a gentleman, and is merely being polite.'

'And what you seem to forget, Miss Em,' Martha retorted, not slow to administer a counter-thrust, 'is that one needs to be a man before one can be considered a gentleman. And no one could dispute the fact that Mr Benedict Grantley is every inch a male. I noticed the look he cast you before he left the inn this morning. I'm not blind.'

'Oh, don't be ridiculous!' Emma scoffed, while secretly wondering just how he had looked at her. 'Gentleman of Mr Benedict Grantley's station in life are not interested in people like me.'

'I don't see why not,' Deborah announced. 'You're exceedingly pretty, Em. Mama has frequently remarked upon it. Oh, and speaking of Mama…she wishes to know if you would care to join us for dinner tomorrow evening. Apparently the new doctor arrived today. She has already made herself known to him, and has invited him to dine, and says there'll be an odd number sitting down at table if you do not accept.'

Ordinarily Emma would not have needed to consider the matter. She always enjoyed the evenings she spent with the Hammonds. Not once had Lavinia or her daughter made her feel in any way inferior, simply because she now lived and worked in an inn. Sadly, this time, she felt she could not neglect her obligations and felt she must forgo the pleasure.

'Naturally, I'd love to come, Deborah. Only with guests staying, I don't—'

'Of course you can go,' Martha interrupted. 'My cooking might not be up to your standard, but I won't poison Mr Grantley, or his precious nephew.'

In view of the fact that Mrs Rudge did not wholly approve of a certain gentleman, Deborah decided not to reveal that both Mr Grantley and Harry would be amongst their guests the following evening. 'Oh, yes, and speaking of Mr Grantley...' Delving into a large, drawstring bag, Deborah drew out a slightly shabby, leatherbound book. 'Mama asked me to give this to him. It's Papa's old diary. Can't imagine why he should wish to read it. But would you see that he gets it, Em?'

Receiving the assurance she required, Deborah soon afterwards departed, leaving Emma to ponder over what to serve at dinner. It certainly didn't cross her mind for a moment, as the afternoon wore on, to suppose that she was giving any undue consideration to what tempting delicacies to create for the evening meal. It most certainly did occur to her, however, that Martha had no intention of relaxing her guard where one of the inn's newest arrivals was concerned, for shortly before the food was due to be placed in the various dishes, the landlady appeared in the kitchen, with the serving-maid at her heels, announcing that Lucy was to wait at table that evening.

'Really?' Emma refused to argue the point, even though she considered that Martha was spreading that protective mantle a little too wide. 'Well, let us hope the dishes don't end in the gentlemen's laps, or on the floor, for that matter.'

She wasn't being entirely facetious. Although Lucy Lampton was an immensely likeable and hardworking young woman, she was built on very generous lines, and on occasions had the unfortunate tendency to be clumsy.

Martha's expression betrayed faint unease, as she watched the inn's popular serving-maid return to the kitchen, one fleshy elbow banging against the laundry door as she tied the strings of a clean apron about her ample curves.

'Yes, see that you don't drop anything, Lucy,' she warned, casting a critical eye over the plump, rosy-cheeked young woman whose fondness for masculine company was famed. 'And fasten up that blouse! And no leaning over the table neither! The gentlemen will have ample breast to satisfy their needs on the chicken served at dinner, without being offered any more!'

Emma almost choked. 'Come along,' she said to a chortling Lucy. 'I'll give you a hand to set the table.'

After collecting fresh table-linen, Emma went out into the coffee room in time to see Lucy's wide hips brush against one of the tables, knocking a sketch-pad to the floor. 'Oh, Lucy, do be careful!' she cautioned, bending to retrieve the pad which she had observed Mr Fencham carrying out to the carriage earlier in the day.

Being something of a keen painter herself, she allowed curiosity to get the better of her and couldn't resist a quick peek inside the cover, her expression turning swiftly to one of comical dismay as she studied the results of Mr Fencham's labours.

'Well,' she murmured, 'perhaps dear Martha is quite right to be suspicious. Without doubt Mr Benedict Grantley is a rank deceiver!'

Chapter Four

Something about his body's clock was most definitely malfunctioning since his arrival at this inn, Benedict decided, making his way as silently as he could down the narrow staircase to the coffee room. As he had informed Lavinia Hammond the day before, he had never experienced the least difficulty in adjusting to country hours. He hadn't experienced the least hardship in falling asleep in that very comfortable bed the moment his head touched the pillow, either. The trouble was, though, he seemed to be waking at a ridiculously early hour. Yesterday he had been wide awake at six o'clock and today it was five. If he carried on at the present rate, there would be little point in going to bed at all!

Deciding that an exploratory stroll round the inn's exterior, and many outbuildings, would be a more pleasurable way of passing the time than sitting in the private parlour waiting for Harry to rise, he carefully drew back the substantial bolts, and stepped outside to discover yet another lovely late spring morning, the

air pleasantly fresh and scented with the fragrance of
the roses that grew around the front door.

When he had wandered into the tap the evening
before to enjoy a tankard of mine host's fine home-
brewed ale, before finally retiring for the night, he had
discovered from the very amiable landlord that the inn
was fairly self-sufficient. Besides managing to grow
most of the vegetables they required, they kept a cow,
pigs and a variety of poultry. There was even a dairy
where the less than friendly landlady produced butter
and cream.

Benedict smiled to himself as he walked past the
barn, and proceeded along a slightly overgrown path
into a long meadow, sparkling with early morning dew
and adorned with a wide variety of pretty wildflowers.
Never could there have been a couple so dissimilar as
the very amiable Master Rudge and his grim-faced
wife. Yet, to be fair, perhaps there was reason enough
for the landlady to maintain the strict vigil over a certain someone and continue to remain a little aloof herself.

If he were honest, he would be forced to admit that
he had been more than just mildly disappointed when
the delightful Miss Lynn had failed to appear in the
private parlour the evening before to furnish them with
port. None the less, the novel experience of being
waited upon by that buxom serving-wench had certainly produced its lighter moments, most notably
when the soup had very nearly ended in poor Harry's
lap, and the trout had skidded across the table to col-
lide with his own wine glass, spilling most of its contents over the pristine cloth.

The sight of a large house, surrounded by early

morning mist and nestling in a slight valley, caught his attention and he stopped by a rustic gate to study the aspect in more detail. Although set in a picturesque landscape, the building was undoubtedly one of the ugliest he'd ever seen. The original part of the house, he suspected, was Elizabethan, but it had been enlarged considerably over the centuries, without much thought to either symmetry or style, resulting in a monstrosity which had long since lost what architectural beauty it might once have possessed.

The sound of sweetly melodious humming reached his ears, and he turned his head in time to see a slender figure emerge from the woodland area at the far end of the meadow. The young woman's silky brown hair, hanging loosely about her shoulders, caught the sun's rays, highlighting the golden tints in the rich chestnut locks, as she stepped from beneath the last of the shading branches.

He found himself quite unable to draw his eyes away as she moved along the path towards him. Swinging the basket she carried to and fro, she seemed to float just above the ground, like some fragile, unearthly creature one read about in fairy-tales. Only she was very real; as real as his body's immediate reaction when she caught sight of him, and paused for a moment, a lovely smile of instant recognition curling her delectable mouth.

'Why, Mr Grantley! You're up and about very early this morning.'

As she approached him the golden tints in the lustrous hair were even more noticeable, matching those flecks in her strikingly lovely eyes. 'I could say the same about you, Miss Lynn,' he responded, momentarily wondering why his chest should suddenly feel as though it were being constricted by encircling bands of steel, making breathing faintly laboured.

'Oh, I'm usually up bright and early in the spring and summer. I always think it is the best time of day. Besides which, I had a very good reason for rising particularly early.' She raised a cloth, revealing the contents of her basket. 'Mushrooms for your breakfast. I also took the opportunity of drying my hair whilst I was out. So you must forgive my slightly—er—informal appearance.'

Although she was doing her level best to conceal the fact, he knew she was feeling faintly discomposed at being discovered in this less than perfectly groomed state. He, on the other hand, considered Providence had favoured him, and was not in the least disappointed to have come upon her in such an unexpected way. Her crowning mane was a wonderful warm brown, flowing, and silky soft. So very different from the short, crimped styles worn nowadays by the vast majority of fashionable ladies, he reflected, whilst manfully resisting the urge to reach out and run his fingers through the shining strands.

'Your hair is beautiful, Miss Lynn. I would suggest you never cut it,' he advised, thereby making her appear for a moment so deliciously flustered that a sudden desire to kiss her breathless almost overwhelmed him, but not quite.

'Tell me,' he remarked, desperate to give his thoughts a new direction. 'Who lives in the house, there, in the valley below?'

'That is Ashworth Hall.' Although unable to prevent that telltale glow from suffusing her cheeks at the unexpected compliment, Emma was relieved to discover her voice continued to remain wholly dependable. 'Apart from the servants, only Miss Ashworth and her niece, Clarissa, live there now. Lord Ashworth died last summer.'

She could see at once, by his expression, that he was decidedly unimpressed. 'I must admit that it is an eerie place, especially at this time of year when it's shrouded in early morning mists. I'm reliably informed that it is quite elegant within, and sumptuously furnished. The Ashworth family is a wealthy one.'

'Have you never seen inside it yourself, Miss Lynn?'

'Hardly, Mr Grantley,' she responded, wondering if he was being facetious. 'I'm not the sort of person who would ever be asked to pay a visit there.' For a moment she thought she could detect a flicker of annoyance in his eyes, but then decided she must have been imagining things. After all, why should he care whether the Ashworths considered her completely unworthy to sit at their table? 'I have, however, been allowed inside the kitchen. The Ashworths' cook and I frequently exchange recipes. More often than not Mrs Wright calls at the inn on her afternoon off.'

His expression now totally unreadable, he transferred his gaze once again to the mishmash of brick and stone in the valley below. 'Are you acquainted with all the servants there?'

'Most of them, yes,' she answered, suddenly wondering why he should be so interested in the domestic situation presiding at the Hall.

'Were you by any chance on friendly terms with the young maid who died there not so many months ago?'

'No, I cannot recall that I ever saw her. She was there a few weeks only. And, as I've already mentioned, Mrs Wright more often than not calls to see me at the inn, if ever she tries a new recipe which she thinks I might like.'

She regarded him in silence for a moment, the suspicion that he had a definite purpose for visiting Ashworth Magna increasing rapidly. 'Mr Grantley, why have you come to this out-of-the-way place?' she asked, rank curiosity overcoming her natural reserve. There was no response. Undeterred, she added, 'You may tell me to mind my own business if you wish, but please do not insult my intelligence again by repeating that farrago of nonsense about visiting the sights in order that your nephew might indulge his artistic bent. To be blunt—he hasn't one. Indeed, he cannot even draw a straight line!'

The faintly harsh contours of his face were softened by a spontaneous smile. 'So, you have glimpsed the result of his efforts yesterday?'

She had the grace to look a little shamefaced. 'Lucy knocked the sketch pad on to the floor when she was crossing the coffee room.'

'Oddly enough, I do not find that too difficult to believe.'

The dry response stretched Emma's self-control to its limits. Evidently Lucy had not impressed the guests with her serving skills. 'Yes, well,' she muttered, a little unsteadily. 'Anyway, to continue, the truth of the matter is that sketching happens to be one of my favourite pastimes. So after I'd retrieved the pad, I couldn't resist a quick peek.' The look she cast him was full of gentle mockery. 'I assume it was supposed to be the famous circle on Salisbury Plain. It resembled nothing so much as a rockfall to me!'

The rich rumble of masculine laughter was just too infectious, and Emma found herself chuckling too, until his laughter faded and she was subjected to yet another of those suddenly intense and penetrating stares.

'Yes, I rather fancy that I can trust you, Miss Emma Lynn, and so shall tell you precisely what has brought me to this village of yours... I am far from certain yet, but I'm beginning to feel increasingly that Dr Hammond's death was quite deliberately planned. The attack upon him, unless I much mistake the matter, was carried out in a deliberate attempt to silence him.'

Benedict was not slow to note the rather pensive expression flitting over the delicate features. 'You will forgive me for saying so, but you do not appear unduly surprised, Miss Lynn.'

'In truth, sir, I am not.' Her frown grew more marked. 'I have always felt myself that there was more to that incident than an attack by thieves which ended in tragedy. I know that, since the end of the war with France, incidents of robbery have been more frequent. So many men unable to find work, and still needing to feed their families, it is little wonder that instances of lawlessness are on the increase. But most attacks take place in the larger towns and cities, not in rural places like Ashworth Magna, and certainly not on quiet country lanes, seldom used. The villains might have lain in wait all night and not glimpsed a prospective victim.'

'Do you know precisely where the incident took place?'

'Yes…yes, I do, as it happens.' An overwhelming impulse to be of some service in his endeavours silenced completely that cautionary little voice which had already warned her that it might be wise to avoid the company of this enigmatic stranger throughout the remainder of his stay at the inn. 'I need to travel to Salisbury later this morning to buy certain provisions. I can show you the exact spot if you wish me to?'

He reached out one shapely hand to grasp the handle of her basket, and Emma found herself automatically releasing her hold, as they walked slowly back along the path towards the inn.

'Obviously Lavinia Hammond is suspicious about her husband's death. Is that why she asked you to come here?'

He nodded. 'I do not, however, wish to cause her more distress than she's already suffered, so I will accept your kind offer to show me the precise location of the attack, and would ask you too, for the present, to keep the reason for my being here to yourself.'

Emma did not hesitate to give her word, but after a moment's thought asked, 'I assume that Mr Fencham is in your confidence?' At his nod of assent, she found it quite beyond her to suppress an impish little smile. 'In that case I may be able to assist you in more ways than one. At least I can add a certain credence to the story you are putting about for being in Ashworth Magna.'

'I shall be immensely grateful for any assistance you can lend me, Miss Lynn,' he assured her, handing back the basket as they arrived at the kitchen door. 'In the meantime, I shall occupy my time whilst waiting for my breakfast by reading the late doctor's diary. One never knows, some clue might come to light.'

When Harry entered the private parlour quite some time later, it was to discover his uncle with his nose in the shabby, leatherbound diary, and to see the remains of what looked to have been a very hearty breakfast pushed to one side. His favourite relative, who normally ate quite sparingly, was beginning to behave in a most uncharacteristic manner!

'I must say, Ben, I don't know what's come over you of late,' he announced, not reluctant to voice his perplexing thoughts. 'Since we've been at this place, there's simply no keeping track of you at all! I bumped into Emma on the landing, and she told me you were up again at some ungodly hour.'

Benedict momentarily abandoned his deciphering of the appalling scrawl to cast his nephew a faintly surprised glance. 'Emma...? I didn't realise you were on such friendly terms.'

'Wouldn't say that we are, exactly... But dash it all, Ben! There's no need to be so rigidly formal. Besides, I've decided I rather like Miss Lynn. She's a deuced pretty woman!'

One black brow was raised in a decidedly mocking arch. 'Surprisingly enough, I had made that observation myself.'

Chuckling at the dry response, Harry seated himself at the table and began idly to glance through the sketchbook pressed upon him a few minutes earlier. 'I assume you've taken Emma into your confidence.'

'Yes, I have. And it just so happens that she had considered there was something suspicious about

Hammond's death. She's kindly offered to show me
where the attack took place.' Benedict abandoned his
reading for the present, and set the late doctor's diary
to one side. 'And whilst I'm out, you can do your duty
by paying a call on Mrs Hammond and her daughter.
But do be careful what you say in Deborah's presence.
Lavinia might be suspicious about her husband's
death, but I'm not at all certain that she's shared her
concerns with her daughter.'

'Understood,' Harry responded, before continuing
to inspect Emma's sketches. 'I say, Ben, these are
dashed good! A great deal more impressive than those
atrocities my sisters insist on showing me.'

'Which isn't saying very much.' Reaching across
the table, Benedict grasped the pad his nephew held
out, and nodded his head in approval, before the door
behind him opened and he distinctly detected his
young relative's faint sigh of relief.

'Thank heavens it's you, Emma!' Harry announced,
as she placed fresh coffee and rolls on the table. 'I
won't now need to don body armour. What a clumsy
wench that Lucy is!'

She cast him a look of comical dismay. 'Oh, dear.
I hope nothing ended in your lap.'

'No, but it wasn't for the want of her trying!'

'Stop complaining, boy!' Benedict chided, whilst
quite unable to suppress a twitching smile. 'You'll be
spared the need to dodge dishes this evening. Which
reminds me…' He turned to Emma, arresting her progress to the door. 'We'll not be requiring a meal. We've
received a dinner invitation.'

Although she managed to conceal the fact, she was
relieved to hear it. At least now she could dine with

Lavinia and Deborah, and enjoy the evening with a clear conscience, knowing that she hadn't left poor Martha to cope alone.

She then bethought herself of something else. 'Would you be ready to accompany me in half an hour, Mr Grantley? I need only change my attire. I'll meet you in the yard.'

It was a rare experience for Benedict to be driven about by a female. The vehicle was certainly not quite up to the fashionable standard in which he was accustomed to travelling about the country. Nor by any stretch of the imagination could the single animal pulling the light carriage be described as a fiery steed. Nevertheless, Emma soon proved that she had a pair of light hands, and that she was more than capable of handling the one-horse gig.

As she expertly turned off the main village street and into a narrow lane, he casually remarked that they might have made the journey in his own carriage, which immediately earned him a quizzical glance.

'You are most generous to express such confidence in my ability, sir, but I rather fancy that I'd require a little extra tuition before attempting to handle a carriage-and-four. Or were you proposing that I should keep your groom company upon the box?'

He was fast coming to realise that the delightful Miss Lynn had a rather wicked sense of humour which, surprisingly enough, was not so dissimilar to his own. 'Neither, you abominable girl!'

Far from chastened, she gurgled with laughter. 'Well, abominable I might be, but I'm not completely ignorant of the ways of the polite world. It is most improper, as well you know, for an unmarried female to travel in a closed carriage with a gentleman who is not a close relative. Even at my age a female must take care of her reputation.'

'Believe it or not, Miss Lynn, preserving your good name is swiftly becoming of prime importance to me.'

It wasn't so much the admission itself which instantly wiped the smile off her face, and almost had her gaping like a half-wit in astonishment, as the sincere note she couldn't fail to detect in the deep, attractive voice. Utterly confused, she could think of absolutely nothing to say in response. Nor could she understand for the life of her why he should concern himself over her welfare. Consequently she experienced no small degree of relief when they approached the place he was so keen to examine, and she was able to steer the conversation in a completely different direction.

'That is where he was found.' Drawing the carriage to a halt, Emma pointed to the exact spot in the ditch, close to a large gap in the hedge, and then watched as he jumped nimbly down from the gig in one smooth, lithe movement.

She could not fail to observe the lines creasing that high forehead, as he cast those strikingly coloured eyes over the ground. She could not fail to notice, too, the wonderfully fluid way he moved: surprisingly graceful for a man of his size.

Very likely this natural elegance of movement extended to the dance floor, she reflected, where he must constantly be sought as a partner by those beautifully attired, wealthy young ladies. Had she ever been blessed to enjoy a Season in town, she would certainly have wished to see his name written more than once on her dance—

Suddenly realising he had addressed her, she swiftly abandoned her foolish musings. 'I'm sorry, Mr Grantley, I wasn't attending. What did you say?'

'I said that it isn't hard to see why Hammond's attackers chose this precise spot.' Having returned through the gap in the hedge, Benedict cast a glance up and down the narrow lane. 'Anyone travelling along this road, and at that time during the evening, would have been taken completely by surprise. The poor unsuspecting devil didn't stand a chance. The miscreants would have been upon him before he knew what was happening.'

Emma gave a sudden start. 'Of course! Lavinia mentioned weeks and weeks ago that her husband had intended visiting Sir Lionel that night. His attackers must have been aware of that fact, and were lying in wait for the good doctor. How exceedingly stupid of me not to have realised that long before now!'

Some perverse imp of mischief held him mute, refusing to allow him to assure her that he considered her anything but foolish, and he found himself on the receiving end of a faintly suspicious glance as he clambered up beside her once more.

'How far is Sir Lionel's place from here?' he enquired, somehow managing to preserve his countenance.

'Just round the next bend. It is the only property along here. That is why the lane is so infrequently used.'

Reaching out, he placed his hand over hers a few moments later, when she attempted to turn the gig in the imposing gateway leading to Sir Lionel's estate. 'There is no need to take me back to the inn. I have decided to accompany you to Salisbury. Providing you've no objection, that is?'

Surprised but certainly not unhappy to have him bear her company, Emma continued down the narrow lane which eventually led to a much wider road. Effortlessly turning the gig in the direction of Salisbury, she swiftly earned herself a word of praise from her very impressed companion for the very neat and stylish way she overtook a lumbering coach.

'Oh, Peg takes little handling. He's a very sensible and reliable animal. He knows his way without receiving instruction from me.'

'Peg?' Benedict arched one black brow. 'An unusual choice of name for a gelding, wouldn't you say?'

'It is short for—er—Pegasus,' Emma enlightened him, lips twitching. 'Yes, well may you laugh. I'll admit he's not precisely a flyer. Samuel became addicted to mythology after he had learned to read, hence the name.'

'Did you teach Master Rudge to read, by any chance?'

'No, Martha did. And she was taught by my mother.'

'Ah, yes! I remember. Martha was at one time your nursemaid.' He received a surprised glance. 'You may have gathered by now, Miss Lynn, that I have a penchant for solving mysteries. You intrigued me, so I took the liberty of discovering from Lavinia Hammond why I should find a girl of evident genteel birth working in a tavern.'

Emma shrugged. 'There's no mystery about me, Mr

Grantley. After my father died, I was offered the opportunity of living with my uncle's widow in Bristol. Unfortunately I gained the distinct impression that she wasn't so keen to acquire my company as the money her late husband had kindly left me in his will. I believe she wished for nothing more than to cement an alliance between me and her son, Edwin. And I could never bring myself to marry a man whose full-lipped mouth puts me in mind of nothing so much as a pig's snout. One would not wish to spend the rest of one's life with someone who not only resembled a boar, but also possessed the manners of one.'

'No, indeed,' he agreed a trifle unsteadily, 'but surely there were other avenues open to you? A girl of your obvious intelligence and refined manners would have had no difficulty in attaining some genteel position.'

'As a governess or companion, you mean?' She was unable to suppress a wry smile as she shook her head. 'Thank you for the compliment, sir, but I assure you that wouldn't have suited me at all! Poor Miss Spears held just such a position, and I saw, firsthand, what it did to her. God rest her soul!'

'Ah!' He regarded her with keen interest. 'So, you were acquainted with the late Miss Spears, were you?'

'Not very well, no,' she freely admitted. 'We passed the time of day after church on Sundays, that is all. Poor downtrodden creature! She always appeared so fidgety, almost afraid of her own shadow. Understandable enough when one considers the spoilt nature of her charge. And before you ask—no, I am not acquainted with the divine Clarissa Ashworth. But I've heard enough about her to be very certain that I wouldn't have been at all content as her governess. If you wish to learn about the Ashworths, you must ask Sir Lionel. He, I understand, has been a friend of the family for years.'

Thus adjured, Benedict decided not to probe further for information which, plainly, she was unable to give. So he changed the subject completely by recounting anecdotes of his past, and disclosing certain facts concerning the more colourful members of Society, which succeeded in keeping her in a high state of amusement. Just occasionally, however, before she pulled into the yard of one of Salisbury's more prosperous inns, leaving her gig in the care of a friendly ostler, he glimpsed a fleeting, wistful expression which betrayed clearly enough that, had her circumstances been different, she would not have been averse to enjoying a Season in town.

Swiftly extracting the large basket from beneath the seat before she could do so, Benedict accompanied her along the busy street, surreptitiously studying her attire as she paused to stare in a shop window. Here in this busy, thriving community she did not appear in the least out of place. She wore her neat blue gown and matching pelisse with an air, and the fetching bonnet, offering a tantalising glimpse of those gorgeous chestnut locks, was neatly secured by matching blue ribbon tied in a bow to one side of that delightfully determined little chin. She looked utterly charming, and as neat as wax. Yet no amount of new trimmings on either bonnet or gown could disguise the fact that her attire was not in the prevailing mode, and had been fashioned from materials which had been chosen, he suspected, primarily for their hard-wearing qualities.

Quite unexpectedly he found himself experiencing a stab of annoyance. Such a lovely young woman ought to be arrayed in the finest silks and laces, with her hair arranged by some skilful abigail. Thus groomed, she could enter any fashionable drawing-room, and he would defy anyone else present who was not familiar with her circumstances to suppose for a moment that such a well-mannered, well-spoken young woman was not the daughter of some highborn gentleman.

Catching sight of his disgruntled expression reflected in the shop window, Emma spun round in time to glimpse the disapproving furrows etched in that intelligent forehead before they vanished. 'Sir, please do not feel obliged to remain by my side. I'm certain you would find it vastly more pleasurable exploring the town,' she suggested, quite naturally supposing boredom to be responsible for the look of discontent. 'We could meet back at the inn later.'

'I'm sure we could, Miss Lynn, but I would much prefer to accompany you.'

She was unconvinced, but when she tried to reach for the basket, he whisked it out of reach, thereby making any further attempt to retrieve it impossible without an undignified struggle. 'Very well, sir,' she relented. 'You may accompany me if you wish, but I'm certain you will be heartily bored.'

'And I can assure you I will not,' he countered. 'I am never bored in your company, Miss Lynn. It is most refreshing.'

Suspecting him of mere gallantry, but deciding not to pursue the matter, she changed the subject by enquiring what he would be most likely doing at this time of day if he were still in the capital.

He consulted his fob watch. 'Oh, browsing through the latest edition of the *Morning Post*, I suppose. I do not permit my butler, Fingle, to admit visitors before two in the afternoon. Consequently the door-knocker is never still one minute past that hour.'

'Truly?' Emma gurgled with laughter, much to his intense surprise. 'How very singular! Are you usually unsociable in the mornings? I know some people are.'

'Certainly not!' he countered brusquely; and had it not been for the betraying little twitch she clearly detected at one corner of that shapely masculine mouth, she might have supposed that he was genuinely miffed at the mere suggestion. 'I would have you know, Miss Lynn, that I have the reputation of being one of the most sociable and even-tempered gentlemen in polite society. No, it is merely that, over the years, I have developed a partiality for a strictly regulated lifestyle, and I seldom deviate from my customary practices. I rise at precisely the same time each morning, retire at precisely the same time at night, and only rarely during the hours between do I vary my daily routine.'

Her sudden gurgle of mirth induced more than one passer-by to glance in their direction. 'Now, I am convinced that you are bamming me, sir! Only a devilish dull dog would choose to live such a humdrum existence. And that you are not!

Torn between amusement and indignation, he stared down at her mischievously smiling countenance. 'So you do not approve of punctuality and an orderly lifestyle, Miss Lynn?'

'I didn't say that, sir, precisely. I very much abhor

unpunctuality, but I would never allow myself to be ruled by the clock.' She began to walk on, and he automatically fell into step beside her. 'My situation demands that I perform certain tasks at certain periods during the day. But at other times I am at liberty to do as I please. A little spontaneity can supply the leaven to what for many is life's tediously heavy dough.'

Much struck by this viewpoint, Benedict followed her into the various shops, where she made her purchases swiftly, proving that, although she might not favour a strictly regimented lifestyle, she certainly possessed an orderly mind.

After making the last of her purchases, Emma led the way outside. It took a moment or two for her eyes to adjust to the bright sunlight once more, then she noticed the two figures strolling towards them on the same side of the street. 'It would appear, sir, that this is your lucky day. None other than the Ashworth ladies are approaching.'

She cast a surreptitious glance up at his profile, and was astonished to discover that he appeared quite unimpressed by Miss Clarissa Ashworth's undeniable beauty. This apparent lack of appreciation struck her as most odd, for whenever Clarissa attended the village church on Sundays, the majority of gentlemen in the congregation seemed quite unable to take their eyes off her. She was held to be one of the most beautiful girls in the county. Yet Mr Grantley, amazingly enough, appeared far more interested in her companion.

Emma watched him doff his hat politely as the ladies drew nearer, and noticed the slight inclination of Miss Isabel Ashworth's head in response, before her niece remarked, just as they passed by, 'Who on earth do you suppose that was, Aunt Isabel, with that female who resides at the inn?'

Inclined to be more amused than anything else, Emma shot a further glance up at her very amiable companion to discover him looking surprisingly grim. His good humour, thankfully, had not deserted him completely, for by the time they were heading back to Ashworth Magna, he had already begun to regale her once more with humorous tales of his many Seasons in town.

No sooner had Emma turned into the inn yard than Josh took charge of the horse and gig, and Benedict took charge of the heavy basket once more, escorting her into the kitchen, and earning himself a disapproving look from the innkeeper's wife for his trouble.

'You'll find your nephew awaiting your return in the private parlour, sir, if you'd care to go through,' Martha informed him, making it abundantly clear that she didn't approve of guests invading her private domain.

Thankfully, he took the hint and quickly departed, leaving Martha to focus her attention on a faintly dreamy-eyed Emma. Alarm bells began to sound louder than ever. 'You oughtn't to bring guests in here. You should know that.'

Concern had made her sound sharper than she had intended, but the scolding tone appeared to have had little effect on her former charge. Emma removed her bonnet and began to swing it to and fro by its ribbons, her eyes still retaining that dreamy, faraway look.

'He carried my basket for me…he carried it for me all the time.'

Martha shook her head, as she watched Emma wander out into the passageway. The sooner Mr Benedict Grantley left the Ashworth Arms the better for all concerned!

Chapter Five

Benedict had not been far wrong when he had suspected that the materials for Emma's dresses were, on the whole, purchased for their hard-wearing qualities rather than an eye for the latest mode. None the less, Emma did possess a few stylish gowns, some of which she kept for wearing to church on Sundays, and one or two others which she donned when she was invited out in the evenings. As these were rare events indeed, the gowns had had very little wear, and looked as fresh and elegant as the day they had received those final little touches added by Martha Rudge's expert hands.

After placing her one and only silk shawl about her shoulders, Emma took a final look at her appearance in the full-length mirror, and was not displeased with her reflection. She had taken more care than usual over the arrangement of her hair, and was wearing the gold locket presented to her by her dear uncle on the occasion of her twelfth birthday. She didn't try to delude herself that she looked every inch the fashionable young lady, but she felt that at least she didn't appear quite the country dowdy.

Not that either Lavinia or Deborah would care a whit how she was attired, she mused, as she left the bedchamber. If she turned up wearing a scullery-maid's apron she would still be most welcome to sit at their table.

Since her arrival at the Ashworth Arms they had both been wonderfully supportive, and Deborah, almost five years her junior, had swiftly become her closest friend. Perhaps that was one of the reasons why Lavinia, not so many weeks ago, had suggested that if she sold the house and moved to Bath, Emma might consider seriously making her home with them. Although Emma had not dismissed the idea out of hand, she had no intention of becoming Lavinia's pensioner. When she came into her inheritance, and could pay her way, she would certainly give the matter some serious thought.

Having flicked a duster round the private parlour, Martha went out into the coffee room in time to see Emma descending the last few stairs. There was a noticeable softening of her dark eyes as she cast an approving glance over the pink silk gown which she had lovingly made the previous year.

'So you're off, are you?' There was no noticeable softening of her tone. 'Well, don't you be leaving late,' she warned. 'I don't want you walking back here in the dead of night. There's been some mightily peculiar goings-on in recent months.'

Emma regarded her thoughtfully for a moment, wondering whether she ought not to disclose the reason why their guests had decided to put up at the inn, but then decided against it. If Mr Grantley wished to take others into his confidence then he would do so himself. She could not suppress a slight smile as something else occurred to her. It just might succeed in softening Martha's attitude towards him if he did eventually choose to do so.

'No, I shan't be late, dearest,' Emma assured her, placing a loving kiss on one thin cheek. 'I'm certain that Lavinia will ensure that her manservant escorts me home. She usually does.'

It was only a matter of a five-minute walk to the late doctor's house, but it took Emma rather longer as she was forced to pause on three occasions to pass the time of day with friendly villagers. When she eventually arrived at Lavinia's front door, she heard the church clock chime the hour. As the clock was invariably slow, she knew she was late, and was not in the least surprised, when she was admitted by the manservant, Gregory, to hear voices raised in cheerful discourse as she approached the parlour.

The instant Emma stepped into the room, Lavinia was on her feet and moving forward to greet her in her usual, affectionate way, grasping her hands and saying how lovely she looked.

'She certainly does,' a deep voice drawled in her ear, making Emma start. 'But that is no excuse to keep us all waiting for our dinner. It rather gives the lie to your admission earlier in the day, does it not, young lady?'

Having nowhere near recovered from the initial shock of discovering him there, Emma forced herself to gaze up into those wickedly teasing masculine eyes, cursing herself for every kind of a fool for not realising at once that Mr Grantley's dinner invitation must also have come from Lavinia. Her only excuse, she supposed, was that after their return from Salisbury, when she had gone upstairs to her room to change her attire, and had caught sight of her dreamy-eyed schoolgirl look in the mirror, she had done her utmost not to think about him at all. If she were honest, though, she would be forced to concede that she had not been wholly successful in her endeavours.

'Don't pay him any heed, Emma dear,' Lavinia advised, coming to the rescue of her delightfully flustered young friend. 'You have not kept us waiting at all. Dinner is not until seven-thirty. Come, let me introduce you to my other guests—Harry you know, of course, and this is Dr Fielding, our new practitioner.'

Emma found her right hand taken in the firm, warm clasp of a man she judged to be more or less the same age as the far too personable Mr Grantley. 'Well, Miss Lynn, if all the young ladies in the village and surrounding area possess your healthy bloom,' he announced, his keen gaze quickly noting her heightened colour, 'I shall never become a rich man.'

Emma quickly withdrew her hand before he detected her pulse, which was behaving in a foolishly erratic manner yet again. Coming face to face with Mr Grantley so unexpectedly had completely overset her for some obscure reason, and she felt slightly foolish for so easily losing her self-control.

Fortunately by the time they had sat down to dinner, and she was enjoying the several mouth-watering dishes on offer, she had succeeded in regaining her poise, though she could have wished that Lavinia had not placed her next to Mr Grantley, who sat at the head of the table.

'Yes, I am content to rent the cottage for a few

weeks, Mrs Hammond,' Dr Fielding, sitting on Emma's left, responded to Lavinia's enquiry. 'Naturally I will need to look about for a larger residence once my wife and children join me at the end of next month. I'm afraid poor Elizabeth has been left to deal with organising the storage of our furniture and the selling of our home in Bath.'

'Ah, yes! I remember hearing that your old practice was in that city,' Lavinia responded. 'I myself am seriously contemplating taking up residence there.' She cast a meaningful glance in the direction of another of her guests. 'And am hoping that a certain someone can be persuaded to make her home with us, if and when I do.'

Although Emma realised she was the focal point of everyone's attention, only that violet-eyed gaze disturbed her. 'And as I've already mentioned, Lavinia, I intend to give the matter some very serious consideration.'

'Can't stand the place myself,' Harry put in. 'Too dull by half. Why, there's hardly a person there under the age of seventy.'

'A slight exaggeration, my boy,' Benedict countered, before turning to the doctor. 'I expect you'll find somewhat different conditions to treat round here, Fielding.'

'Yes, you're right. In Bath ailments brought about by overindulgence are the norm. That is one of the reasons why I decided to come here. I shall find it more rewarding helping those less fortunate.'

Benedict nodded in approval, before turning his attention to Emma. 'And are you seriously considering moving away from here?'

'Oh, yes. I never intended it should be a permanent arrangement. Originally I had planned to stay only for a few weeks, until I could obtain some position whereby I could support myself.' She shrugged. 'I don't know. I just never found anything that I thought would suit me, and so remained.'

'Yes, it is quite easy to get oneself into a rut,' he astonished her by remarking. 'One can be fortunate enough to be in a position whereby one can command almost any luxury, and still not be perfectly contented.'

'But surely you cannot be dissatisfied with the life you lead, sir?' She found this very hard to believe. 'You give the impression of being completely relaxed and happy.'

'Do not be fooled by appearances, my dear Miss Lynn.' He reached for his glass of wine, and gazed down at it thoughtfully for a few moments before sampling its contents. 'It most certainly gives one pause suddenly to discover that the life one has taken great pains to build for oneself is not so very fulfilling, after all.' His smile was a trifle crooked. 'Fortunately I have not quite reached the stage where I'm so set in my ways that I cannot change.'

Lavinia then drew his attention by enquiring after the various members of his family, and his less than flattering remarks, most especially concerning his sister, Lady Fencham, succeeded in keeping everyone in a high state of amusement until Lavinia invited Emma and Deborah to return to the parlour, leaving the gentlemen to enjoy their port.

Benedict, the first to rejoin the ladies, entered the room to discover one noticeable absentee, and moved directly across to the French windows, which had been left open to allow the pleasant evening air, sweetly perfumed with the fragrance of roses, to freshen the room. Lavinia, sitting close by, distinctly heard him muttering something under his breath, but could not quite catch the words. The unguarded look in his eyes, however, was unmistakable, and she turned her head slightly in the direction of his openly admiring gaze to see Emma, framed in a garland of delicate pink roses, almost exactly the same shade as her dress, standing beneath the wooden archway.

How very, very gratifying, she mused, before hurriedly deterring Harry, who had suddenly appeared in the room, from following his uncle's example by taking a stroll out into the garden.

Emma turned the instant she detected the approaching footsteps. 'Are these not amongst the most perfect specimens, sir?' she remarked while striving to regain some control over her pulse rate, which had suddenly seemed to have acquired a will of its own and a tendency to behave erratically at frequent intervals.

'Quite exquisite,' he responded, his gaze never wavering from her face.

The evening air seemed suddenly filled with more than just the powerful scent of flowers. 'Dr Hammond was very fond of his roses.' She raised her eyes fleetingly to his, then promptly wished she had not. What on earth was the matter with her? Anyone might suppose that she was unaccustomed to the company of the opposite sex. Which was simply untrue! What was totally alien to her were these peculiar sensations she seemed powerless to control whenever Mr Grantley was near her.

'I do hope, sir, that you are successful in your endeavours,' she continued, determined not to lose her poise entirely for a second time that evening, and took heart from the control she somehow always managed to maintain over her voice. 'He was a good man who always put the welfare of others before himself. He did not deserve to die in such a way.'

'With your help, Miss Lynn, perhaps I may solve the mystery.'

'As I've already mentioned, I shall willingly help in any way I can. But I do not immediately perceive how I can assist you further.'

Emma raised one hand in a helpless gesture, and quick as a flash it was captured in long fingers, and pulled through the crook of one well-muscled arm so that she had little choice but to accompany him, as he began an exploratory stroll about the beautifully maintained garden.

She was immediately conscious of the firmness of the biceps beneath her fingers; conscious too of the latent strength in every line of his perfectly proportioned, muscular frame. From the first moment she had set eyes on him she had been struck by his air of refinement. Undeniably he was every inch the well-bred gentleman, dignified and courteous. Beneath the fashionable trappings, however, he was without question also every inch the powerful male. There was little point, she swiftly decided, to ignore the truth any longer—she was, and had been from the very first, more than just faintly attracted to him.

She was not so naïve as to suppose that he was

indifferent to her, either. A virtual innocent she might be, but she had recognised the raw longing in his eyes, which he had seemed incapable of concealing, or had simply chosen not to do so, when he had first joined her in the garden. Yes, he desired her—that was patently clear. But what niche was there for a female like her in the life of such a man? His mistress, perhaps? Yes, common sense told her, that was possibly all she could ever hope to achieve. It would mean her ruin, of course, if she were ever foolish enough to contemplate such a course of action. Yet, if these feelings she could no longer ignore were to deepen, and she ever came to—

'I believe you mentioned you were on friendly terms with the Ashworths' cook,' he unexpectedly announced, and she forced herself to concentrate on what he was saying, pleased to be given the opportunity to abandon her unsettling reflections and to channel her thoughts in a less disturbing direction. 'When do you expect to receive another visit from her?'

'Tomorrow, early in the afternoon.'

'Excellent! Find out as much as you can about this young maid who died up at the Hall. Try also to discover the state of the late Miss Spears's mind before she left to visit her sister in London. I know I can rely on you to be discreet. Whilst you are busy prising information out of the estimable cook, I shall be attempting to coax Sir Lionel, who has, so I have discovered, returned home today, after spending several days with a friend, to give me all the information he can on the history of the Ashworth family.'

Puzzled, Emma drew her fine brows together.

'Surely you don't imagine that the Ashworths had anything to do with Dr Hammond's death?'

'At the moment, my dear, I'm still groping in the dark, searching for that one lead which might shed some light on this business. From reading Hammond's diaries, I have gathered that he was suspicious over some aspect of that maidservant's death. If it wasn't an accident, then I'm afraid—'

'She too may have been murdered,' she finished for him. Emma shook her head, at a loss to understand why anyone should wish to dispose of an insignificant maid, and echoed her thoughts aloud.

'Yes, it does seem hard to imagine, I know, but we must strive to keep an open mind. She had worked there, I understand, for a short time only. So I can only assume that she must have discovered something that someone in that house feared becoming common knowledge. With any luck, we should have a clearer idea tomorrow.'

He raised a warning finger. 'It would seem the others have decided to follow our example by taking a breath of fresh air,' he murmured, and Emma could not decide, as he led her across the lawn towards the house, whether she felt relieved or disappointed at having what for her were rapidly becoming very precious moments alone with him brought to an abrupt end.

Sir Lionel Brent betrayed no little astonishment when he cast his eyes over the visiting-card his butler handed to him early the following afternoon. Nevertheless he didn't hesitate to instruct his servant to show his surprising visitor in at once.

'My dear Grantley, this is an unexpected pleasure!'
He came forward to shake his fellow member of
White's warmly by the hand. He then frowned slightly
as he noticed a second figure appear in the doorway,
and it was left to Benedict to perform the introductions.

'I do not know, sir, whether you are acquainted with
my nephew, Harry Fencham.'

'No, I cannot recall that we have ever met before,'
Sir Lionel admitted candidly, before shaking the
younger man's hand no less warmly. 'But I do know
your father quite well. How is he keeping these days?'

'Oh, he's in fine fettle, sir, although not at all happy
to be in town. He ain't one for a deal of socialising
these days. He much prefers the peace and quiet of
the country.'

'Well, town life doesn't suit everyone,' Sir Lionel
remarked, after inviting his guests to sit down and instructing his butler to furnish them with some refresh-
ments. 'Like to spend some time in the capital each
year myself, but I must confess I'm always glad to get
back here.'

Making himself comfortable in his favourite chair,
Sir Lionel waited only for his butler to perform his
duties, and leave the room, before asking in his usual
forthright manner, 'So, what brings you to these parts,
Grantley?'

Although he took a moment to sample the excellent
burgundy, Benedict saw little point in trying to avoid
the issue. 'I'm here at the request of Lavinia Hammond.' His eyes never wavered from his suddenly
alert listener's face. 'She is not wholly convinced that
her husband's death was simply the result of being

in—how shall I phrase it?—the wrong place at the wrong time. In other words, she believes his death was planned. And I have to say that from what I've managed to uncover thus far, I'm inclined to agree with her.'

'I see,' was the only response forthcoming, before Sir Lionel leaned back in his chair, his bushy grey brows snapping together above the bridge of the prominent, hawk-like nose. Then, 'I am aware that you have had no little success in solving certain puzzling events which have confounded the authorities, Grantley— your locating the whereabouts of the famous Penticote pearls, to name but one of your achievements. So I shall not dismiss your suspicions out of hand, but would ask on what grounds you base them?'

Just a hint of reserve had crept into Sir Lionel's manner. Understandable in the circumstances, Benedict considered, for the Baronet must have tried everything humanly possible to discover the identities of his friend's murderers.

'Before I answer that, may I ask you a question, sir? Were you perfectly satisfied that Hammond's death was purely and simply a tragic mischance?'

A grudging smile tugged at one corner of Sir Lionel's thin-lipped mouth. 'Confound you, Grantley! No, I was not. But what I fail to understand is why he should have set out to visit me in the first place when he knew I wouldn't be at home. I'd written to him, cancelling the arrangement. And before you ask,' he went on, 'I know for a fact that my letter was delivered to his home. Alice, the young maid I employ here, swore that the note was pushed under the door, and I have no reason to suppose she would lie.'

Sir Lionel paused for a moment to stare down into the contents of his glass. 'Naturally I questioned Lavinia's servants, and was assured that neither of them had picked up any note from the mat. So I can only assume that Hammond himself must have discovered it there, swiftly apprised himself of its contents, and then threw it away. Influenza was rife in the area at the time. I had only just recovered from a bout myself. Half the county had been affected by the outbreak, and poor Hammond was rushed off his feet. With so much on his mind, I can only imagine that he forgot our Friday evening had been cancelled.'

'That's certainly a possibility, Ben,' Harry agreed, thereby earning himself a mild look of approval from their host.

'I might wholeheartedly agree with you,' Benedict responded, 'if I was not fairly sure that his attackers were lying in wait for him, certain that he would be keeping that appointment with Sir Lionel.'

Reaching into his jacket pocket, Benedict drew out the late doctor's diary, opened it at the page containing the very last entry, and then handed it over to their host. 'And that, sir, is why I believe your friend was murdered.'

The look of astonishment on the Baronet's face, after reading the last words written in his late friend's hand, was too spontaneous not to be perfectly genuine. 'But—but…this is ridiculous! What on earth was suspicious about the maid's death? She died as a result of a fall—simply tripped and fell down the main staircase at Ashworth Hall.'

'Did you happen to see the girl's body, Sir Lionel?'

'No, Grantley, I did not,' he freely admitted. 'I was

staying with my sister in Bath at the time, recovering from that bout of influenza I mentioned earlier, and taking those confounded waters. Not that they did me much good. I was pretty knocked up.' He shook his head sadly. 'I wish Lavinia had come to me about this, though perhaps it's understandable why she did not. I have been deliberately keeping my distance.'

He caught the faint glimmer of surprise in Benedict's eyes. 'Good Lord, man! You know what small places like this are for wagging tongues. Lavinia Hammond's a damn fine woman. I've never made any secret of the fact that I admire her immensely. But I had no intention of adding to her distress by visiting her regularly and giving rise to gossip. This, however,' he added, handing back his late friend's diary, 'is a different matter entirely, and must be looked into.'

'I could not agree more, sir.' Benedict returned the diary to his pocket. 'And might I suggest that for the time being, at least, you leave it to me… Yes, I know, strictly speaking, the matter should be left in your hands,' he continued, when Sir Lionel looked about to protest, 'and I have no intention of attempting to undermine your authority as the local Justice of the Peace. None the less, if you begin to make further inquiries, suspicions will instantly be aroused, whereas a stranger asking questions might be considered as nothing more than merely inquisitive. Give me a week, two at the most, and if I uncover nothing, then I shall willingly leave the whole matter entirely to you.'

The Baronet appeared to debate within himself for a moment or two, then nodded his head in agreement. 'Very well, Grantley. But on the strict understanding that you report any findings straight back to me.'

After receiving this assurance, Sir Lionel looked gravely across at his visitors. 'If only for Lavinia's sake I'd like this business cleared up. She's a lovely woman, and little Deborah is a sweet girl.' He frowned heavily. 'I just wish I could say the same about my ward!'

'I did not realise that you had a ward, sir,' Benedict remarked, not out of any undue interest, only as a means to prolong the visit. There was much more he needed to uncover from Sir Lionel. 'Does she reside with you?'

'No, thank the Lord! It's Ashworth's gel, Clarissa. I have joint guardianship with Isabel Ashworth. The chit lives with her aunt up at the Hall—an arrangement which suits me very well, I might add. Beautiful girl, but spoilt to death.' He shrugged. 'Still, I suppose it's understandable in the circumstances. Initially Roderick Ashworth blamed the child for her mother's death. Clara Ashworth died of childbed fever, you see. It was touch and go for a while whether Clarissa herself would survive. It was only thanks to her aunt that she did. Isabel returned, took charge of the household again, and arranged for a new nursemaid to take care of the infant. It certainly did the trick. The baby lived, but it was quite some time before Roderick would have anything to do with her. Time, as they say, though, is a great healer and eventually, after two or three years, his attitude began to change and he simply doted on his daughter, possibly because she had in-herited her mother's fair hair and blue eyes. But I can't say she resembles either of her parents to any great extent. With the possible exception of George, the younger brother, the Ashworth family were never famed for their good looks.'

'You are evidently very well acquainted with the family,' Benedict remarked, not slow to make use of the opening offered, and Sir Lionel, thankfully, appeared willing to satisfy his curiosity.

Benedict listened carefully to the reasonably detailed account of the Ashworth family history, while committing certain interesting details to memory. 'So, the family automatically assumed that George Ashworth had died when he failed to return to the ancestral home?' he prompted when Sir Lionel eventually fell silent. 'Did the late Lord Ashworth make no attempt to discover what had happened to his young brother?'

'I believe he did make certain inquiries, yes, but when he discovered that even George's closest friends had received no communication from him, after he had arrived in America, he assumed his brother had died. Which, I'm afraid, was typical of Roderick. He was never one to bestir himself unduly if he could possibly avoid it. Why, his sister Isabel has run the house, and managed the estate for years! They were twins, you see, Isabel and Roderick. She was born half an hour before her brother. I've always maintained that it was a pity she hadn't been born the boy. She was undoubtedly the one with the brains and determination.'

'The fact that George Ashworth not only survived, but married and produced a son must have come as something of a—er—shock to certain members of the family,' Benedict suggested, bringing a grim smile to Sir Lionel's mouth.

'Yes, it was definitely a bitter blow to Cedric who,

I might add, has made frequent visits to Ashworth Hall since Roderick's demise. But there's no denying the fact that George's son, Richard Ashworth, is the rightful heir. I've recently discovered that contact has been made with him, and he is now on his way back to England. He was, in fact, born in this country,' Sir Lionel went on to divulge, thereby confirming what Benedict had discovered from Lavinia Hammond. 'George returned, with his American wife, and settled in Yorkshire, where Richard was born. Sadly, twelve years later, both George and his wife died in a small-pox epidemic, and young Richard was sent back to America to be raised by his maternal grandfather.'

Benedict frowned. 'It is rather odd, don't you think, that George never attempted to make contact with any member of his family, after his return to this country?'

'Yes, I certainly do,' Sir Lionel agreed. Then he shrugged. 'But as I've already mentioned, George wasn't close to either his brother or his sister. I just hope that young Richard, when he eventually does arrive here, proves to be a little more amiable, though Isabel and Clarissa have been well provided for in any event.'

He turned to stare out of the window, as he detected the sound of a carriage pulling up outside his house. 'Ah! Most opportune! If you have not as yet met the Ashworth ladies, gentlemen, then you are about to be granted the opportunity to do so.'

Benedict was not unduly surprised to see his young nephew's jaw drop perceptibly when Clarissa Ashworth, accompanied by her aunt, entered the room a few moments later. Although he had masterfully concealed the fact yesterday, when he had first set eyes on her during his visit to Salisbury, he had been forced to own that Miss Ashworth was one of the most outstandingly pretty young females he had ever clapped eyes on in his life. Large, cornflower-blue eyes, set in a heart-shaped face, the whole framed in a riot of shining, golden curls, was enough to take the most hardened gentleman's breath away. It was certainly a face that one could not easily forget. If there was a slight flaw, then it was that sweet bow of a mouth about which there was just the faintest hint of sulkiness when she was not smiling.

There was not the smallest hint of sullenness now, however, as Sir Lionel made the introductions, and she found herself the focal point of a handsome young man's openly admiring regard. Benedict's attention, as before, was most definitely focused on the older female, whose surprisingly direct gaze betrayed a keen intelligence.

'Am I correct in thinking, sir, that we have met somewhere before?'

'We have never been formally introduced, ma'am,' Benedict answered, resuming his seat once the ladies had made themselves comfortable on the sofa, 'but our paths did cross in Salisbury, late yesterday morning. That is perhaps why I seem familiar.'

'Oh, yes, I remember!' Clarissa put in. 'You were with that person who resides at the village inn.'

Perhaps no one else noticed, but Sir Lionel thought he could detect just the faintest hardening of the muscles along a square, powerful jaw, and hurriedly intervened. 'And to what do I owe the pleasure of this unexpected visit, Isabel?'

'Oh, we came here to remind you not to forget my

party on Friday week, sir,' Clarissa answered, before
her aunt could do so. 'If you do not come there will
be hardly anyone there!'

'Clarissa, my dear, that simply is not so,' her aunt
countered, thereby proving that she was quite capable
of edging in a word when she chose to do so. 'Nearly
all those who were sent invitations have accepted.'

'I'm referring to people of consequence,' her niece
returned, peevishness increasing. 'A great many of the
notable families are still in London, enjoying the Season. And why you felt the need to invite the Vicar and
his family, Colonel Meecham and his wife, and the
Hammonds, I'll never know!'

Benedict noticed the look of admiration swiftly fad-
ing from his nephew's eyes; glimpsed, too, an expression on the Baronet's face which suggested that it
would have afforded him the utmost pleasure to slap
his ward, and Benedict, for one, could not have
blamed him if he had.

'I shall have you know, young lady,' Sir Lionel
snapped, 'that Mrs Hammond and her daughter are
well respected in these parts. Their behaviour is always impeccable.' He did not add, 'Which is more
than can be said for yours', but the sentiment hung in
the air all the same.

'They are, indeed, very refined,' Miss Ashworth
agreed, hurriedly stepping into the breach. 'It is understandable, however, that Clarissa is feeling a little
disgruntled. Had her dear papa not passed away last
year, she would be celebrating her eighteenth birthday
at a ball in the capital, instead of having to be content
with a small country party to mark the event. None
the less,' she added, turning her surprisingly astute

gaze in Benedict's direction, 'perhaps if Mr Grantley and Mr Fencham will still be in the area, they might consider favouring the occasion with their presence.'

'As we have many more places of interest to visit, we have made no immediate plans to move on just yet, and so shall be delighted to accept, ma'am,' Benedict responded, before a glint of sheer devilment brightened his eyes. 'Would your generosity, I wonder, extend to a third party, if I should care to invite a—er—friend?'

Easily gaining her consent, Benedict then rose to his feet, and took his leave of the Ashworth ladies. Sir Lionel saw them safely into their carriage, extracting a promise from Benedict that he and his nephew would return that evening to dine with him.

'I say, Ben,' Harry remarked, as the carriage turned out of the drive and into the lane where the late Dr Hammond had met his death, 'I'm glad you didn't hesitate to accept Sir Lionel's invitation to dine this evening. I rather like him. He's a bit of a dry old stick, but at least he has a sense of humour.'

'Possibly just as well. One would need to possess one, being the guardian of such a girl.'

'Dear me, yes,' Harry agreed, smiling wryly. 'I must confess when I first clapped eyes on her, I was pretty well bowled over. But her manners are deplorable! Mama would never allow any of my sisters to behave in such a fashion.'

'No. I cannot help wondering for how much longer Sir Lionel will be able to suppress his desire to school her.'

Harry frankly laughed. 'I'm rather surprised you accepted the invitation to her birthday party. Not that I object to putting in an appearance as Debbie and her mama will be there.' He frowned as a thought suddenly occurred to him. 'And who the deuce are you intending to bring along to make up one of our party?'

A smile hovered about Benedict's mouth, as he leaned back against the plush velvet squabs and closed his eyes. 'Someone who has more refinement in one of her hardworking little fingers than Miss Clarissa Ashworth will ever attain.'

Chapter Six

Although Emma had always considered herself to be a very level-headed and even-tempered member of her sex, she would never have presumed to describe herself as a born optimist. None the less, she had striven never to give way to despondency. Today, however, her sunny disposition seemed to have deserted her completely, and no one working at the Ashworth Arms was in any doubt whatsoever that she was in a rare ill humour.

She had slept badly the night before, lying awake for much of the time, endeavouring to suppress ever-increasing emotions that she feared could only end in heartache. Consequently she had risen much later than usual, and had been behind in her work ever since.

It certainly had not helped the situation having to spend some considerable time gossiping to the Ashworths' cook, trying to discover what she could about the servant-girl's death. Then, no sooner had Mrs Wright eventually taken her leave than Lucy, behaving true to form, had brushed against the tray of freshly baked bread cooling on the table, sending the half-dozen loaves rolling in various directions across the kitchen floor; and now, in the full heat of a very oppressive June afternoon, a fresh batch was having to be made.

Oh, but she couldn't blame Lucy for this bout of ill humour, Emma chided herself, pausing in her kneading of the dough to flick some unruly strands of hair away from her eyes. Her present troubled state was entirely of her own making. She ought to have possessed more strength of character, and resisted right from the start the charm of a certain very personable, violet-eyed gentleman. But how could any female withstand such charisma? she wondered, remembering too clearly the way, after he had escorted her back to the inn the previous evening, he had kissed her hand in very much the grand manner, before they had finally parted company on the landing. That portion of flesh where those lips had fleetingly touched had tingled for an age afterwards, leaving her longing for further and very much more intimate contact.

Silently cursing herself for a weak-willed fool, Emma gave the dough a further vicious thump with her small fist. Undoubtedly gentlemen of Mr Benedict Grantley's stamp posed a real danger to inexperienced females, most especially those like herself who might foolishly suppose that common sense might offer some protection against peerless displays of masculine gallantry. Try as she might, though, she could not in her heart of hearts regret that he had come into her life. No, her main concern, if she were honest, was that she was finding it increasingly difficult to come to terms with the fact that he would one day walk out of it, and she very much feared that no other man would ever succeed in filling the void.

'Now who, I wonder, could possibly have aroused such disapprobation that you feel the need to vent your barely suppressed ire on a harmless lump of dough?'

Startled, Emma swung round to discover the being responsible for her present highly irrational state framed in the doorway, his smile of wry amusement making him more appealing than ever. The mere sight of him was sufficient to induce her foolish heart to beat a tattoo against her ribcage. Fortunately, though, her disgruntled mood came to her aid.

'You shouldn't be in here, Mr Grantley!'

Much to her intense dismay the testily uttered rebuke had the reverse effect from what she had intended. Refusing to admit defeat, however, as he calmly sauntered into the kitchen, she added for good measure, 'The landlady of this hostelry doesn't approve of guests invading the inn's private areas.'

'And by the sounds of it, my girl, she's by no means the only one.' With the speed of a striking snake, he had her chin imprisoned in his long fingers, giving her little choice but to meet his all-too-perceptive gaze. 'What's wrong? And kindly do not try my patience by suggesting that nothing has occurred to upset you,' he went on when she was about to do just that. 'When we parted company last night you appeared—how shall I phrase it?—ah, yes, perfectly contented. And yet today I find you—'

'Out of all reason cross,' she finished for him, managing to extract her chin from that disturbingly arousing clasp. 'And so would you be annoyed if you were forced to bake on an afternoon like this one. This kitchen is like a confounded furnace!'

Thankfully he appeared to accept the peevish explanation readily enough, before he once again moved in that smoothly elegant way of his across to the door leading to the yard, and threw it wide. 'Then let us attempt to make things a little more comfortable for you, my little love,' he said, and she could only hope that her suddenly increased bloom at the unexpected endearment might be attributed to nothing more significant than her renewed pummelling of the dough.

'If you sit there, you'll likely end up covered in flour,' she warned, resorting again to a waspish tone in a valiant attempt to conceal her rapidly increasing disturbed state. Not surprisingly the tactic was no more successful than before, and he calmly seated himself at the table, smiling up at her in a way that would have had a less determined female's knees instantly turning to jelly. 'Well, don't say I didn't warn you!'

'Be assured I shan't do that, my sweet scold.' Benedict noted the swift return of added colour with intense satisfaction. 'Why, if it isn't a foolish question, are you baking on such a warm afternoon?'

'Because Lucy knocked the first batch of loaves over the floor.'

He manfully suppressed a smile. 'In that case you should be grateful to me for saving you yet more work. I managed to prevent the breakfast rolls from skidding across the parlour floor this morning.'

'Oh, dear Lord! She gets worse!' Emma raised her eyes ceilingwards before reaching for the flour jar, only to discover it annoyingly empty.

Proving that he was not utterly useless in a kitchen,

Benedict picked up the earthenware vessel, and offered to refill it. No sooner had he disappeared into the depths of the huge and well-stocked larder then Emma was forced to swallow a protracted groan, when an all-too-familiar cheery voice announced, 'The sight of those lovely bare arms of yours covered in flour sends me all of a tremble, my little darling!'

Emma raised her eyes to discover, as expected, the plump figure of Colonel Meecham entering by way of the stable-yard. Since her arrival at the inn, almost half a decade ago, he had managed to find reasons to pay thankfully short but all-too-frequent visits. With all the guile of an experienced campaigner, he always succeeded in putting in an appearance when her self-appointed chaperon, Martha Rudge, was nowhere in sight to send him packing.

Emma was certainly in no mood for his harmless flirting today, but refrained from making this abundantly clear. After all, there was no possibility that she would ever lose her foolish heart to a portly ex-army officer whose florid complexion betrayed his fondness for the port and brandy. How she wished she could say with any conviction that she wasn't in the least danger of losing it to a certain raven-haired gentleman of her acquaintance!

All things considered, it might be wise to offer her loyal admirer a little encouragement to stay on this occasion, she swiftly decided, glancing briefly in the direction of the larder, before bestowing a smile of such dazzling brilliance upon her ageing swain that he blinked his small, round eyes several times in astonishment.

'Emma, you utter darling,' he announced in a soul-

ful sigh, while ineffectually striving to capture the
floured hand which was brushing away those unruly
strands of hair again. 'When are you going to put me
out of my misery and marry me?'

'I would be only too delighted to oblige you, Colonel, if it wasn't for the fact that it might make your
charming wife just a trifle peeved.'

Benedict's deep rumble of laughter, as he emerged
from the larder, had the Colonel swivelling round on
the heels of his boots. 'And who the devil might you
be, sir!' he demanded, resorting to the barking tone he
had used to terrify the raw recruits under his command
during his days in the army.

'Thank you.' Emma relieved Benedict of the filled
earthenware jar, before taking it upon herself to make
the introductions.

'Grantley?' The Colonel's bushy brows snapped to-
gether as he shook the proffered hand. 'Not one of the
Kentish branch of the family, by any chance…? Ah!
Met your father once, many years ago,' he added, at
Benedict's nod of confirmation. 'Charming rogue, as
I recall.'

'Ha! Must be a family trait,' Emma muttered,
thereby earning herself a painful nip just above the
elbow, as Benedict passed behind her to resume his
seat. She cast him a darkling look before plunging her
hand into the earthenware jar and sending a cloud of
flour into the air. 'Mr Grantley is here on a sightseeing
tour with his nephew, Colonel.'

Unlike Benedict, who remained stubbornly seated
next to the table, the Colonel took the precaution of
edging his chair back a trifle. 'Are you, by gad! Well,
if you're at a loss one evening, you're most welcome

to sample the victuals served at my table. Can't miss the house—first in the village, set a little way back from the road.'

'The Colonel and Mrs Meecham moved into old Squire Penlow's house some sixteen years ago,' Emma informed Benedict, as her little stratagem of casting flour about with gay abandon had quite failed to induce him to leave the kitchen, though the look he had cast her, after brushing his sleeve, boded ill for her if she pursued the tactic. 'The villagers often tell tales of the wild goings-on that took place in that house.'

'Pity there ain't any now,' muttered the Colonel, disgruntled, which surprisingly elicited a chuckle from Emma, the first that day.

'Now, you know you don't mean that,' she countered. 'Both the Squire and his son died as a direct result of their wild ways, so I'm reliably informed. You're much better living a quiet life with Mrs Meecham.'

'Aye, I suppose you're right,' he answered, but not sounding wholly convinced. 'And talking of Harriet, I ought to be getting back.' He eased his large bulk off the chair. 'Besides which, I don't want the dragon-woman discovering me here. Where is she, by the way?'

'Mrs Rudge is busy in the dairy, Colonel,' Emma informed him, whilst casting a disapproving look, which he blithely ignored.

'Fiendish female, that, Grantley. I wouldn't let her catch you in here, if I were you,' he warned, pausing at the door. 'And don't forget to come and dine with me one evening.'

Assuring him that he would be delighted to accept the kind invitation, Benedict turned his attention back to Emma the instant they were alone. 'Well, at least the Colonel's visit appears to have put you in a better humour, you provoking little witch. Come, hurry and finish that, and sit down! I wish to know what you've discovered from the Ashworths' cook.'

Although very much resenting the faintly dictatorial tone, she succeeded in swallowing her chagrin. After all, the sooner she told him what he wanted to know the sooner he would leave her to her own devices. Which, of course, was precisely what she wanted, wasn't it?

'I'm afraid I didn't discover that much,' she freely admitted, seating herself opposite and desperately striving not to allow the warmth of that wholly masculine smile to weaken further the half-hearted resolve to be rid of him. 'The young maid, Sally Pritchard, hadn't worked at the Hall for very long, as you already know. Apparently she wasn't well liked by the majority of the staff.'

'Was there any reason for this, do you suppose?' he asked, evidently finding this snippet interesting.

'Difficult to say.' Emma shrugged. 'Her presence might have been resented simply because she wasn't a local girl. Country people tend to band together. They don't like it when outsiders are offered situations which can easily be filled by local people looking for work. Sally, it seemed, came to live with her married sister in Andover only a week or two before attaining the position up at the Hall.'

'Did you manage to find out the name of the sister?'

'As I thought you might wish to know it—yes, I

did. Her name is Tyler. Mrs Wright remembered it particularly because it happened to be her own mother's maiden name.'

'And was anyone up at the Hall suspicious over the girl's death?'

'I didn't gain that impression from Mrs Wright, no,' Emma was forced to concede. 'Everyone at the house seems to suppose that she died as a result of that fall. She was discovered by the butler, Troughton, lying in the hall at the foot of the main staircase. However, Mrs Wright did mention that she thought it strange that the maid had been using the main stairway. Only the higher-ranking servants were permitted to use it. The rest were instructed always to use the back stairs.'

She couldn't prevent a smile. ' "But being something of an uppity girl, as you might say, and thinking far too much of herself, besides, she possibly thought she could do just as she pleased." Mrs Wright's words, not mine, I hasten to add.'

The masterly mimicry of the local dialect brought a further smile to Benedict's lips. 'When was the body discovered?'

'Early in the morning.' Her eyes widened in mock horror. 'And stone-cold dead she were, too.'

'Assuming she was—er—stone cold, she'd obviously been dead for some time.'

'Dr Hammond, so I'm reliably informed, seemed to think that she had died late the previous evening.'

Black brows rose in surprise. 'Obviously he was called in to confirm life extinct?'

'Oh, no,' Emma corrected him. 'He called mid-morning, as previously arranged, in order to pay another visit to Clarissa Ashworth. She had been suffer-

ing from influenza. Apparently, when he discovered
what had occurred, he asked to see the body, which
had by that time been placed in one of the outhouses.
Mrs Wright clearly remembered that he had asked a
great many questions after examining the body—
wanted to know precisely where the girl was found,
and how she was lying. Which certainly suggests that
he wasn't completely happy about something.'

Benedict nodded in agreement. 'What were the extent of her injuries?'

'According to Mrs Wright, apart from the right side
of Sally's head being ''all smashed in'' from the fall,
there wasn't a mark on her.'

'From a fall, I wonder?' he muttered, frowning now.
'Or was she perhaps bludgeoned to death?'

Emma didn't attempt to conceal her dismay at the
awful possibility. 'Surely not?'

'Extensive bruising and broken bones are not uncommon when a person takes a tumble down a flight
of stairs,' he reminded her. 'Injuries to the neck and
head are not uncommon, either.' His frown grew more
pronounced. 'But just injuries to one side of the head,
and perhaps no others…? I wonder if it was this that
made Hammond suspicious.'

'What you suspect, in fact, is that Sally was killed
elsewhere, and then placed at the foot of the stairs to
make her death appear an accident, don't you?' she
prompted, flicking away the annoying strands of hair
that were continuously flopping over her forehead,
adding to the irritations of the day.

The gesture appeared to please him, because his
smile returned as he conceded, 'It's a possibility, cer-

tainly. Did you manage to discover anything about the late Miss Spears?'

'I gained the distinct impression that the servants never did have very much contact with her, even though she had been employed by the Ashworth family for some years. Governesses and companions,' she reminded him, unable to resist a wry little smile, 'are in that unfortunate category where they do not fit in anywhere. They are above the general order of domestics, and yet they are still forced to earn a living and are at the beck and call of their employers.

'One very interesting snippet I did discover, however,' she continued, after a moment's thought. 'Mrs Wright remembers that one of the other maids overheard Sally Pritchard talking to Miss Spears on the day before Sally died. Apparently, Sally was in one of her ''uppity'' moods, and was telling Miss Spears that she would soon be in a position to better herself, and that she wouldn't be spending the rest of her life in service.'

'Interesting,' he murmured.

Emma shrugged. 'If it wasn't just wishful thinking on the girl's part, then, yes, it does suggest that she was expecting some good fortune to come her way in the near future,' she agreed, before changing the subject slightly by asking if he'd discovered anything of interest during his visit to Sir Lionel.

'I learned something about the Ashworth family's history, but I require confirmation of certain details.'

'Why?' She was genuinely surprised. 'Surely you don't suppose that Sir Lionel would lie?'

'Well, no, not exactly,' he responded, his tone guarded. 'You must remember, though, that Sir Lionel has been a friend of the family's for a number of years, and naturally might feel he was being disloyal if he betrayed too much. I believe what he told me was true enough, but I suspect there is much more to discover.'

'In that case you could do no better than to take Samuel and Martha Rudge into your confidence. They were both born in the village, and would have heard, or would be in a position to discover, anything you might wish to know. Furthermore they can be trusted to be discreet.'

A loud clatter from the direction of the dairy, quickly followed by Martha's scolding voice, was sufficient to inform Emma, at least, that Lucy had had another mishap.

'I think I shall put this batch of dough out of harm's way, before Lucy returns to the kitchen.'

'Very wise, Emma,' he agreed, and noticed that delightful little chin lift fractionally.

'I cannot recall giving you permission to address me by my given name.'

'No, you didn't. And very remiss of you too, I might add, since you gave my nephew leave to address you in that manner. My name is Benedict, by the way. Most of my friends call me Ben. I don't mind which you use.'

Whilst striving to formulate some withering response, Emma caught sight of a stalking figure crossing the yard. 'I did warn you that Martha doesn't take kindly to interlopers invading her kitchen,' she reminded him, with a certain grim satisfaction. 'You're on your own, Mr Grantley.'

Not noticeably abashed by the dagger-look he received from the landlady the instant she perceived him seated at her table, he forestalled any blistering remark she might have been about to utter in masterly fashion by announcing, 'Ah, Mrs Rudge, the very person I wished to see! I know you are exceedingly busy, but would you and your husband be kind enough to spare me a few minutes of your time? There is something I wish to discuss with you both.'

'Of course, sir.' She was momentarily taken aback, and it showed. 'I sincerely trust that everything is to your—'

'No complaints whatsoever, Mrs Rudge,' he interrupted, before rising to his feet in one smooth movement. 'Perhaps if you would grant me the opportunity to don fresh linen, we could meet in the parlour in— say—half an hour,' and with that, and the cheekiest of winks cast in Emma's direction, he disappeared down the passageway, leaving Martha, for perhaps the first time in her life, with absolutely nothing to say.

The man was a marvel! Emma was forced silently to concede as, following his example, she too decided to go up to her room to freshen up, and change her attire. She had a sneaking suspicion that dear Martha didn't quite know what to make of the very gentlemanly Mr Grantley. She was a woman who very much appreciated good manners, and Emma suspected that his polite behaviour, clean habits and evident appreciation of the service he was being offered at the inn was slowly beginning to melt darling Martha's ice-cool reserve.

Entering her bedchamber, Emma could not prevent yet another wry smile. Well, he had certainly succeeded in chipping away all of hers! Not that she had ever attempted to erect a barrier between them which, with hindsight, she was forced to own, might yet prove a grave error of judgement on her part. But how could she possibly have known that here, of all the unlikely places, she would meet someone who was…oh, so very right for her in every respect? Had she had an inkling of what was to befall her, she might have been more able to deal with the situation in which she now found herself.

Experiencing scant pleasure, she gazed about the prettily decorated room which had been her own private little sanctum for so many years, and was forced to accept that for the first time in her life she was utterly dissatisfied with her lot. It wasn't that she was ashamed of the work she did—nothing could have been further from the truth. She had earned her keep and had been able to hold her head up, secure in the knowledge that she had been a burden to no one. Somehow, though, this undeniable fact no longer brought the satisfaction it once had.

Perhaps foolishly during these past few days she had begun to dwell more and more on how very different her life might have been if her father had not been quite so philanthropic, had not turned his back on the trappings of wealth, and had not ostracised himself from the other members of his wealthy family. Might she then have gained entry into Benedict's world? Might they have met at some ball or rout, and become better acquainted during the dizzy whirl of a London Season? She had never known that world where the rich and famous gathered in fashionable salons, privileged to enjoy the very best that life could offer. Yet when Benedict was with her she was experiencing increasingly the rather foolish fancy that she belonged there, and not here. He possessed the most wonderful ability to make her feel in no way inferior, but his equal in every respect.

The fact of the matter was, of course, she just very much enjoyed being with him; much preferred his company to that of anyone else she had ever known. Sadly, though, unless she was very sensible, and swiftly erected a barrier between them, she might easily find herself falling hopelessly in love with a gentleman who in reality was far beyond her touch. Or had she, a taunting little voice queried, left it rather too late even to make the attempt?

With this very real possibility weighing heavily on her mind, Emma set about the task of making herself look more presentable, and gained a modicum of satisfaction, as she left the bedchamber a short time later, from the fact that, on the surface at least, she appeared as neat as wax, even if her thoughts and emotions remained an untidy, jumbled mass of contradictions.

As she descended the stairs, she clearly heard that attractive masculine voice bidding both Martha and Samuel to enter the private parlour. She hoped to be excluded from the meeting. Someone else, however, had other ideas, and arrested her progress across the coffee room by bidding her join the little gathering.

Having swiftly come to the conclusion that attempting to avoid all contact with him would be a complete waste of time while he remained at the Ashworth Arms, especially as he had proved already that he was not above seeking her out when he chose to do so, and that trying to distance herself was not the solution to her present predicament, she acquiesced to his request, but made it clear, as she entered the parlour, that she would be unable to remain for very long, as she must return to the kitchen shortly.

'Lucy's keeping an eye on the bread,' Martha assured her, at her most grim. 'And I've warned her that if she dares to ruin a second batch she'll receive a sound box round the ears!'

No one appeared to doubt that the landlady would carry out the threat, least of all Benedict who drew out the chair next to his own, and waited for Emma to oblige him before seating himself at the table. He then wasted no further time in confessing his real reason for putting up at the Ashworth Arms.

'So that's why you're here, sir!' Samuel brought his massive fist down on the table, very nearly spilling the contents of the two filled tankards he had placed on the shiny surface only minutes before. 'I knew it! I told Martha there was more to poor Dr Hammond's death.'

'And what made you think so, Mr Rudge?'

'Because that very day Tom Pike sees two men skulking in the lane, sir, and that night, while he were about his—er—business, as yer might say, he spied 'em again, skulking behind the hedge, waiting like.'

Benedict had a pretty shrewd idea of precisely what occupation Mr Pike was engaged in, which possibly explained why he had not come forward to volunteer any information. Emma had been absolutely right when she had suggested it would be beneficial taking these two into his confidence!

Deciding it might be wise at this early stage not to probe too deeply into the affairs of the enterprising Mr Pike, he said, 'Which would suggest they knew the doctor, or someone, would be travelling along that infrequently used lane on that particular night.' He then went on to relate what he had learned from Sir Lionel earlier in the day.

'Alice happens to be my niece, sir,' Martha informed him, looking faintly troubled. 'If she said she delivered Sir Lionel's note, then I for one wouldn't doubt that she did. She finishes at Sir Lionel's place most evenings at six, or thereabouts. I'll pop along to my sister's house and have a talk with her, when I have the time.'

'That would be of immense value, Mrs Rudge, thank you,' he responded, thereby very nearly winning a smile from the austere landlady. 'I understand from Emma that both of you were born in the village, and have lived here most all your lives. Perhaps you would be kind enough to tell me what you know about the Ashworth family.'

Although he betrayed mild surprise, Samuel didn't hesitate to confirm what Benedict had already discovered from Sir Lionel that day, 'Well, that's true enough, sir. Miss Isabel Ashworth and the late Lord Ashworth were twins.' He chuckled to himself. 'And Sir Lionel weren't spinning no yarn when he told you everyone in these parts always thought it were a great pity that Miss Isabel weren't a boy. Happen she were first born, too. She were the one with the brains, and the love of the land. Why, it were she who mostly looked after the house and the estate. Everyone's always felt she's looked upon it as her own.'

Martha nodded in agreement. 'I've been told, although I myself weren't here at the time, that that was why she was so put out when her brother upped and married, after a whirlwind romance, as you might say.'

Benedict's brows rose. 'The marriage was not planned?'

'No, sir.' Samuel took up the story. 'Seemingly, after a brief courtship in London, Lord Ashworth married and brought his young bride back to Ashworth Hall. Miss Isabel were right put out about it by all accounts.'

'Understandable, when you come to consider it,' Emma put in. 'Isabel no doubt considered herself mistress of the Hall, after virtually running the estate for so many years. Then for a perfect stranger to come along and usurp her position...well, it would be bound to make her peeved.'

'Aye, there you have the right of it, Em,' Samuel agreed. 'Began to behave quite unlike herself after Lady Ashworth arrived at the house. There were talk at the time that she paid regular visits to Squire Penlow's place. Which she never did before.'

'Ah, yes,' Benedict murmured, memory stirring. 'I believe I did hear mention of some wild goings-on at the late Squire's abode.'

'Disgusting, some of the tales I've heard!' Martha resembled nothing so much as an outraged hen. 'The Squire's son frequently had his friends to stay. And indecent women visiting the place at all hours too!'

'You can't call Miss Isabel indecent, m'dear,' Samuel pointed out. 'And even if it were true that she did fall in with bad company, she didn't do so for long. She upped and left and went to live with some maiden aunt, as I recall.'

Lines of deep thought etched Benedict's high, intelligent brow. 'And only returned when she learned that her sister-in-law had died giving birth to Clarissa Ashworth, I understand?'

'Aye, that's right, sir,' Samuel confirmed.' And took charge again, just as though she'd never been away. Which, I might add, was a blessing. I heard tell the baby weren't expected to live, neither. But Miss Isabel, well, she gets a new nursemaid to look after the child, though whether it were this that saved the little mite, or that Dr Hammond arrived in the village at about that time, I couldn't rightly say. I do know that Miss Isabel called on his services not long after he arrived.'

'And she has taken care of the girl ever since,' Benedict murmured.

'Like her own daughter, as you might say,' Samuel responded, and Emma noticed a distinctly speculative gleam appear in Benedict's blue eyes.

'Can you recall exactly how long Isabel was absent from Ashworth Hall?' Benedict asked, after a moment's silence.

Samuel rubbed his fingers back and forth across the slight stubble on his chin. 'Five or six months, or thereabouts, I'd say.'

'I see,' Benedict responded, the speculative gleam increasing marginally before he changed the subject by asking about the younger brother.

'Oh, everyone in these parts liked Mr George,' Martha didn't hesitate to confirm. 'He were a real nice young gentleman. A bit wild, I suppose, but not like the Squire's son.'

'I gained the impression from Sir Lionel that he didn't get along too well with his elder brother and sister.'

'Well, that I couldn't say, Mr Grantley,' she responded, scrupulously truthful. 'But it's been my experience when there's twins in a family that they do tend to stick together. And there was some six or seven years between Mr George and the other two. All I do know is that if the son is anything like his father, the new Lord Ashworth will be most welcome here. I overheard Mrs Wright mention earlier that there was to be a party up at the Hall to celebrate Miss Clarissa's eighteenth birthday next week. It would be nice if he arrived in time for that.'

'Ah yes, a timely reminder, Mrs Rudge!' Eyes still glinting, only this time with an unmistakable hint of mischief, Benedict turned to Emma. 'You have been invited to attend that celebration.'

She didn't attempt to hide her astonishment. 'What? You cannot be serious!'

'And I cannot imagine why you might suppose I should lie,' Benedict returned, deliberately sounding haughty. 'But if you require confirmation, you may ask Harry when he returns from his trip to Andover with the Hammonds. Which reminds me,' he added, turning to Mrs Rudge whose expression was now faintly troubled. 'Do not be afraid that Emma will not be suitably chaperoned for the occasion. Both Lavinia Hammond and her daughter, Deborah, will also be travelling in my carriage, so everything will be quite in order.'

A look of approval instantly erased the worried frown. 'Well, that's all right then, sir.'

'No, it is not all right!' Emma countered, feeling as if she were being swept away into terra incognita on an unstoppable tide. 'How can I possibly attend? I would be totally out of place at such an occasion and with such people.'

'Do not be ridiculous, girl!' It was difficult to say who was most startled by the steely element in Benedict's voice. 'You are the daughter of a gentleman, and you are closely related, unless I much mistake the matter, to one of the most respected and influential families in Derbyshire.'

'Why, I do believe you're right, sir,' Martha announced. 'I recall the late Reverend Lynn, God rest his soul, mentioning once that his family lived in that part of the country.'

'Well, and what of it?' Emma responded, having at last recovered from the shock of discovering that there was a surprisingly hard, determined streak in the personable Mr Grantley's nature. 'If you suppose for a moment that I would trade on the fact that I have some influential relations to gain entry into polite society, you are far and away out.'

'No one who knows you would ever suppose any such thing,' Benedict assured her. 'You will attend the party because I wish it, and will be there under my protection.'

Much moved by this assurance, Emma hovered for a moment, tantalised by the prospect of being amongst those at a fashionable event, before fear of the unknown shattered the pleasurable vision her mind's eye was conjuring up of her swirling about a dance floor on a certain gentleman's arm.

She shook her head. 'No, impossible. Besides, I have nothing suitable to wear. And before you suggest I don the dress I wore for Lavinia's dinner-party,' she added in response to the faintly sardonic lift of one dark brow, 'you may save your breath. It would not be in the least appropriate to wear for such an occasion as a formal evening party.'

'But I could make you something that would be,' Martha surprised everyone by announcing. 'I asked Mrs Hammond if she would kindly purchase a length of silk for me when she made her recent trip to London. I intended to make up a new dress for you as a surprise, Emma. I've got almost a week to do it, which ought to be ample time. You might be gifted where cooking is concerned,' she added, 'but you're no match for me with a needle.'

Emma was about to protest further when she distinctly detected a certain highly suspicious odour. 'If that is my bread burning…' she muttered, before disappearing into the coffee room.

Benedict rose also. 'Then I shall leave her attire in your very capable hands, Mrs Rudge,' he announced, looking very well pleased with himself.

Martha watched him pick up his tankard and leave the room, before turning to her husband, the troubled look once again back in her eyes. 'I wonder if I did the right thing, Sam, offering to make the gown.'

'Course you did, m'dear. You'll do a splendid job.'

'I wasn't meaning that, exactly.'

He reached out his arm to clasp thin shoulders. 'I know you weren't, but you can rest easy. Just because I'm a man don't mean I don't notice things. And I'll tell you this, Martha—our Emma will never come to any harm at that gentleman's hands.'

Chapter Seven

'You might think it marvellous, Deborah, but I most certainly do not!' Emma's nerves were very much on edge, and she wasn't attempting to conceal the fact. 'I am being coerced by that wretched man into accompanying him to the party. And by Martha, too, would you believe? It was she who insisted I come here this morning to borrow your mother's most recent fashion journals. I really cannot understand what has come over her. She's determined I shall be the belle of the ball.'

'And so you shall be,' Deborah assured her, striving not to add to Emma's obvious vexation by laughing. She simply couldn't understand why her dear, and normally sensible, friend should appear so flustered, and echoed her thoughts aloud. 'After all, Em, it isn't as if you've never attended such affairs. I clearly recall your mentioning once that you frequently accompanied your father, after your mother had died, to numerous parties.'

Emma had almost forgotten that. It seemed such a long time ago now, when she and her father had attended social evenings held by the more affluent families in the parish. 'But that was different, Debbie. My father was a well-respected gentleman, and I was his daughter.' She shrugged. 'Now, I'm just—'

'And you still are respected by those who know you well,' Deborah interrupted, refusing to allow Emma to belittle herself further. 'No one meeting you for the first time would have the least difficulty in appreciating your gentility. Mr Grantley evidently doesn't think any less of you because you have been forced to make your own way in the world. When you came here to dine the other evening, I could tell at once that he admired you, Em. And I was by no means the only one to notice, either. Why, even Harry remarked that he'd never known his uncle display such a marked partiality for a particular female's company before.'

Emma had little difficulty in quelling the pleasurable sensation which this intelligence engendered by silently reminding herself that Mr Grantley's displays of attention stemmed from nothing more meaningful than a desire to enlist her aid in uncovering the truth surrounding Dr Hammond's demise. That, in all probability, was the sole reason why he was so keen for her to attend the party at Ashworth Hall. No doubt he thought that she might be more successful in quizzing the servants further than he would be, should the opportunity arise. It would have been flattering to suppose that Benedict wished to squire her to the party because he found her company agreeable, but she refused to delude herself, and swiftly turned her thoughts to something which had continued to puzzle her, before her sombre reflections had a chance to depress her still further.

'I would dearly love to know how he managed to persuade Miss Ashworth to include me among her guests.' She sat bolt upright as a dreadful possibility suddenly occurred to her. 'I'll wager she doesn't even know! Oh, that wretched man! I'll lay a monkey he quite brazenly asked if he might bring a companion, knowing full well that Miss Ashworth is far too well bred to enquire precisely whom he wished to escort.'

Deborah's shrug betrayed the fact that she didn't consider this very real possibility in the least important, even before she said, 'Well, and what of it?'

'What of it?' Emma echoed, fearing her friend might well have fallen victim already to a certain black-haired gentleman's pernicious influence. 'I should have thought it obvious to anyone possessing a ha'p'orth of sensibility. I simply won't go if it turns out to be—'

Emma caught herself up abruptly as the door opened and Mrs Hammond, carrying a substantial pile of the requested journals, returned to the parlour.

It swiftly became apparent, as they began to scan the pages for dresses that would compliment a young woman who was not precisely straight out of the schoolroom, that Lavinia, like her daughter, was keen for Emma to attend the party, and for a while Emma was able to forget those niggling reservations as she was swept along on the tide of her friends' enthusiasm. Unfortunately her conscience was not quite accommodating enough to allow her to dwell overlong on the delightful prospect of being dressed for once in her life in the prevailing mode, for no sooner had she left the Hammonds' house, armed with three of the journals, than those wretched misgivings returned to plague her, and she determined to discover the truth about her surprising invitation.

She was destined not to remain in ignorance for much longer. When she arrived back at the inn a few minutes later, entering by way of the kitchen door, it was to discover the being admirably capable of satisfying her curiosity seated at the kitchen table, happily conversing with the landlady like some lifelong bosom bow.

This in itself came as no great surprise to Emma. Martha's attitude towards Mr Grantley had undergone a dramatic change since he had taken her and Samuel into his confidence the previous afternoon. Now she simply could not do enough for him. It really was quite nauseating!

'Ah, so there you are, Emma!' Martha was swiftly proving to one and all that she could smile just as readily as anyone else when she was of a mind to do so. 'And you've managed to discover something you like in Mrs Hammond's journals. Excellent! I can make a start on your new gown today!'

'There may be no need for you to put yourself to the trouble.' Emma wasn't immediately aware that her evident lack of enthusiasm had dimmed Martha's smile, for she was staring fixedly at the other occupant of the table. 'Tell me, Mr Grantley, would I be correct in thinking that Miss Ashworth is not aware that it is I you wish to escort to her niece's birthday party?' she demanded to know, desperately striving not to permit the warmth she perceived in his blue eyes to diminish her resolve.

Broad shoulders rose in a shrug. 'I really couldn't say whether she does or not, Emma.'

'No, I thought not.' After carelessly tossing the journals down on the table, she went across the room to collect a clean apron. 'There's no need for you to cut out the dress, Martha,' she added, pausing by the kitchen door. 'I shan't be going to the party.'

Benedict easily prevented Martha from following by placing a gently restraining hand on her arm as she made to rise. 'No, I'll talk to her. You take the opportunity to browse through those fashion journals. She may yet come to appreciate a new gown.'

He discovered his quarry busily engaged with the butter churn in the dairy, and knew at once by the stubborn set of that delightful little chin that he was going to find it no easy task to persuade her to change her mind. Undeterred, he made use of the door jamb by leaning his broad shoulders against it, before folding his arms across his chest, and studying her in silence, his expression clearly betraying a combination of amusement and faint exasperation.

Emma didn't feign ignorance of his presence; nor did she attempt to ignore the look he was casting her. 'I don't know why you're standing there, regarding me as though I were some unruly child, Mr Grantley. You must realise why I cannot possibly accompany you to the party on Friday.'

'No, I'm afraid I don't. Pray, do enlighten me.'

The blasé response almost had Emma gaping in astonishment. Surely he was being deliberately obtuse? Yet, she was forced to own that there was nothing in his expression to suggest that he was being anything other than totally sincere. She sighed, much

moved by the fact that he evidently considered her
worthy enough to attend the party, but refused to permit this to sway her.

'I would not be welcome there, Ben, that is why,'
she said softly, in an attempt to make him understand
that others would never come to view her in such a
favourable light. 'Miss Ashworth would never dream
of inviting someone like me to her home. I suspect
that when she acquiesced to your including another in
your party, she supposed that you would be escorting
someone of undeniable quality, someone of your own
class.'

'And that is precisely what I shall be doing.' Bridg-
ing the distance between them in three giant strides,
Benedict grasped her arms just above the elbows, and
administered a slight shake, while forcing her to face
him squarely. 'So I want no more of this foolish talk,
understand?'

Although his hold was secure, it was not ungentle,
unlike the steely edge Emma could clearly discern in
his voice, a further example had she needed one that
the amiable Mr Grantley could be quite ruthlessly determined when he chose. To her surprise she didn't
find this display of male dominance in the least dis-
tasteful. In fact, much to her intense amazement, she
discovered she rather liked it, most especially the wonderful feeling of security the touch of those long-
fingered hands was beginning to engender. Undoubtedly this man would know well how to guard his own.
It would be a fortunate lady indeed who succeeded in
winning his regard, and who would then experience
the sheer joy of being protectively held in those strong,
muscular arms. Oh, how she wished…

Aghast at where her wayward thoughts were leading, Emma broke free of his clasp, before forcing herself once again to meet a faintly quizzical gaze which left her with the uncomfortable feeling that he wasn't totally ignorant of what had been passing through her mind.

Her first impulse was to flee the dairy, to put as much distance as she could between them, but she curbed it. After all, she couldn't possibly hide from him indefinitely; worse still, she could never hope to escape from her own rapidly increasing regard.

Somehow summoning up sufficient courage to stand her ground, she said, 'I have already mentioned, sir, that I would never stoop so low as to trade on my kinship with the wealthy Derbyshire Lynns, none of whom I have ever met, in an attempt to gain acceptance into polite society.'

'And as I have already assured you that would never cross my mind for a moment. I have, however, taken it upon myself to write to Charles, informing him of your existence.' He could not forbear a smile at the look of utter bewilderment which took possession of her delicate features. 'Charles Lynn, unless I much mistake the matter, is your cousin, Emma, and the head of that particular branch of your family. It just so happens that he's a very good friend of mine. We were up at Oxford together.'

'And you've written to him about me?' Indignation replaced bewilderment. 'The devil you have, sir!'

'Now that is not the sort of language I expect to hear passing a young lady's lips!' he didn't hesitate to inform her sternly, waving an admonishing finger. 'And I want to hear no more of it, understand? Nor do I wish to hear any more feeble excuses why you shouldn't attend this party. Of course you'll go!' he went on masterfully, suppressing a smile as her expression changed yet again to one of indignant outrage. 'Deborah and her mother would be most disappointed if you did not take your seat in my carriage, not to mention Harry. Furthermore, I refuse to be denied the pleasure of escorting the only female I have any desire to have on my arm.'

With which he sauntered from the dairy, leaving Emma with absolutely nothing to say, and not quite knowing whether to feel annoyed by his high-handed attitude, or deliriously happy because he truly did wish to escort her to the party.

As Benedict, for reasons best known to himself, had decided to accept Colonel Meecham's invitation to dine, Emma was destined not to see him for the rest of the day. This, however, did not prevent him from intruding into her thoughts all too often, and although she tried desperately hard to check those ever-increasing romantic images of herself locked in a pair of well-muscled arms, she was, by the time the evening was well advanced, no longer foolishly striving to convince herself that she had not, for the very first time in her life, fallen hopelessly in love.

The sound of a carriage pulling up in the yard had her foolish heart turning a somersault, and Benedict's sudden appearance in the doorway a few moments later did little to improve that ungovernable organ's increasingly wayward behaviour. Well, she might now be powerless to suppress tender feelings towards Mr Grantley, she told herself sternly, but at least she could attempt to keep them well hidden. He had a purpose in coming here to Ashworth Magna, and she must strive not to lose sight of this fact, and make his situation uncomfortable by revealing her feelings, no matter how difficult that might prove to be.

Fortunately help was at hand on this occasion in the form of Martha who, unlike Emma, did not attempt to disguise her delight at his early return. 'Why, Mr Grantley! I didn't expect to see you back here for another hour at least.'

Benedict transferred his gaze from the young woman who was busily cleaning the surface of the table, and who had acknowledged his presence with the merest nod of her head, to the more welcoming landlady.

'The Meechams dine early, and as my time could be better spent here than whiling away the evening hours playing billiards, I decided to leave Harry to challenge the Colonel.' Narrow-eyed, he glanced again in the direction of the table. 'I perceive young madam here hasn't got over her sulks yet?'

Martha was unable to suppress a chuckle. 'I wouldn't go as far as to say that, sir, but she's certainly been in an odd mood all day. In a world of her own, as you might say.'

'Would you two mind very much not discussing me as though I were not here!' Emma snapped, managing to encompass them both in a darkling look. 'And didn't you have something to tell Mr Grantley, Martha?' she reminded her.

'Ah, yes! So I did,' she confirmed, thereby instantly regaining his full attention. 'I paid a visit to my sister earlier, sir, and managed to have a private word with my niece Alice. It turns out that she didn't deliver that letter to Dr Hammond herself. It was Lucius Flint who pushed it under the door.'

Memory stirred. Benedict distinctly recalled Sir Lionel mentioning that particular name on the night he had dined at his house. 'Am I correct in thinking that Flint is the Ashworths' steward?'

'Aye, that's right, sir.' The firm set, which had been less noticeable of late, returned to Martha's mouth. 'And he's not well liked in these parts, I can tell you. Still,' she shrugged, 'I don't think anyone who took Mr Granger's position would have been well received. Now, he was a nice gentleman. Everybody liked him, and no one believed that he'd been lining his pockets with profits from—'

'I'm sorry, Mrs Rudge,' Benedict interrupted, 'I do not perfectly understand. Could you explain a little more fully? Firstly, by telling me exactly who Mr Granger is.'

'He held the position of steward up at the Hall before Flint took over. He'd been there for about five years, and doing an excellent job by all accounts. The next thing we heard was that he'd been dismissed because of some discrepancies Miss Ashworth had discovered in the estate books, shortly after she came back to live at the Hall, and that there weasel-faced Flint had taken Mr Granger's place.'

Emma watched those strikingly coloured eyes narrowing speculatively. 'You think that might be in some way significant?' she prompted, when he continued to gaze fixedly at the floor. 'I don't see how it could possibly have any bearing on Dr Hammond's death. It all happened so long ago.'

'True. But one should always take into considera-tion that which might at first seem the most insignif-icant detail.' Benedict then addressed himself to Mar-tha. 'Let us return to the matter of Sir Lionel's letter. What exactly did your niece tell you earlier?'

'She said that Sir Lionel's butler gave her the letter to deliver, as she needed to walk into the village that morning on an errand. She came upon Lucius Flint in the lane. Fortunately Alice, like Emma here, don't of-fer him any encouragement, but seemingly she didn't object to him bearing her company. When they reached the doctor's, he offered to take the note up to the house. She said that she didn't actually see him knock, on account of one of the villagers stopping to pass the time of day, but she clearly remembered see-ing him bend to push the letter under the door.'

'Which doesn't necessarily mean that he did so,' Emma remarked, reading Benedict's thoughts with re-markable accuracy, and thereby earning herself a warm look of approval. She frowned as something else occurred to her. 'I think it's safe to assume that Alice probably knew that her master would be delayed in Salisbury that evening. It is also possible that she knew what Sir Lionel's letter contained.' Her frown grew more pronounced. 'I wonder if, at some point during their walk to the village, she happened to tell Flint that Sir Lionel was having to cancel the chess evening with his good friend the doctor.'

'I never thought to ask her that,' Martha freely ad-mitted, looking faintly annoyed with herself for this oversight. 'But I'll make a point of doing so the next time I see her.'

'I would be grateful if you would, Mrs Rudge, be-

cause it might prove of real significance,' Benedict
assured her, before wandering across to the door leading to the passageway. 'And I, in the meantime, with
your assistance, will further my acquaintance with
your patrons in the tap.'

As Emma watched them leave, she found herself
once again taking stock of her far-from-idyllic situation. No matter how welcome he was now being made
to feel, it was unlikely that Benedict would wish to
put up at the inn for longer than was absolutely necessary. Therefore she might as well enjoy his company
for the week or two he might possibly remain.

She wasn't so foolish as to suppose that she would
find it easy to conceal the depths of her feelings for
the duration of his stay, and maintain the wonderful
camaraderie which had surprisingly existed between
them from the first. None the less, any attempt at
avoidance on her part would, she felt sure, swiftly alert
that large brain of his to the true state of her heart.
Which would inevitably lead to her suffering the hu-
miliation of rejection. Gentlemen of Benedict's station
in life, she reminded herself, did not foolishly fall in
love with tavern wenches. When they looked about for
a wife, they searched among those highborn ladies of
the *ton*.

Desperately striving not to allow this unpalatable
truth to send her plummeting to the depths of despair,
Emma turned her attention to the pies she had made
a little earlier and, after piling them neatly on a large
plate, carried them through to the tap, where she discovered Benedict propped against one end of the
counter, already deep in conversation with several regular customers. She did not find this in the least sur-

prising, for although his dress alone proclaimed his vastly superior status, he possessed the innate ability to converse easily with people from a lower station in life than his own, without making them feel in any way inferior.

While making herself useful by pouring several tankards of Samuel's very popular home-brewed ale, Emma noticed the arrival of a new customer, and began to edge her way down to the end of the counter without, she hoped, making her intentions obvious.

'You might be interested to know,' she said, easily managing to gain Benedict's attention, 'that Lucius Flint has decided to honour us with one of his rare visits.'

Casually glancing over his shoulder, Benedict took quick stock of the wiry, middle-aged man making his way towards the counter, and was not unduly amazed to find himself on the receiving end of a narrow-eyed, assessing look.

'It is hardly surprising you have gained his interest,' Emma remarked in an undertone, as she too noticed the swift appraising stare from a pair of hard, dark eyes. 'You don't precisely blend in with your surroundings. It isn't often we have such fashionably attired gentleman propping up our counter. Your presence here is bound to give rise to a degree of speculation.'

This singularly failed to extract any response and, as he continued to regard her in silence, without any vestige of that wonderful smile which she had grown accustomed to receiving, she gained the distinct impression that he was not wholly pleased about something this evening.

'Did you not manage to discover anything of interest from our regulars?' she ventured, naturally assuming that this must be the reason for his faintly disenchanted state. 'It's early days yet, remember. It might take some time before you win their confidence.'

'Oh, I learned the odd interesting snippet. Discovered something of interest earlier, too, when I dined with the Meechams. One or two of the Colonel's servants worked in the house when the property was owned by Squire Penlow, and remember well the dreadful goings-on. Which reminds me,' he added, after sampling the contents of his tankard. 'The Colonel's pleased to hear that you intend to be among the guests at Ashworth Hall on Friday, and instructed me to inform you that he expects you to save him a dance.'

'Oh, Lord!' Her expression clearly betrayed dismay. 'That will undoubtedly prove an interesting spectacle!'

This did induce a smile. 'It is quite amazing the effect a very pretty countenance can have on the most case-hardened male.' His eyes strayed to the door behind her as it opened. 'Ah, Mrs Rudge! And not a moment too soon!'

Martha's smile faded the instant her eyes fell upon Emma. 'And what, may I ask, are you doing in here, young lady? Sam and Lucy can manage perfectly well on their own. We're not busy this evening. Your time would be better spent with me upstairs, helping to make your new gown.'

If Emma supposed the glance of earnest appeal she instinctively cast in his direction would gain his support, Benedict swiftly disabused her. 'I could not agree with you more. A common tap is no place for you, young lady.'

It was not so much the strong, masculine hand pressed against the small of her back forcibly ejecting her from the room that Emma very much resented as the taproom door being firmly closed against her a moment or two later.

Smouldering with resentment, she stalked down the passageway towards the kitchen. The wretched man was taking far too much upon himself. She might have unwittingly allowed herself to fall desperately in love with Benedict Grantley, but be damned if she would allow him to dictate what she might or might not do!

Chapter Eight

It was while she was seated before the dressing table early on Friday evening, having her hair arranged in a more elaborate style by Martha for the party, that Emma began to appreciate just how much authority Mr Benedict Grantley was now beginning to wield at the Ashworth Arms.

The very day after the wretched creature had had the sheer effrontery to evict her forcibly from the tap, Samuel had tactfully requested her not to venture in there again, because, as he explained a little sheepishly, 'Mr Grantley don't rightly think it fitting for a lady to be working behind the counter.' And if that were not bad enough, later that very same day, Martha had informed her that she wasn't to serve any further meals in the private parlour either, as his high-and-mightiness preferred Lucy waiting at table, although he had no objection whatsoever to her continuing to prepare their food.

Inwardly she had fumed at this crass interference, and had been on the verge of seeking him out to take him roundly to task for daring to dictate what she may or may not do, when wiser counsel had prevailed. Swallowing her pride, hard though it had been at the time to do so, she had accepted these dictates with as much grace as she could muster, simply because it would inevitably mean that she would see less of him. Which, as things had turned out, certainly proved to be the case.

Silently she was forced to concede that at least during the past week she had not been precisely stretched to the limits in endeavouring to keep those more tender feelings from surfacing. Benedict had been away from the inn for much of the time. He had received several dinner invitations. One, surprisingly enough, had been penned by none other than Isabel Ashworth, which he had promptly accepted.

Just what he had managed to discover Emma had no way of knowing, for she had not seen him since he had set out in the carriage for Ashworth Hall the previous evening. Nor had she had the opportunity to discover from Harry how well his uncle's investigations were progressing, for he too had been out and about for much of the time, either bearing his uncle company, or taking advantage of the kind invitation issued by Sir Lionel to fish his well-stocked trout stream.

On the few occasions Emma had seen Benedict during recent days, she had somehow managed to overcome the temptation to gaze at him like some lovesick schoolgirl. None the less, his sudden appearances in the kitchen never failed to send her pulse racing and her foolish young heart pounding so loudly that she felt he must surely hear it. Undoubtedly tonight would turn out to be her greatest test thus far. She could only hope that both Lavinia and Deborah's presence would prove beneficial, and that she would not find herself too frequently in the sole company of that gentleman who, with precious little effort it seemed, had succeeded in winning her love.

'Now, Miss Em, tell me what you think of that.'

Thus adjured, she raised her eyes to see the spray of artificial flowers, cunningly fashioned from the same material as the dress, nestling amongst the riot of shining curls. 'You have lost none of your skill, Martha. I have tended to forget during these past years just what an accomplished lady's maid you used to be.'

Whilst Martha, looking very well pleased with herself, went over to the wardrobe to collect the primrose-coloured dress which she had worked on with such loving care for so many hours in order to have it finished for the party, Emma donned the pearl necklace and earrings which had once belonged to her mother, before finally stepping into the gown.

Once the last button had been securely fastened, Martha coaxed Emma across to see the finished result in the full length mirror. Never had she seen her one-time charge look more lovely. The gown fitted the slender figure perfectly, its colour enhancing the tints in the rich brown hair and the golden flecks in the striking eyes. Consequently she was rather taken aback to see a slight frown marring the perfection of Emma's forehead.

'What is it, dear? Is something not quite to your liking?'

Bitterly regretting now that she hadn't shown more interest in selecting the exact style for her new dress,

Emma continued to gaze at what she considered to be an indecent amount of cleavage erupting from the square-cut neckline. The exquisite pleating on the bodice, and the intricate detail on the delicate puff sleeves, the dress's only adornments, quite naturally focused one's attention on the upper part of the gown.

'It is beautiful, Martha…except…well…I cannot help wondering whether it is not just a—er—trifle immodest.'

'Nonsense, child! I have it on the best authority that ladies in London frequently wear their gowns much lower.'

An appalling possibility suddenly occurred to Emma. 'Whose authority, may I ask?' she demanded to know, eyes narrowing suspiciously.

No response was forthcoming, but Martha's faintly guarded expression was answer enough. 'Do you mean to tell me that—that man had the final say in the fashioning of this garment?' It was bad enough having to kowtow to his edicts on what she might or might not do about the inn, without having to suffer the indignity of being instructed on how she must dress. 'Well, really! That wretched man is taking far too much upon himself!'

'Now, now, Emma dear. He was only trying to be helpful,' Martha soothed, before hurriedly arranging a white shawl, beautifully embroidered with gold-coloured thread, about Emma's slender shoulders and placing a delicately painted chicken-skin fan in one gloved hand.

Momentarily forgetting her grievances, Emma gazed at the exquisite accessories in wonder. 'But these are not mine. Where did they come from?'

'The fan is a gift from Samuel and me. And the shawl is a little something from—er—Mr Grantley. He made a special trip into Salisbury earlier in the week to buy it for you, and was kind enough to choose the fan too. He assured me that it is perfectly in order for young ladies to receive such small trifles when attending their first ball.'

'Hardly trifles, Martha,' Emma corrected. 'And I'm not attending my first ball.' She was having to do battle with her conscience. 'I really shouldn't accept such—'

'Of course you should!' Martha interrupted. 'It's only a little thank-you for all the hard work you've done for us over the years. Sam and I would be very upset if you spurned our gift.'

Emma wasn't precisely thinking about the fan. She could hardly accept that, however, and reject the shawl. Mr Grantley, it seemed, was not above resorting to cunning tactics to achieve his aims.

Bending forward a little, Emma placed a kiss on one faintly lined cheek. 'Thank you, Martha. It is lovely, and I shall cherish it always.'

She detected what sounded suspiciously like a sniff before being shooed from the bedchamber, and adjured to go directly down to the coffee room, where she discovered both her escorts awaiting her. As they were both standing with their backs to the stairs, and were deep in conversation with Samuel, neither was immediately aware of her presence, which granted her the opportunity to take stock of their attire without their knowing.

She did not suppose for a moment that either of them had come to Ashworth Magna expecting to attend any formal evening engagements, and quite naturally the amount of apparel they had been able to bring with them had been limited. Nevertheless both uncle and nephew were never less than immaculately attired, and this evening was no exception.

Undeniably Lucy Lampton ought to be given much of the credit for the superb condition of their clothes, for although Martha was frequently heard to scold her for her clumsiness, she was the first to admit that one would have to go a long way to find anyone more skilful with a flatiron, and the excellent care Lucy had taken of the gentlemen's apparel was certainly testament to this. There was not so much as a single crease, as far as Emma could detect, in either pair of tight-fitting pantaloons, and the long-tailed dark coats had been pressed to perfection.

Samuel, suddenly catching sight of her, broke off what he was saying. 'Why, Miss Em,' he announced, thereby alerting his companions' attention to her presence at last, 'you're as pretty as a picture! A real lady you look.'

'You most certainly do,' Harry agreed, appearing faintly surprised, as though he might have expected to see her clad in a dairymaid's apron.

Much to her dismay, Benedict came forward to assist her down the last two stairs. The feather-light touch of those warm fingers on her arm was hard enough to withstand, but the slow appraising glance, much more like an intimate caress, left every inch of her flesh tingling with such a wealth of sensations that she could only hope that the colour stealing into her cheeks might be attributed to dipping too deeply into the rouge-pot.

Unwittingly Harry came to her aid by reminding his uncle that they had best be on their way if they were not to be late, and then promptly led the way outside to the waiting carriage.

Emma would have much preferred not to have had Benedict sitting directly opposite, for she was very conscious, even after the Hammond ladies had joined them, of those wonderful violet eyes too frequently turned in her direction. Nevertheless she strove not to allow this to mar her delight in travelling in such a wonderfully comfortable conveyance. Sadly the treat was over all too quickly, and it seemed no time at all before one well-shaped masculine hand, reassuringly placed just above her elbow, was guiding her through the impressive stone entrance at Ashworth Hall.

If the aged butler was surprised to see her fashionably attired, and entering by way of the main entrance, he possessed good manners enough to conceal the fact. Which was more than could be said for Miss Clarissa Ashworth who, after one startled glance of recognition, could hardly bring herself to respond to Emma's polite greeting.

To some extent the warmth of Sir Lionel's welcome, and Miss Isabel Ashworth's politely worded greeting, more than made up for Clarissa's distinctly frosty reception. None the less Emma might have wished that the young woman in whose honour the party was being held had waited until they were out of earshot before exclaiming, 'What in the world is that creature doing here? Surely you didn't invite her, Aunt? Why, she's that serving wench from the village inn!'

Emma distinctly felt the tall figure beside her

stiffen, and glanced up in time to glimpse those masculine features hardened by a rare expression of anger.

She was by no means the only one to observe the suddenly tense set of those powerful shoulders. Sir Lionel, too, had not been slow to note the sudden stiffening in a certain muscular frame, and could quite cheerfully have throttled his ward.

'I shall take leave to inform you, Clarissa,' he took the opportunity to say, as they waited for the next group of guests to make their way across the hall to the salon, 'that your behaviour on occasions leaves much to be desired, unlike that of Miss Lynn, whose innate good manners are testament to her genteel birth. I shall also take leave to inform you that the young woman you have just so thoughtlessly maligned is closely related to the Derbyshire Lynns, a wealthy and most respected family.'

Clarissa appeared singularly unimpressed to learn this. Her aunt, on the other hand, betrayed mild interest. 'You seem very well informed, Sir Lionel.'

'I have learned something of that young woman's history from Grantley during these past days, Isabel. Naturally I have met her on several occasions before, when I have visited the Hammonds, and have always considered her a well-mannered young woman. I did not realise until recently, however, just how well connected she is.'

'If she is so well connected,' Clarissa put in, her lips curled in an unpleasant smirk, 'what in the world is she doing working in a common tavern?'

'She is there, young woman, through no fault of her own!' Sir Lionel answered, his sharp tone clear evidence of his continued displeasure. 'And you can think yourself lucky that you will never find yourself in a position whereby you are forced to earn a living. Your situation, however, might not be as secure as you imagine.'

The smirk was instantly wiped off her face. 'What—what do you mean, sir?'

'Merely that your continuing to reside in this house is far from certain. The estate now belongs to your cousin, Richard Ashworth. He would be well within his rights to request both you and your aunt to remove yourselves from under this roof.'

Having been escorted to the far side of the large salon by Benedict and left in Lavinia's care, Emma had been idly glancing about the room, when she had happened to catch a disturbing expression on a certain face which had sent an icy shiver feathering down the length of her spine.

'I hope you were not too upset by Miss Clarissa Ashworth's tactless remarks,' Lavinia ventured gently, after noting the direction in which Emma's troubled grey eyes were fixed. 'She's nothing but a silly, spoilt child.'

'W-what? Oh, no, no,' Emma hurriedly assured her, finally drawing her gaze away from the trio by the door, and managing a wry smile. 'Well, to be truthful, Lavinia, it was no more than I expected, and I'm determined not to allow it to lessen my enjoyment of the evening.'

Which was surprisingly enough perfectly true, and she began to look about her with renewed interest, spotting among the ever-increasing throng the odd person here and there whom she recognised.

Emma didn't suppose for a moment that the vast majority of guests present would rate this party as anything more than a small country affair, a pleasant way to spend an evening, but in no way grand. Yet to her it seemed such a splendid occasion, with all the ladies dressed in their finest laces and silks, and the gentlemen looking so very smart in their long-tailed coats and crisp, intricately tied neck-cloths.

She took a moment to glance down at her own gown, suddenly feeling rather foolish now for supposing that she might be considered indecently clad. Her *décolletage* was relatively modest compared to certain others on display that evening, a particular that Lavinia was not slow to point out when Emma voiced her former misgivings.

'I wouldn't go so far as to suggest that I would approve of such a gown for a chit straight out of the schoolroom, Emma,' Lavinia went on to admit, 'but you are hardly that, my dear. Furthermore, your figure is excellent, so I see no reason why you should attempt to conceal the fact.'

She too took a moment to cast a glance down at her own charming pearl-grey gown. 'If anyone's apparel is likely to be frowned upon this evening then it will undoubtedly be mine, but I shall not concern myself unduly over that. When I decided to accept the invitation, I had no intention of either Deborah or myself turning up in mourning attire.' A rather wistful little smile flickered about her mouth. 'Besides which, dear Henry wouldn't have wished us to deprive ourselves of a little pleasure from time to time. In fact, he did not approve of strict mourning at all, considering it a meaningless gesture of respect.'

For her part Emma certainly did not think any less of Lavinia for appearing in public so charmingly clad. The widow had undoubtedly grieved over her husband's untimely demise, and although she had just spoken about him quite without reserve, no one could mistake the lingering sadness in her voice.

It was a timely reminder, and Emma was determined to continue to aid Benedict in his endeavours. She didn't immediately perceive of what further use she could be to him; nor indeed why he should suppose that Dr Hammond's death was somehow linked with that of the servant-girl's. He was certainly suspicious about something, though, she decided, raising her eyes and easily locating his tall figure among the group of gentlemen who had congregated in the far corner of the room. So if the opportunity arose to have a little conversation with any one of the Ashworths' servants, she would certainly do her best to discover something which might be of help.

'You must not feel obliged to remain with us all evening,' Deborah remarked, swiftly gaining Emma's attention. 'Although I was very happy to attend the party, I promised Mama that I would not dance, but I expect to see you on the dance floor.'

'Oh, you shall,' Emma assured her. 'I've already promised to stand up with both Harry and his uncle.' She chose not to add that she had accepted one invitation very willingly and the other with the strongest misgivings, most especially as it had been a request for the first waltz, where bodily contact was unavoidable.

'And it would appear that your hand is about to be demanded for the first set of country dances,' Deborah

did not hesitate to inform her, ineffectually suppressing a chuckle, and Emma turned her head in the direction of her friend's wickedly mischievous gaze to
discover Colonel Meecham heading purposefully in
her direction.

Benedict too had followed the amorous Colonel's
progress across the room, and had glimpsed the look
of comical dismay flit briefly over Emma's delicate
features. It came as no great surprise to see Emma rise
instantly to her feet, and graciously accompany her
portly admirer to that area in the salon set out for
dancing. Her nature was such that she would never
hurt anyone's feelings if she could possibly avoid it.

Edging away from the small cluster of gentlemen
who were very content to lament the ills of the world,
Benedict continued to study the progress of the dance.
It came as no great surprise to him, either, to discover
that Emma performed the steps with effortless grace,
as light on her feet as any professional dancer. Which
was possibly just as well, he mused, for she was going
to need to be swift of foot if she was to stand the
remotest chance of avoiding a collision with her en-
thusiastic partner, whose performance was not short
on verve, but was lamentably lacking in elegance.

'She is a charming young woman, Grantley,' a
voice unexpectedly announced, and Benedict turned to
discover Sir Lionel at his side. 'I wish I could say the
same of my ward. I hope Miss Lynn was not too upset
over Clarissa's thoughtless remarks.'

'She didn't appear unduly concerned, no.'

This in all probability might have been the case, but
the tone in which the response had been uttered left

Sir Lionel in little doubt of Benedict's continued annoyance.

He glanced beyond one well-muscled shoulder to where his ward, looking remarkably smug, now sat surrounded by a group of foolishly languishing young men, and experienced a return of his own ire.

'During my years on the Bench I have been forced to listen to numerous accounts of violence. Quite sickening, some of them, most especially those perpetrated against the weaker sex. Yet I would be less than honest, Grantley, if I didn't acknowledge that there have been occasions when the palm of my hand has quite itched to administer a slap to that ward of mine.'

A reluctant smile tugged at one corner of Benedict's mouth. 'I applaud self-restraint as a rule, sir. But I too would be less than honest if I did not own to the fact that I might have wished that you had yielded to temptation on occasions.'

Sir Lionel's deep rumble of appreciative laughter vanquished the faint atmosphere of restraint which had needlessly arisen between them, and for a few minutes they spoke quite without reserve, until the Baronet recalled the reason he had abandoned his position by the door in order to have a private word with the gentleman who had swiftly earned his respect.

'By the by, I received a communication from Richard Ashworth this morning. He's at last arrived in this country, and is at present in the capital. He plans to travel to Wiltshire in the very near future, although he did not specify precisely when.'

He saw the faint lines appear across the high, intelligent brow, and experienced a twinge of mild irritation. 'I wish you would take me fully into your confidence, Grantley,' he urged, having sensed the younger man's unwillingness to do this. 'I made it clear at the start that I wished to be kept informed of any small details which you might have unearthed concerning Hammond's death. Yet I have felt increasingly that you are reluctant to trust me.'

'Disabuse yourself of such a notion, sir. It is far from the truth,' Benedict assured him, his worried expression still very much in evidence. 'It is just that I am disinclined to point an accusing finger at anyone unless I am very sure of my facts. As yet I am far from certain, and, until I am, I would prefer to keep my suspicions, for that is all they are, to myself.'

He regarded the older man intently for a moment. 'There is one task, however, that you might undertake when the young Lord Ashworth eventually does arrive here... Watch over him.'

'God damn it, Grantley!' Sir Lionel exploded. 'If you believe the boy's life might be in danger, then I demand to know on what grounds you base this judgement!'

Although he could appreciate the older man's wrath, Benedict remained doggedly determined not to commit himself quite yet. 'Sir, I do not believe for a moment that you would ever pass judgement on a fellow human being without first being very certain that the person standing before you had indeed committed some crime. And so it is with me. I have my suspicions—yes. But as yet that is all they are. A hazy picture is beginning to build up in my mind,' he felt obliged to admit in an attempt to soothe the Baronet's understandable ire, 'but there are still areas, many salient details, still to be uncovered before everything becomes perfectly clear.'

That winning smile, which even the vast majority of his own sex found hard to withstand, successfully induced a nod of assent from Sir Lionel. 'The truth of the matter is, sir,' he continued, 'I have suffered something of a highly pleasurable distraction since my arrival at Ashworth Magna which has tended to occupy my thoughts—a rare occurrence, believe me, but one that I shall never regret having experienced to my dying day.'

Benedict then turned his attention once again to those taking part in the dance in time to glimpse a second expression of dismay flit over a delicately featured face, and guessed at once what must have occurred. 'Yes, it is high time I successfully settled the matter of the delightful distraction. Then I shall be more able to concentrate on the business which prompted my visit to your county.'

Benedict's suspicions were correct: her energetic partner's less-than-perfect footwork had succeeded in wreaking the inevitable damage to the hem of her dress, and the instant the set came to an end, Emma sought the aid of the Ashworths' aged butler.

He cast her a glance of fatherly concern as he accompanied her from the salon. 'Don't you worry, Miss Emma,' he advised, leading the way across the lofty hall, and into a small parlour. 'You wait in here and I'll send Mary to you. She'll have the gown put to rights in a trice.'

Left alone, Emma made herself comfortable in one of the chairs, and looked about the room with interest. There were none of the elegant silk-covered sofas and fine Sheraton chairs which lined the walls of the salon, where the party was taking place, to be found in here; only an old-fashioned, low-backed sofa, festooned with an assortment of cushions, and three slightly worn winged chairs. Undoubtedly this room was used by the family when not entertaining guests as a place where they could sit in comfort and relax of an evening.

As the door opened again she withdrew her attention from the area of threadbare carpet near the hearth, and looked up to see Mary, her wide eyes clearly betraying astonishment, enter the room.

'So it is you, Miss Em! Why, I couldn't hardly believe it when Mr Troughton said as how it was you that had torn the hem of your dress.'

Emma could not forbear a smile at this somewhat artless disclosure. 'I can hardly believe I'm a guest in this house myself, Mary,' she confessed. 'And it was Colonel Meecham who tore my gown.'

Mary, having knelt on the floor to examine the rent, raised her eyes ceilingwards. 'You'd have thought a man of his age would have given up prancing about a dance floor long since. I only hope he don't ask Miss Clarissa to stand up with him again. Tore her gown at the party here last Christmas. And what a commotion she set up over that! Still,' Mary shrugged, 'it were a judgement on her is what I say. Shouldn't have been dancing at all, what with her father not six months in his grave.'

Emma's interest in Clarissa Ashworth was lukewarm at best. None the less, she wasn't prepared to waste the golden opportunity the damage to her dress had given her to discover something which might be of interest to Benedict.

'Miss Clarissa is something of a troublesome young mistress, is she, Mary?'

'She can be contrary at times, and no mistake. But she ain't as bad as certain people make out…providing she gets her own way, that is.'

Once again Emma found herself smiling at the young maid's honesty. 'I'm rather surprised to find you here. You're usually back home by this time, aren't you?'

'I always stays in the house when there are guests here, Miss Em. Miss Ashworth has her cousin, Mr Cedric, and his family staying here at present. So I'll remain here until they go next Thursday.' She paused in her sewing of the hem to cast Emma a swift glance. 'Mind you, what I says is it's high time Miss Isabel employed some extra staff. She always gets one or two of the village women to help out from time to time, but we're in desperate need of another maid, and a footman.'

The opening was there and Emma did not hesitate to take advantage of it. 'Ahh, yes! I remember Mrs Wright mentioning something about that. Miss Ashworth never did replace the maid who died here, did she?' No response was forthcoming this time, so she adopted a different tack. 'You must find the house somewhat changed these past months, Mary—what with Lord Ashworth's demise, the servant girl's—er—accident, and then poor Miss Spears's death. The place must seem quite empty.'

'It do that. Though I did hear tell that Miss Spears wrote Miss Isabel a letter saying that she had no intention of coming back here as she were going to stay in London with her sister. Which didn't surprise me none.' Mary cast a brief glance over her shoulder before adding in an undertone, 'Overheard Miss Spears talking to Sally one day. Sally were saying as how she wouldn't be here much longer on account of her coming into some money. And Miss Spears said that she didn't intend remaining neither, and had been looking for a new position. Mind, I don't know who were going to leave Sally money. Her father were only a farm labourer, like mine. She used to keep house for him until he died. If she did have some rich relations, why didn't she go and live with them, instead of coming down here? I reckon it were all talk myself.'

'Yes, you might be right,' Emma agreed, before remarking on the fact that it was strange Miss Spears should suddenly take it into her head to leave, after working for the Ashworth family for so many years.'

'Ahh, well, she were a funny old stick, and no mistake! Forever creeping about she were, and you'd never know she were there. Remember one occasion late last summer when Miss Isabel came out of the library, after she'd been talking with the steward in there, and caught Miss Spears hovering in the hall near the library door. Took her roundly to task, Miss Isabel did. Which ain't like her. She's so calm and quietly spoken as a rule, but she weren't then.'

Interesting, Emma thought, but said, 'Perhaps Miss Spears resented the reprimand and that was why she was so determined to leave at the first opportunity.'

'That I couldn't say.' Mary set a last neat stitch, before snipping the thread and rising to her feet. 'I can tell you something, though—Miss Ashworth ain't been quite herself since her brother died. She certainly weren't best pleased when she found out that her cousin, Mr Cedric, weren't the heir.' Again Mary cast a swift glance over her shoulder towards the door. 'Between you and me, Miss Em, I reckon Miss Ashworth were hoping to marry Miss Clarissa to Mr Cedric's son. There's been talk of it for years. Miss Ashworth's always had her niece's best interests at heart. Why, Miss Clarissa's own mother couldn't have taken better—' Mary broke off as the door opened, and none other than Miss Ashworth herself entered the room.

After discovering the urgent repair had been completed, she dismissed the maid, and then turned to Emma. 'I am here at Mr Grantley's behest, Miss Lynn. He wishes to remind you that you have promised him the first waltz, which is due to begin shortly.

'Such a charming gentleman, Mr Grantley,' she added, surprising Emma somewhat by accompanying her from the room, and pausing in the hall, which forced Emma to do likewise. 'Have you been acquainted with him for very long?'

'Only since his arrival at the inn, ma'am.'

'You must find life at the inn far different from the life you led in a vicarage, my dear,' Miss Ashworth remarked, thereby betraying the fact that she had at some point during the evening taken the trouble to discover something about her unexpected guest.

But why this sudden interest? Emma wondered. During the past five years Isabel Ashworth had never betrayed the least desire to get to know her a little better. Why, she had never once offered even to pass the time of day when they had attended the same service at church on Sundays!

'Indeed, it is vastly different, ma'am.'

'You must be kept very busy at present with two guests staying.' A slight frown added more lines to the high, intelligent brow. 'I wonder why Mr Grantley chose to put up at the inn, when he might have stayed with Lavinia Hammond? He is a close friend of hers, I understand?'

'They are certainly acquainted, ma'am, but I think it would be more accurate to say that Lavinia is a close friend of Mr Grantley's sister, Lady Agnes Fencham.'

Although her hostess appeared satisfied with this, Emma remained on her guard when the penetrating dark eyes continued to regard her rather searchingly. 'What, I wonder, can have brought him to this part of the world? Such a fashionable gentleman is usually to be found in town, enjoying the Season.'

Whether or not Benedict truly suspected that someone residing at Ashworth Hall might in some way be connected with Dr Hammond's death, Emma wasn't sure, but she did feel certain that, had he wished her to know his reason for being in the area, he would have taken Isabel Ashworth into his confidence on the evening he had dined here. Patently he did not wish her to know.

'Did he not mention, ma'am, when he dined with you the other evening, that he's on a sightseeing tour with his nephew? I understand they intend to move on to Somerset quite soon,' she responded, improvising quite beautifully, and wondering just at what point in her life she had learned to lie so convincingly.

Once again her hostess appeared satisfied with the explanation, for she gave a faint nod of her head before moving towards the salon, where they discovered the subject under discussion hovering near the entrance.

'I have brought her to you as I promised I should, Mr Grantley,' she announced, as he turned at their approach, that wonderful smile which never failed to send Emma's foolish young heart fluttering coming effortlessly to his lips.

'And perfectly restored to order, I see,' he responded, with a slight bow in their hostess's direction, before entwining Emma's arm through his.

'Was it perhaps my reason for being in the district that our esteemed hostess was endeavouring to discover a moment ago, my little love?' he astonished Emma by asking the instant they had moved a safe distance away.

His perspicacity was quite frightening on occasions, Emma was forced silently to concede. The dreadful possibility that he might already have penetrated her most secret thoughts crossed her mind before she confirmed his suspicions. 'Needless to say I didn't reveal anything. But I cannot imagine your real motive will remain a secret for very much longer. You've been asking a good many questions. People are bound to become suspicious.'

'Unless I very much mistake the matter our hostess is already suspicious. Do not underestimate her, Emma. Behind that quiet reserve lurks a keen intelligence and a deal of ruthlessness and cunning.'

She wasn't granted the opportunity to ponder over whether this was an accurate assessment or not, for the musicians hired for the evening struck up a chord, and her thoughts were suddenly turned in quite a different direction, as they took up their positions for the commencement of the waltz.

Although powerless to control the suddenly erratic behaviour of her pulse, as one masculine hand slid to her waist and the other captured her fingers, Emma was determined not to disgrace herself by missing a step, and resolutely focused her attention on the neat arrangement of the well-starched neckcloth, as they began to swirl about the room.

'The top of your head is quite charming, and your hair is looking particularly lovely tonight,' the faintly amused voice from above drawled, 'but I rather think I would prefer to look at your *beaux yeux*, my darling.'

How she wished he would not use such sweet endearments when addressing her! Raising her head, she looked into those dark blue eyes which had so swiftly melted her foolish young heart. And she was foolish to feel as she did, she silently reminded herself. Incredibly so! What possible future could they ever have together? It was madness even to suppose it might happen.

'What is it?' His gaze was suddenly searching. 'What has occurred to upset you?'

'Why, nothing…nothing at all!' The sceptical arch of one black brow proved that he was patently unimpressed by this assurance. 'Well, if I do seem a little preoccupied it is simply because I am determined not to step on your toes. Tell me,' she went on hurriedly, in an attempt to prevent him from probing further, 'have you stood up with the belle of the ball yet?'

'I am standing up with her.' He smiled at the telltale surge of colour. 'I rarely dance these days, Emma, and never with spoilt children.'

She did not pretend to misunderstand, and glanced fleetingly in the direction where Clarissa sat, still surrounded by several ardent admirers. 'I was not offended by what she said,' she declared. 'It was no more than I expected.'

'Be assured it will not occur again,' he pledged, his lips set in a grim line, and she swiftly changed the subject by asking him if he was acquainted with certain other members of the Ashworth family.

He allowed his gaze to stray momentarily to that spot in the room where a portly, middle-aged gentleman stood beside a chair, upon which a sallow female in a fussily adorned puce gown was seated. 'I take you to mean the abominable Cedric Ashworth, his insipid wife Caroline, and their obnoxious son Percy.' His brow rose. 'What is your interest in them, my sweet life?'

Once again forcing herself to ignore the endearment, she related what she had discovered a little earlier, and was surprised to find herself the recipient of a rather disapproving look.

'I did not bring you here this evening so that you might question the servants, and you will cease to do so forthwith,' he informed her in a tone which brooked no argument. 'You are here to enjoy yourself, my girl.'

Although she discovered herself once again very much resenting the dictatorial tone, the command itself was not in the least difficult to obey, and all too soon, it seemed, Emma found herself seated once more in the comfortable carriage, heading back towards the village.

Lavinia and Deborah did not linger over their farewells, and Harry too appeared eager to seek his bed, for no sooner had they entered the coffee room at the Ashworth Arms, where some considerate soul had left a lamp burning low, than he picked up one of the candles, lit it and did not delay in bidding a swift goodnight.

Once the sound of his footsteps along the passage-way above had died away, the inn seemed strangely quiet, and Emma was intensely aware that the man standing silently beside her was staring fixedly at her profile. She had never once experienced the least reticence in being alone with him, and she certainly wasn't the least uncomfortable now. Yet the atmosphere since Harry's departure seemed quite different, charged with something almost tangible.

'I think it is time we too sought our beds, sir,' she suggested, and reached up to throw the top bolt across the door, only to have her hand captured and held in a firm clasp.

'No, not yet,' he countered, his attractive voice thickened by a strangely husky note. 'There is something I wish to say to you first.'

As she found herself being turned to face him squarely, the shawl slipped a little off her shoulders, drawing her attention, and reminding her of a lamentable oversight on her part. 'And there is something I wish to say to you, sir. Firstly, I would like to thank you for perhaps the most pleasurable evening I've ever spent in my life.'

'The first of very, very many, I trust.'

She doubted it very much. It was highly unlikely that the Ashworths would ever honour her with a further invitation, but she chose not to remark upon that.

'And, secondly, I would like to thank you for this lovely shawl. I shall treasure it always.'

'Merely the first of many gifts I have every intention of bestowing upon you, Miss Emma Lynn.'

Thinking she must surely have misheard, she slowly raised her eyes to his, and almost found herself gasping at the depth of tenderness she could not fail to recognise in those striking blue depths, before the heavy lids lowered, successfully concealing the heart-melting glow, and she found herself very willingly imprisoned in two strong arms.

If the thought did cross her mind that she ought to stop this before it went any further, it certainly didn't remain there for very long. The instant his lips met hers, gently persuasive and forcing hers apart, she was suddenly prey to a rapidly increasing and unfamiliar need. It sprang from she knew not where, and swiftly gained complete mastery over both mind and body, so that when a moment later she found herself held fast against that powerful frame, she experienced not the least inclination to deny the response the increasing pressure of his mouth demanded.

She emerged from her first experience of masculine passion breathless, and not a little dazed, but not so much that she could not instantly recognise a gleam of triumph in the eyes which stared down at her, and the hint of satisfaction in that deeply attractive voice, as he remarked, 'Well, now, that was more than just a little revealing, was it not, Miss Emma Lynn?'

For his part Benedict had little difficulty in identifying both the embarrassment and bewilderment her expression clearly betrayed. He pulled her back against him so that she could not fail to detect the powerful beating of his heart, a heart that he experienced no reluctance at all in admitting belonged to her.

'Yes, I love you, Emma Lynn,' he reiterated, as she gazed up at him in awe-struck silence. 'Believe me, it came as no small surprise to me to discover that I had succumbed to an emotion I had begun to believe I was incapable of experiencing.' He brushed his lips across a brow that was betraying dawning wonder. 'And now I am sure that you love me too, so please do not mar this poignant moment by attempting to deny it.'

She could not suppress a slight smile at this. There was undeniably more than just a touch of arrogance in his nature, but this only seemed to enhance his charm. 'I wouldn't dream of doing anything so foolish,' she assured him, finding such blessed release in at last being able to acknowledge openly feelings which she had found increasingly difficult to conceal. She raised her hand to touch his cheek. 'Yes, I love you, Ben. Yet it has happened so quickly that it has left me a little bewildered, I suppose. I wouldn't have thought it possible to feel as I do on so short an acquaintance.'

There was an unmistakable tender note in his surprising rumble of laughter. 'And I never hoped to find a girl so much after my own heart. But I have, and I mean to keep her.' He gazed down at features which clearly revealed everything he needed to know. 'Will you allow me to take care of you? Will you leave here and place your future in my hands?'

Her lips parted, but the response he longed to hear was checked at the clearly discernible click of a door from somewhere above, swiftly followed by a whispered demand to know if Emma was there.

Although faintly irritated by the untimely interruption, Benedict found it impossible to suppress a crooked half-smile. 'Yes, Martha. She's here, and coming up directly.'

Evidently she seemed satisfied, for they detected the light tread on the landing before a further click announced the closing of the door. 'That woman would have made a formidable duenna,' he murmured, before turning to light their candles. 'But it is possibly just as well that she did remind me that I was born a gentleman.'

Handing Emma one of the candles, he placed his lips gently to one corner of her mouth. 'Yes, you go to bed now, my darling, whilst I still retain sufficient control to let you go. We shall talk again in the morning.'

Chapter Nine

By the time Emma had woken to discover what promised to be yet another perfect early summer's day, the cloud of happiness on which she had floated up to her bedchamber the night before, if not completely dissipated, had certainly developed rather large holes.

After sliding into bed, she had lain awake for quite some time, turning over in her mind what had passed between her and Benedict, and marvelling over the fact that the man she loved was every bit as much in love with her. Again and again she had recalled his declaration of love, cherishing his each and every word, until eventually it had occurred to her that it wasn't so much what he had said which might prove of vital importance to her future as that which he had yet to disclose.

A sigh escaped her as she turned over on her back to stare blindly up at the ceiling. She could only wonder at herself for being so unworldly as not to have realised at once that Benedict's offer to take care of her was tantamount to an invitation to become his mistress. After all, what else could it have been? A proposal of marriage? She shook her head. No, she would be foolish to attempt to delude herself. To be his mistress was the most she could ever hope to achieve.

The problem besetting her now, of course, was that, although she loved him beyond words, was she prepared to give up everything to be with him until he grew tired of her, and searched about for a replacement? Was she prepared to set aside all her rigid principles? Was she willing to risk losing the respect and friendship of those she held dear? Hard though it was, she must face the fact that, if she allowed her heart to rule her head, she would be forever an outcast, looked upon with scorn, and never accepted in polite company. Worse still was the heartrending possibility that, even if their association should prove lasting, Benedict in all probability would one day marry. Would she then be willing to share him with another woman?

Her stomach gave a painful lurch at the mere thought, yet she knew there was little point in not facing this very real possibility. Nor indeed was there any use in trying to avoid the fact that she had a heart-breaking decision to make—either she gave up her self-respect, or she risked losing completely the man she loved.

Tossing the bed covers aside, she swung her feet to the floor, and quickly washed and dressed. After arranging her hair in a neat chignon, she took a moment to glance at her overall appearance in the full-length mirror. The plain gown seemed dowdy compared to the beautiful silk evening dress she had worn the night before. If she did become Benedict's mistress, all her gowns would be of the finest. Gentlemen, she had heard, were never unwilling to dig deep into their pockets to ensure that their birds of paradise were beautifully clad. Strangely enough, though, the prospect did not bring much joy. It wasn't jewels, carriages and fine clothes she wanted. Material possessions had never meant very much to her, and she doubted that they ever would.

Slipping her feet into a pair of soft shoes, she left the room, and was surprised, as she descended into the coffee room, to see Lucy emerge from the private parlour, carrying a pile of used dishes on a tray.

'Good heavens!' she exclaimed, casting a glance in the direction of the long-case clock in the corner. 'I didn't imagine the gentlemen would be up this early.'

'Only Mr Harry. He's been up an hour since, and has taken himself off to do a spot of fishing up at Sir Lionel's place,' Lucy disclosed, leading the way through to the kitchen, where Martha was busily baking.

She glanced up as they entered, surprised to discover Emma in Lucy's wake. 'I didn't expect to see you for a while yet, my dear. Why on earth didn't you have an extra hour in bed? You must be tired after last night.'

'What was it like?' Lucy, agog with curiosity, demanded to know. 'Were all the ladies wearing fine jewels? And did you dance and drink champagne?'

'I certainly did, but not at the same time. Most of the wealthier families in our community were present.' She couldn't suppress a smile of wry amusement. 'There were certainly a few raised eyebrows when I walked in.'

'Probably thought you were Mr Grantley's fancy woman,' Lucy suggested, with more honesty than tact, thereby earning herself a darkling glance from her mistress.

'Of course no one thought any such thing!' Martha snapped. 'No one with sense would take her for anything other than what she is—a lady.'

Oh, dear God! Emma inwardly groaned. Poor Martha would be devastated, utterly heartbroken, if she ever suspected that the person whom she looked upon as a daughter was even so much as contemplating becoming a kept woman. What on earth was she to do?

'As you both seem to have everything here under control, I rather fancy I'll go for a walk before I have breakfast,' she announced, and swiftly departed before either Lucy or Martha could offer to bear her company.

She needed to be alone with her thoughts, but swiftly discovered that the more she considered her dilemma the more confused she became.

Stopping by the gateway where she and Benedict had stood contemplating Ashworth Hall nestling below in the slight valley, she placed her elbows on the roughened wood, and rested her chin on the backs of her hands.

Was it really just two short weeks since Benedict had arrived at the inn? She felt as if she had known him all her life. And how her life had changed in so short a time! Never in her wildest dreams had she ever imagined that she would one day enter Ashworth Hall as a guest. Most of those present last night had treated her as their equal, with the utmost respect. None the less respect, sadly, was something she would need to forgo if ever…

Her sombre reflections dwindled as she detected approaching footsteps, and she turned to discover the being responsible for all her soul-searching striding down the track towards her, that wonderful smile, which never failed to send her pulse racing, curling his lips before he pressed them over hers in a lingering kiss, which left her in little doubt that he considered her wholly his already.

'That was by way of "good morning", my darling.' Grasping her shoulders, he held her a little away from him. 'Martha informed me that you'd gone for a walk.' His perceptive gaze, raking her face, easily detected the touch of uncertainty in her expression. 'What is the matter, my love? You're not having second thoughts, I trust, because I'll tell you plainly I'll not permit you to change your mind.'

Emma did not doubt for a moment that he was being totally sincere, and now that he was with her she could not deny that much of her disquiet was beginning to ebb. Undoubtedly he was a passionate man who would choose to visit her often. She would be deliriously happy at such times. But what of those numerous other occasions, the lingering voice of doubt reminded her, when he wasn't there to offer comfort and support?

'I—I think you must allow me a little time to consider, Ben. It's a big step for me to take, and it will mean my leaving all my friends here.'

'It's a big step for me too, my darling,' he surprised her by admitting. 'And you won't be that far away. Hampshire, after all, is the next county. You can visit Samuel and Martha as often as you like.'

'Hampshire?' She did not attempt to hide her astonishment. She would have been the first to admit that she was quite ignorant of the ways of gentlemen in polite society, but she had understood that it was common practice to set their mistresses up in discreet little houses in the capital. 'But I thought you would want me to live in London?'

'And so you shall at certain times of the year. But for the most part we'll be at Fairview.'

Emma was utterly bewildered now, and it showed in both expression and voice as she said, 'You mean you wish me to live in your country house with you?'

He appeared genuinely nonplussed for a moment. 'Of course, silly girl! Where else does a wife belong except at her husband's side?'

'Y-your wife?' It was as much as Emma could do to stop herself from gaping up at him like a demented fool. 'But I thought…' Words failed her and she had the grace to blush, a circumstance which did not escape Benedict's all-too-perceptive gaze.

'Yes…and what precisely did you think?' he prompted, eyeing her narrowly. The truth hit him with stunning clarity. 'You have not, by any chance, been foolishly imagining that I was offering *carte blanche*?' The rapidly deepening crimson hue was answer enough. 'You really do deserve to be soundly shaken, Emma Lynn! Let me assure you, my girl, that gentlemen do not as a rule ask virtuous young females to be their mistresses.'

As he watched the tiny white teeth begin to gnaw the sweetly curving bottom lip, he abandoned the pose of mock-annoyance. 'And would you have become my mistress, Emma?'

He was nothing if not ruthlessly direct on occasions. She peered up at him through her long lashes. 'I was certainly giving the matter some very serious consideration,' she conceded. 'But marriage? Ben, are you sure? We've known each other for such a short time…'

'I'm certain of my own feelings, Emma.' He pulled her back into his arms. 'And I know that you love me too. So why should we wait? All I need to know is whether you'd like a large London wedding, or would you prefer a quiet ceremony in the village church near Fairview?'

Her mind was in such a deliriously happy whirling state that it was impossible to think straight. 'A quiet wedding, I suppose.'

'Good, because that is what I should prefer. I can arrange it quickly, as soon as I've finished this business here.' Regretfully he held her at arm's length again. 'I must complete the task I've undertaken on Lavinia's behalf, but as soon as it's over I shall journey to London to obtain a special licence, and we can be married at once. We'll honeymoon in Paris, and then in the autumn we'll pay a round of calls on various members of my family and friends. How does that sound?'

'Perfect,' she murmured, once again swathed in layers of blissful contentment. 'Anywhere would be perfect so long as you were there, Ben.'

He rewarded her for her sound good sense by kissing her again. Then catching her hand, he led the way down the narrow path towards the inn yard, where Emma discovered his groom in the process of harnessing the fine team of horses to the carriage.

'Are you going somewhere?'

'I'm afraid I'll be away for several days, perhaps as long as a week, but I hope no longer.' He looked down at her, his expression suddenly troubled. 'I hate leaving you, Em, especially now. But I'm determined to clear up the mystery surrounding Hammond's death. And I rather fancy the answer may lie in a certain village in Worcestershire where, I recently discovered during my visit to her sister, the young serving-maid, Sally Pritchard, hailed from.'

'Then of course you must go,' she agreed, desperately striving not to betray her acute disappointment. 'I just wish there was more I could do to help.'

'There is, my darling.' His tone was gentle, so Emma was a little surprised to detect a flicker of annoyance in his eyes. 'That confounded nephew of mine has taken himself off fishing, I understand, so I must entrust you with a message. I discovered from Sir Lionel that Richard Ashworth is expected to arrive here any day now. If he should do so during my absence, I want Harry to go out of his way to befriend him, and keep an eye on young Ashworth.'

The reason was obvious. 'You think he might be in some kind of danger, don't you?'

'I think he may well be, yes, if what I suspect is true,' he responded grimly, before bending a concerned look in her direction. 'Also, for the time being, my darling, I would prefer that you keep our betrothal secret. I have my reasons for requesting this, which I shall share with you on my return.'

He glanced over his shoulder to see his groom clambering up on the box. 'And now I must leave if I'm to complete the better part of the journey before nightfall.'

Emma was not slow to note the return of the concerned look before he climbed into his carriage. Waving a final goodbye, she remained in the yard until the carriage had pulled away, certain in her own mind that something was troubling him deeply, and that it was far more than concern over the new Lord Ashworth's welfare. Undoubtedly he would confide in her on his return. By which time, she sincerely hoped, she might have come to accept that she, against all the odds, had been awarded the dearest wish of her heart, and was very soon to become Mrs Benedict Grantley.

Midway through the afternoon, when she was arranging some roses in a bowl, Emma received a visit from Deborah, bringing with her two letters for Harry.

'I'll leave them in your care, Emma,' she said, after seating herself at the table and learning that Mr Fencham was still over at Sir Lionel's place. 'One, I think, is from his father and the other, I suspect, was forwarded by him. Though why in the world Lord Fencham should have supposed his son was staying with Mama and me, I cannot imagine.'

Having been informed by Lavinia herself on the night of the pleasant dinner-party, held at her house the previous week, that her daughter remained ignorant of the real reason for Benedict's visit to Ashworth Magna, Emma had been very careful what she had said in her young friend's hearing. Deborah had been heartbroken when her father had died. They had been so very close. Only now was she beginning to recover, and Lavinia, understandably, did not want her daughter upset further by constant reminders of the tragedy which had struck their lives.

'As you and your mother are such close friends of the family, it was a natural assumption to make, I suppose, as Lord Fencham must have known his son was visiting the area.'

'Yes, I suppose so,' she conceded, but doubt still lingered in the brown pansy eyes. 'I still think it odd that they should have come here in the first place, though. There are far more interesting places to visit, and they seem to have been here for a long time. Surely they've seen all the sights by now?'

As no response was forthcoming this time, she glanced up at Emma, who had begun to hum a merry little tune as she continued arranging the flowers. 'You appear full of the joys of spring today.'

Emma didn't attempt to deny it. She would dearly have loved to share her wonderful news with her friend, but having given her word, she refrained, merely saying that she had every reason to be happy. She had very much enjoyed herself at the party the previous evening.

'Yes, it was pleasant,' Deborah agreed, before casting her a further arch look. 'I cannot help wondering whether you would have enjoyed the event quite so much if Mr Grantley had not been there, however.'

'If he had not been there, my dear, neither would I,' Emma was quick to point out. 'It was he, might I remind you, who managed to wheedle an invitation for me.'

'That's true enough, I suppose,' Deborah again conceded, before it suddenly occurred to her that the inn seemed strangely quiet. 'Where is everyone today? Surely you're not here on your own?'

'Not quite. Samuel is upstairs, resting. He's been overdoing it again, moving those hefty barrels in the cellar, and now his back is giving him trouble. Josh has taken both Martha and Lucy into Salisbury in the wagon to buy some urgent provisions. Harry, as I've already mentioned, is over with Sir Lionel and Ben...Mr Grantley has been called away on urgent business.'

'Well, it sounds as if he's returned,' Deborah remarked, catching the sound of a carriage drawing to a halt.

Emma, however, knew that it could not possibly be Benedict, and so went through to the coffee room in time to see a tall stranger enter the inn. He was young, no older than twenty-five or six, she guessed. He was undeniably handsome, and his thick mane of blond hair enhanced the healthy tan of his complexion.

'Good day to you, ma'am.' His voice, like Benedict's, was deep and rich, but unlike Benedict's contained just a trace of an unmistakable accent. A dreadful possibility occurred to her. 'I was informed that I could obtain a room here.'

'Yes, indeed, we do have a room, sir,' she answered, swiftly marshalling her thoughts. 'How long will you be staying?'

'That I couldn't say for sure.' His lips drew back to reveal white, even teeth. It was a dazzling smile by any standards, and strangely reminiscent of a certain other gentleman's. 'At least a week, I should say, although my plans at this stage are uncertain. Does that cause any problems?'

'None whatsoever, Mr...'

'Ashworth, ma'am...Richard Ashworth.'

Deborah, who had followed Emma through to the coffee room, was only partially successful in suppressing an exclamation of surprise, and the strange little sound alerted the young lord's attention to her presence in the shadows, for which Emma was exceedingly grateful. By the time he had cast appreciative, twinkling bright blue eyes over her friend's sweet face and trim figure, and had returned his gaze to her, she had managed to regain sufficient control to prevent her acute dismay from surfacing.

'I am pleased to make your acquaintance, my lord.' After executing a neat curtsy, she held out her hand which was instantly held for a moment in a gentle grasp. 'My name is Emma Lynn. And this,' she added, gesturing to a shyly smiling Deborah, 'is my very good friend Miss Hammond.'

On discovering that his lordship had travelled from London in a hired carriage and, more surprisingly still, with no servants to attend him, she arranged for the post-boys to bring in the luggage, and then led the way upstairs. Fortunately she was not left to cope on her own for very long, for no sooner had she shown Lord Ashworth into the bedchamber next to Harry's than Martha appeared upstairs and took immediate charge, leaving Emma free to return to the coffee room to discover a surprisingly dreamy-eyed Deborah gazing into space.

'Evidently you are impressed, my dear friend,' she teased, wondering how often her own face had worn just such an expression in recent days.

'W-what…?' Deborah finally emerged from her dreamlike state. 'Oh, yes. He's so very handsome.'

That was certainly true. Yet it was strange, Emma mused, as she accompanied her friend to the front door, that the handsome young lord had not caused her own heart to skip a beat.

No sooner had she returned to the kitchen, after seeing Deborah scurrying off down the road, than she caught sight of Harry, dismounting the horse kindly loaned to him by Sir Lionel for the duration of his stay, and rushed outside to have a quiet word with him.

'Harry, thank heavens you've returned! I don't know what on earth we're to do! Lord Ashworth has arrived.'

He appeared mildly surprised. 'Well, what of it? What has his arrival to do with us?'

'Nothing, of course, except...' Grasping his arm, Emma drew him a little away from Josh, who had taken charge of the mount and was in the process of removing the saddle. 'Ben left for Worcestershire this morning. He expects to be away for a week.'

'What the deuce has taken him there, do you suppose?'

'He expects to discover something which might shed light on poor Dr Hammond's death. But that's not important now. Before he left he charged me with a message for you. He seems to think that Ashworth might be in some danger, and wants you to keep an eye on him. Which shouldn't be too difficult an undertaking as he's putting up here.'

Harry's perplexed expression quickly changed to one of surprise. 'Deuced odd, that, wouldn't you say? Why didn't he go to the Hall? He's the rightful owner, after all.'

'Yes, I thought it strange too,' she admitted. 'It even crossed my mind that he just might be an impostor, but Martha's timely arrival quashed that foolish notion. She took one look at him, and said he was the image of his father, whom she remembers well, of course.'

Emma frowned as a thought suddenly occurred to her. 'What did strike me as most odd was that he travelled here in a hired carriage and without any personal servants.'

Harry shrugged. 'Don't see anything strange in that. Ben and I did precisely the same thing. We didn't bring our valets either. And as for the carriage…well, I expect he thought there'd be carriages enough at the Hall, servants too, come to that.'

'Yes, perhaps,' she conceded. 'But I still think it strange that he chose to put up here. You'll need to ask him why.'

His jaw dropped perceptibly. 'Dash it, Em! I can't go asking questions like that! I don't even know the fellow.'

She brushed this objection aside with a wave of her hand. 'That is precisely why you must befriend him. In fact,' she went on after a moment's thought, 'it might prove a blessing in disguise that he has chosen to stay here. It will be a great deal easier to keep track of his movements. You're not dining with Sir Lionel tonight, I hope?' She experienced a certain amount of relief when he shook his head. 'Good. It will offer you the golden opportunity to become acquainted. Ashworth too bespoke dinner.'

'In that case you'd better join us,' he suggested, much to her intense astonishment.

'I can't do that, Harry! It would create a very odd impression.'

'No, it won't,' he argued. 'We'll tell him you're a friend of Ben's. Which is no less that the truth,' he added, when she was about to protest further. 'I know! We'll tell him you're a close friend of the family, or perhaps a distant cousin,' he went on, evidently warming to the notion. 'You're slightly eccentric, and rather than accept charity from any member of the family, you've taken work here. And Ben has come to Ashworth Magna to talk some sense into you, and try to persuade you to return to the bosom of your—'

'Stop, stop!' she interrupted, her expression clearly betraying acute dismay, as she raised both hands in a gesture of defeat. 'All right, you win—I'll join you for dinner. But kindly leave any explanation for my presence, should the need arise, to me!'

If Lord Ashworth did indeed think it most odd that the young woman whom he no doubt imagined to be the daughter of the house should take her seat at the dining table, he possessed good manners enough not to betray the fact when Emma joined the gentlemen in the parlour that evening. More surprising still was that Martha raised not the least objection. Evidently she had taken an instant liking to the young man, possibly because she still retained fond memories of the father he so resembled.

If the young Lord Ashworth had inherited his temperament from his father too, then Emma well understood Martha's fondness for the late Mr Ashworth, for there was absolutely no reserve whatsoever in Richard's manner, and he insisted that all formality was swiftly dropped.

Emma was more than happy to oblige him, but did not hesitate to add, 'I fear that you must accustom yourself to your title, Richard, for most people will insist upon addressing you in the correct manner.'

One broad shoulder rose in a dismissive shrug. 'All depends on whether or not I remain here. We don't have much use for titles back home.'

'Do I infer from that, that you do not intend to make England your permanent home?' she asked, after she and Harry had exchanged startled glances.

'My plans are uncertain at the moment,' he was honest enough to admit, for which Emma admired him greatly.

Whether or not it was an innate dislike of unnecessary formality, or the fact that he was enjoying very much the food and wine, and perhaps the company in which he now found himself, Emma wasn't perfectly certain, but Richard seemed not in the least reticent to talk about himself and his early life, and she found his lack of reserve very refreshing.

Surprisingly she discovered that he had been born in England and had lived here for more than a decade. After tragically losing both his parents in a smallpox epidemic, he was sent back to Boston to live with his maternal grandfather whose wealth had been derived from trade.

'The truth of the matter is, I don't think I would be sitting here now if my grandfather hadn't passed away last year. Although,' he added with a wry smile, 'he surely would have insisted that I saw to my obligations, and at least came over for a short while, even if I didn't choose to remain.'

'You know, Richard, I find it most odd that you had no idea that you were the rightful heir until a few months ago,' Harry put in, his mind dwelling on this one fact, after all that he had learned. 'Didn't you ever meet any of your relations when you lived in England?'

'No, never. I can remember my father telling me that he had a brother and sister, but he never talked about his family much, at least not to me. He told my grandfather once that he didn't think too highly of his brother, considering him a bit of a weak-natured character. And by all accounts he disliked his sister intensely. The story my grandfather told me was that my father caught his sister once tormenting a cat. It had scratched her, and she had captured it and imprisoned it in a box, and was torturing it by prodding a stick through a hole in the wood. He tried to stop her, but he was several years younger than she was, no more than six or seven at the time. Isabel turned on him and beat him with the stick. My father, by all accounts, never forgave her for it.'

Harry looked appalled, and faintly sceptical, but Emma had little difficulty in believing the story, for an image of Isabel Ashworth's expression on the evening of the party, momentarily hard and icily merciless, flashed before her mind's eye. No, she had no difficulty whatsoever in supposing it might be true, and she strongly suspected that, had he been present, Benedict wouldn't have doubted the truth of the tale either. He certainly did not trust Isabel Ashworth, of that Emma felt certain, for had he not referred to her as a coolly ruthless woman?

Swiftly changing the subject, Emma suggested that Harry might take Richard over to meet Sir Lionel in the morning, and then left the gentlemen to enjoy their port, and discuss whatever it was gentlemen chose to discuss when not hampered by female company.

'Miss Emma is sure a fine young woman,' Richard was not slow to remark, after she had left the room. 'Are all the females in these parts so pleasing on the eye?'

'About the same as anywhere else, I should say,' Harry responded, regarding his pleasant new acquaintance over the rim of his glass. 'But I wouldn't get any ideas where Emma is concerned, if I were you.'

Bright blue eyes began to twinkle. 'No...? Wouldn't be treading on your toes, I suppose?'

'Good gad, no!' Harry didn't hesitate to assure him. 'Not that I don't think a deal of her... Emma's a great girl, one of the best!' He gave vent to a wicked chuckle. 'I'm very much looking forward to the day when I can call her "Aunt", for unless I very much mistake the matter it will not be very much longer before my dear uncle Benedict finds himself caught in parson's mousetrap. And very willingly caught too, I might add.'

It took Richard a moment only to digest what he had been told. 'In that case I'll not attempt to encroach on your uncle's—er—territory. I'm sure there's more than just one pretty girl in these parts.' Memory stirred. 'In fact, there was one here when I arrived, a darling little thing, with big brown eyes and dark brown hair, who barely reached my shoulder.'

'Ah! I expect that was my mother's goddaughter, Deborah,' Harry announced, having had little difficulty in interpreting the description. 'I'll take you over to meet her and her mother tomorrow, if you like?'

With a lazy smile tugging at his lips, Richard reached for the port. 'The idea of remaining in this little country of yours is becoming slowly more appealing.'

Chapter Ten

Satisfied that she had carried out Benedict's instructions to the letter, Emma was quite content to leave Lord Ashworth in Harry's care during the following days. She was not in the least surprised to witness an ever-increasing bond of friendship developing between the two young gentlemen. She wasn't in the least surprised, either, to discover from Harry, who always furnished her with a daily report of their comings and goings, that Richard was more than willing to call on the Hammonds whenever they passed the red brick house, and that he was betraying a marked partiality for the sweet-natured Deborah's company. What did leave her somewhat nonplussed, however, was his lordship's seeming reluctance to take up residence at Ashworth Hall.

Apart from one brief visit to his home on the morning after his arrival at the inn, he betrayed no inclination whatsoever to make a return visit to the ancestral pile, although he did accept a written invitation to dine there three days later, informing his aunt that he would be bringing a party of friends. Consequently

Emma, much to her surprise, found herself once again travelling in a carriage, with Lavinia and Deborah Hammond, to Ashworth Hall.

'I must say, I never expected to be making a return visit,' she admitted, after seating herself beside her friend in the smart equipage very generously provided for their use by Sir Lionel Brent.

'No, nor I,' Deborah confessed. 'We are becoming quite fashionable, are we not?'

Emma followed the direction of her friend's soft gaze to see Richard, astride the mount he had hired from a stables in Salisbury, riding alongside the coach, happily chatting away to Harry.

From what she had gleaned thus far, Richard had appeared very contented to accompany Harry and Sir Lionel on visits to various families in the area, and by all accounts he had left a very favourable impression. Emma found no difficulty in believing this, for Richard was undeniably a very likeable young man, amiable and charming. He certainly appeared to be enjoying his visit to the area, though whether he would be content to remain as a permanent member of the community was a different matter entirely.

'I do hope Richard decides to make his home permanently in England,' she remarked. 'I think he would be a great asset to the community.'

Lavinia appeared faintly surprised. 'You think there is a possibility that he might not?'

Emma shrugged, unwilling to commit herself. 'I'm not sure. He doesn't seem in any hurry to take up residence at the Hall, you must admit.'

'I can understand his reasons for not doing so,' Deborah surprised her companions by announcing. 'He explained to me that he would much prefer not to take up residence whilst his aunt and cousin remain under the roof.'

Emma was faintly surprised, and turned towards Lavinia for confirmation, but that lady merely lowered her eyes and began to make a great play of rearranging her skirts.

Well, well, well! she mused. It appeared that little Deborah was on very good terms with Lord Ashworth. It would be agreeable to think that the relationship might deepen, and she did not suppose for a moment that Lavinia would try to prevent any such eventuality. None the less, she knew that lady well enough to be sure that she would never attempt to promote a closer bond developing between them, but would allow nature to take its course.

It was so very sad, Emma reflected, turning to stare out of the window as they passed through the gateway leading to Ashworth Hall's impressive park, that Deborah had been denied the opportunity to enjoy the London Season which had been planned for earlier in the year. Deborah had mentioned on more than one occasion that her godmother, Lady Fencham, was very much looking forward to bringing her out in the spring. Sadly all the well-laid plans had had to be abandoned when Dr Hammond had died in the autumn. It was then, Emma clearly recalled, that Lavinia had begun to think seriously of making her home in Bath, where she hoped Deborah would have a greater chance of meeting personable young gentlemen. Emma did not suppose for a moment that Lavinia ever imagined that a very eligible *parti* would one day be living virtually on her doorstep. She smiled to herself. Early days yet, of course, but one never knew!

As the carriage drew to a halt, Emma abandoned her musings, and accompanied the others into the house. As though he felt his uncle would have expected it of him, Harry positioned himself at her side. She felt moved by the gesture of support, but was forced silently to concede that dear Harry was no substitute for Benedict. She missed him so very much, more than she would have ever believed possible. He had been away for less than a week, and yet it felt more like a year. How she wished he would return!

Fortunately her appearance this time prompted no raised brows. Even Clarissa, who no doubt had been forewarned to be on her best behaviour, managed to utter a polite greeting. The only faintly awkward moment occurred when they entered the dining room. Cedric Ashworth, evidently having been accustomed to doing so whenever visiting the Hall since the late Lord Ashworth's demise, had been about to take the seat at the head of the table, and had had to be reminded by his cousin Isabel that the place now belonged to the head of the family. The embarrassed silence which followed, as Richard seated himself, was quickly broken by Sir Lionel who proffered a mild joke.

Emma was pleased to discover herself placed beside Sir Lionel near the foot of the table, but she was not so delighted to find the Ashworth steward, Lucius Flint, on her left. Initially she assumed he must have been invited so that there wasn't an odd number dining that evening, but she was swiftly forced to revise her opinion. He appeared quite at home, as though he rou-

tinely sat down to dinner with the family, and did not
seem in the least reluctant to have his share of the
conversation.

Isabel Ashworth proved that she was a seasoned
hostess, when she rose to her feet the instant everyone
had eaten their fill of the excellently prepared food,
and invited the ladies to retire to the salon. Much to
Emma's surprise, Isabel chose to position herself beside her on the sofa, and was not slow to raise Mr
Grantley's name by enquiring when he was expected
to return to Ashworth Magna.

'I was most disappointed to discover that he would
not be with us this evening,' Isabel continued, after
receiving only a vague response.

'Perhaps it was just as well.' Very much on her
guard, Emma was determined not to betray Benedict's
trust. Although he had not put it in so many words,
she felt sure that Isabel Ashworth was the very last
person he would want apprised of his whereabouts.
'Had he been invited, there would have been an odd
number at table. Thirteen to be precise—unlucky, I
believe.'

Isabel dismissed this with a wave of one thin hand.
'Oh, we could easily have overcome that problem. I
do hope he does not delay his return too long. Such
an intelligent man! I trust he will condescend to dine
with us again when he does return.'

'I should not suppose for a moment that he intends
to remain away for very much longer, otherwise I'm
certain he would have taken his nephew with him.
Although it is perhaps fortuitous in the circumstances
that Mr Fencham chose not to accompany his uncle.

He and Lord Ashworth appear to have struck up a swift friendship.'

Emma did not doubt for a moment that Isabel had been quick to appreciate this fact. Not much, she suspected, ever escaped the notice of the female whose word had been law in the Ashworth household for very many years.

Undoubtedly her association with Benedict had induced Emma to be far more observant in recent days, and she had certainly not missed the several assessing glances their hostess had cast down the length of the table during dinner. Had Isabel too observed that, although Lord Ashworth had paid a reasonable amount of attention to his cousin, who had been seated on his right, his eyes, more often than not, had strayed in quite a different lady's direction. Yes, she strongly suspected that Isabel had not missed Richard's frequent glances at Deborah.

With this passing through her mind, Emma transferred her gaze to the sofa opposite, where Deborah sat in conversation with Clarissa Ashworth. Her friend was, undeniably, a pretty young woman. Nevertheless, when compared to Clarissa she paled into insignificance. Most gentlemen, Emma didn't doubt for a moment, would be dazzled by Miss Ashworth's undeniable beauty, and yet Emma was acquainted with at least two members of the opposite sex who appeared completely unmoved by the young lady's charms, namely Benedict and Richard.

Isabel, following the direction of those strikingly lovely grey eyes, which had so captured a certain absent gentleman's attention, was not slow to comment that her niece was looking particularly animated to-

night. 'That, I suspect, is because she has been invited
to accompany Cedric and his family to Brighton when
they leave in the morning. I was not certain whether
I should allow her to go, Miss Lynn, but all things
considered, I thought it would be wrong to refuse. Like
Miss Hammond, Clarissa was denied the pleasure of
a Season because of her father's demise. My brother
has been dead now for almost a year, and I thought it
would be cruel to adhere strictly to convention and
deny her the treat.'

Emma found herself easily agreeing with this. 'You
will find the house strangely quiet when they have all
left you, Miss Ashworth. Or do you propose to make
up one of the party?'

'Oh, no. I shall remain here. It will grant me the
opportunity to become better acquainted with my
nephew. I am hoping to persuade him to take up residence here. Which, I might add, he seems strangely
reluctant to do.'

Thankfully Emma was saved the necessity of commenting, for the door opened, and Richard himself surprisingly entered the room. After a swift glance about
him, he came directly across to the sofa in order to
ask her if she would care to accompany him on a tour
of the house. She didn't need to consider the matter,
and was on her feet in an instant. When, however, his
aunt made to rise also, Richard quickly forestalled her,
informing her that he had already secured the services
of the butler to take them on a guided tour, so she was
at liberty to remain with her other guests.

The invitation was then extended to Lavinia and her
daughter, both of whom appeared happy to accept, and

they did not delay in going out into the hall, where they discovered the aged retainer awaiting them.

Lavinia, being a respected member of the community, had visited the house on numerous occasions in the past, and was familiar with most of the ground-floor rooms. Emma, on the other hand, was not, and found much to interest her.

Although, like Benedict, she considered the exterior of the building singularly lacking in architectural beauty, she had no fault to find with the interior. With the possible exception of the comfortable parlour, which she had entered on the night of the party, all the rooms were charmingly decorated and tastefully furnished. So it came as something of a surprise to see that Richard, apart from commenting favourably on the carved wooden panelling in the library, displayed little enthusiasm for his ancestral home.

This surprising show of indifference continued as they explored the charming bedchambers on the upper floor, and it was only when they ventured into the west wing, and began to view the main apartments, that he finally began to betray some degree of interest in his surroundings.

'Correct me if I'm wrong, Troughton,' he remarked, after casting his eyes round the delightful bedchamber, decorated in various shades of pink and rose, 'but did you not say that these rooms are those which have been favoured by past mistresses of the house?'

'That is correct, sir,' the butler confirmed, before gesturing towards a connecting door. 'As you see, sir, it adjoins the master bedchamber.'

Richard focused his attention on the assortment of bottles on the dressing table, and then glanced briefly

at the shawl lying over the back of the plush velvet
chair. 'Would I be right in thinking that this room is
being used at the present time?'

'Why, yes, sir. Miss Isabel moved in here shortly
after her brother was taken ill last year in order to take
care of him. After the late Lord Ashworth's demise,
she remained here whilst her own bedchamber, next
to Miss Clarissa's in the east wing, was being redec-
orated. She has yet to issue instructions to have her
things returned to her old room, my lord.'

'I see,' Richard murmured, opening the connecting
door and leading the way into the master bedchamber,
which in stark contrast to the delicate pink shades of
the adjoining room was strikingly decorated in gold
and crimson.

After approving the solid masculinity of the fur-
nishings, Lavinia suggested that they might take time
to study the paintings that decorated the walls of the
long gallery. Emma, certainly not averse to spending
a few minutes casting her eyes over the previous hold-
ers of the title, was about to follow the others from
the room, when she noticed Richard, clearly troubled
about something, staring rather forlornly out of the
window at the park, and decided to remain to bear him
company.

It was not perhaps the wisest course of action to
remain alone with a gentleman who was not a close
relative, and most certainly not in a bedchamber, but
she did not allow this to deter her from moving back
into the room to join him by the window. She did not
suppose for a moment that it would cross his mind to
take advantage of the situation. Furthermore, unless

she was very much mistaken, he already suspected that her heart belonged to another.

When he continued to stare out across the park, seemingly oblivious to her presence, she reached up to touch his arm with her fingertips. 'What is it?' she asked gently. 'Do you not approve of your ancestral home?'

'I wouldn't go so far as to say that, Emma,' he answered, after a further moment's thoughtful silence. 'I cannot help wondering, though, why the place was erected on this spot. If I had the choice, I would build my house there.' He pointed to a raised area of land which offered a commanding view of the lake and the surrounding countryside.

'Yes, it would be an ideal situation,' she agreed, before returning her gaze to the faintly troubled face of the young Baron. 'Is it that you feel that you would not be contented living here, Richard?'

'I'm striving to keep an open mind, Emma,' he responded, with that innate honesty which she could not fail to admire. 'What I strongly suspect, however, is that I would never be perfectly comfortable living here with my aunt and cousin residing under the same roof.' He cast her a faintly embarrassed smile. 'Does that seem foolish to you?'

'No, not at all,' she assured him. 'I think I can understand how you must feel. Your aunt and cousin have lived here all their lives. The servants might find it a little strange at first having to take their orders from another, which might give rise to a certain amount of awkwardness.'

'Not only that, Emma. My aunt plainly feels that she is mistress here. That role will one day fall to my wife when I marry. Will Isabel Ashworth willingly relinquish her position, and be content to remain here merely as a dependant? Somehow, I think not.'

No, and neither did Emma, but she had no intention of adding to his worries by admitting to it. Instead she said, 'I do not see why she should be dependent upon you, Richard. Unless I much mistake the matter, she has sufficient money of her own to buy a comfortable residence somewhere—perhaps at one of the fashionable spa towns. In the meantime, I see no reason why she should not take immediate steps to move into the dower house. You could always speak to Sir Lionel, or Benedict—I mean, Mr Grantley, when he returns. Either could advise you far better than I can.'

'Ahh, yes! The errant gentleman of whom everyone seems so fond.' He cast her a quizzical glance. 'I very much look forward to making his acquaintance. I have been led to believe he is something of an astute judge of character. It might be interesting to learn his views on the steward here, who appears to have his feet firmly under the table. Is it common practice to invite one's employees to join a dinner party?'

Once more she found herself admiring his perspicacity. 'I wouldn't have thought so, no. But, here again, you could do no better than to ask—'

She checked, as she clearly detected a sound from the adjoining room. In all probability it was merely a maid-servant come to tidy her mistress's bedchamber. None the less, it was a timely reminder, and Emma decided, for appearance's sake, that it might be wise not to remain alone with Richard any longer.

Seemingly he was of a similar mind, for he at once suggested that they rejoin the others whom they discovered contemplating a painting of one of his more notorious ancestors, who had earned the reputation of having been a wild and godless man. After taking a moment to contemplate the clear evidence of dissipation etched into the harsh-featured face, Emma gave way to an imp of mischief by announcing that she could detect a strong resemblance to the present holder of the title, which sent Richard into peals of laughter, before he led the way back down the impressive staircase to the salon in time to catch Clarissa asking her aunt if she had managed to find her handkerchief.

'Yes, dear. I eventually discovered it beside my chair in the dining room.' Appearing slightly breathless, Isabel turned, bestowing a smile upon all members of the returning party, before addressing her nephew. 'Richard, I was wondering if you would have any objections to the household staff attending the annual summer fair held near Andover? It will take place on Friday, and will mean their being away for most of the day and perhaps not returning until the following morning. You see, I thought it might serve by way of a celebration to welcome the arrival of their new master.'

'I have no objections whatsoever, ma'am,' he was quick to assure her. 'But will it not make things a little difficult for you?'

'Not at all. Cousin Cedric will be leaving us tomorrow morning, taking Clarissa with him for a short stay in Brighton. Consequently from Thursday onwards the servants will only need to cater for my needs. I do not have a large appetite. Cook will simply need to prepare my breakfast before she leaves on Friday and leave me something cold which I might eat for my supper, so there will be no problem,' Emma heard Isabel Ashworth respond, before she noticed Harry making frantic gestures, which she took to mean that he wished her to partner him at whist.

As Emma took her seat opposite him at one of the tables set out for cards, she considered what she had overheard, and swiftly came to the conclusion that it had been very generous on Miss Ashworth's part to suggest such a treat for the servants, little realising, as she reached for her cards, that she would in the very near future be forced to revise that opinion.

After overnight rain, Friday dawned bright and sunny, and thankfully remained clement for those making the journey to Andover for the annual fair. Samuel was among the several villagers who had set out at the crack of dawn, for he had decided it was high time he purchased another horse, and was determined to arrive early in order to attain the best bargain. He had taken Josh with him, and Emma thought the inn had seemed strangely quiet throughout the day. Both Harry and Richard had been out for much of the time, and Harry had informed her shortly after breakfast that he would not be returning until late, as he had accepted a second invitation to dine with Colonel Meecham and his wife.

Shortly before six, Emma returned to the kitchen to check on the dinner. As only Richard planned to bear her company in the parlour that evening, she had taken the trouble to prepare several of his favourite dishes, which included asparagus soup, a fricassee of chicken and a lemon jelly. Everything was ready and waiting to be served. Sadly, though, there was no sign of Richard.

She had not been at all happy when she had discovered that he had had every intention of spending the whole morning in Salisbury, and that he had planned to go on his own. However, as Harry had quite rightly pointed out, when she had approached him about it shortly before he himself had left the inn, it was impossible to guard Richard all of the time without his becoming suspicious.

Unfortunately Richard did not share Harry's passion for either fishing or billiards, which was perhaps why he had chosen not to accompany Harry to Sir Lionel's that morning, and had also declined the invitation to dine with the Colonel, who loved nothing better than spending an evening with a cue in his hand. Nevertheless she simply couldn't understand what could possibly be keeping him in Salisbury all this time. She felt certain he had said he intended to return early in the afternoon.

'Are you certain Lord Ashworth hasn't returned, Lucy?'

'Yes, Miss Em. I knocked on his door while you were changing your dress, and when there was no answer, I went in. The coat he asked me to press when he came back earlier is still lying on the bed where I left it.'

Emma's brows rose in surprise. 'I didn't realise he had returned. When was this?'

'Around two o'clock.' The response came from Martha, who had emerged from the laundry, carrying a pile of clean sheets. 'If my memory serves me correctly, it was while you were returning those journals to Lavinia Hammond. He went out again almost at once. Said something about riding over to Sir Lionel's place. Maybe it slipped his mind that he bespoke dinner this evening, and is dining with Sir Lionel.'

'Or mayhap he's still over at the Hall,' Lucy suggested, thereby earning herself a sharp look from a pair of suddenly alert grey eyes.

'Why do you suppose he may have gone there, Lucy?'

'On account of the letter, Miss Em.'

'What letter?'

'The letter one of the estate workers brung up from the Hall this morning. I only just remembered in time that I'd slipped it into my apron, and rushed into the yard to give it to Lord Ashworth before he left.'

Martha did not miss the fleeting look of concern. 'What's wrong, Emma?'

'Oh, nothing—nothing at all,' she answered, but to Martha's ears the response lacked any real conviction.

'He may have decided to dine at the Hall,' she suggested.

'Yes, perhaps he did,' Emma agreed, before memory stirred. 'No, he wouldn't have done that,' she corrected. 'Isabel Ashworth offered the servants the opportunity to go to the fair. I cannot imagine that many, if any, would have declined the treat.' She shrugged. 'In all probability you are right and he is with Sir Lionel, so we shall eat the meal I've prepared for supper when Samuel returns.'

Desperately striving not to allow herself to worry unnecessarily, Emma accompanied Martha upstairs and, after changing back into her old gown, helped to put clean sheets on Harry's bed, before returning to the kitchen to repair the one Richard had inadvertently put his toe through earlier in the week. It was a large rent, and the sewing took her some little time. Unfortunately she found her gaze all too frequently straying in the direction of the kitchen clock, and when the hour hand had slowly moved from seven to eight, she found it impossible to thrust from her mind the dreadful possibility that something untoward had happened to the young Baron.

Oh, if only Benedict were here! she thought, reaching for the apron which Lucy had torn that morning. He would have known precisely what to do. But she had received no communication, not even just a few hurried lines, to suggest when she might expect to see him. A sigh escaped her. Having had both Richard and Harry to bear her company had certainly made the evenings slightly more enjoyable. She liked them both immensely, but neither, sadly, could fill the void. It was Benedict's face she longed to see smiling at her across the dining table, and his voice she longed to hear; even though on occasions it could be quite infuriatingly dictatorial.

'Samuel not back yet?' Martha asked, wandering through from the tap to stare out of the window, where Emma had sat for most of the evening, keeping watch on the yard.

'No, no one has returned,' she confirmed, before coming to a decision. 'Oh, confound the man! Why isn't he here?'

Slightly startled, Martha watched Emma toss the apron aside, and then storm across to the kitchen dresser. 'Oh, I expect he'll be back soon, and it's not as if we're busy in the tap. Surely you don't begrudge Sam a little free time?'

'I was referring to Benedict,' Emma enlightened her, as she began to rummage through the drawers. 'If he were here now, I would be hard pressed not to administer a sound box round the ear!'

'But why?' Martha found it impossible to suppress a chuckle. Emma rarely succumbed to ill humour, but when she did, no one was left in any doubt about it. 'The dear man said he would be away for at least a week,' she reminded her, but Emma refused to be humoured.

'I'll "dear man" him when I get my hands on him!' she muttered darkly. 'Oh, confound it! Where is the dratted thing…? Ah, yes, I remember!'

To her intense dismay, Martha saw Emma reach up to the top of the dresser and draw down the pistol Samuel left within easy reach should the need for its use arise. 'Be careful, Emma, the thing is kept loaded.'

'I know. It wouldn't be a lot of use to me if it wasn't,' she responded, checking the pistol, before slipping it into the pocket of her gown. 'Martha, I'm going out to search for Richard. I'm worried about him. He's too considerate a man not to have sent word if he had any intention of not returning for dinner.'

Holding up her hand against the protest Martha was about to utter, she instructed her to send Lucy over to Colonel Meecham's house immediately to ascertain if Richard was there, and, if not, to ask Harry if he would kindly ride over and see if Lord Ashworth was with Sir Lionel.

'And what do you intend to do?' Martha demanded to know, following Emma outside into the yard.

'I'm going over to the Hall. I'll cut across the fields. It will save time,' and so saying, she hurried away, granting no opportunity for further argument.

Having been swiftly infected with Emma's anxiety, Martha wasted no time in searching out Lucy, and speedily saw her off down the lane in the direction of the Colonel's house. All she could do then was wait. Consequently she experienced no small amount of relief when a few minutes later she clearly detected the sound of a vehicle drawing to a halt in the yard.

Assuming it must be Samuel returning from Andover, she rushed out, almost crying with relief as she watched the tall, immaculately attired figure stepping down from the carriage.

'Oh, Mr Grantley, thank heavens you're back!' She was to wonder ever afterwards how she managed to stop herself from falling upon that broad expanse of chest. 'Young Lord Ashworth has not returned, and we're that concerned.'

Benedict's smile was instantly erased. 'When did he arrive?'

'On the very day you left us, sir. He was supposed to return for dinner, and Emma's gone over to the Hall to search for him.'

Those expressive black brows snapped together. 'The devil she has!'

Uncertain quite how to respond to this totally unexpected explosion of wrath, Martha was somewhat relieved to hear the sound of an approaching horse, and turned to see Harry entering the yard.'

'Hello, Ben! Didn't expect to find you here.' His boyish grin faded when he detected his uncle's grim expression. 'What's to do?'

'Apparently young Ashworth is missing. Obviously he hasn't been with you?'

'No. I've been dining with the Meechams.' Harry too began to betray signs of concern. 'He might be over with Sir Lionel, although he certainly hadn't called there before I left, which was around five.'

'In that case, ride over now, just to be certain he isn't there.'

'Fine. And what are you going to do?'

'Pay a visit to Ashworth Hall to find Emma,' Benedict responded, after instructing his coachman to turn the carriage round.

'And then what?'

'Wring her neck!'

Harry frankly laughed. 'In that case I'll be off now to see Sir Lionel, and then ride over to the Hall afterwards, just in case Emma should feel the need of my protection.'

Chapter Eleven

By the time Emma had arrived within yards of the house there was still sufficient light for her to see reasonably clearly, but this she well knew would not remain the case for very much longer. Feeling the effects of her hastily executed cross-country excursion, she made good use of one of the sturdy elms which edged the drive by leaning her back against the trunk, and taking a moment to regain her breath and look about her.

Since scrambling over the boundary fence, and entering the park, she had been on the watch for any possible estate worker still toiling in the grounds. She had seen no one. This at first had struck her as most odd, until she had recalled that Isabel Ashworth had granted the servants the opportunity to enjoy themselves at Andover's annual fair. The generous offer had possibly been extended to those working on the estate too, and it would be a rare man indeed who would deny himself the pleasure of doing no work and still earning a day's pay.

Earlier in the week she had considered Isabel most

thoughtful to suggest that the servants be given the opportunity to enjoy a rare treat. Now, however, Emma was beginning to feel increasingly that something quite sinister had instigated this surprising show of kindness on Isabel's part. After all, with the house empty of servants, what better time to commit some malicious act? It was just possible, though, that one or two older members of staff had not grasped the opportunity offered to make the trip to Andover. She could not imagine, for instance, the staid butler wishing to visit a noisy fair. Troughton might, of course, have chosen to visit his sister who lived on the outskirts of Salisbury. If not, then it was more than likely that he was still in the house.

Her eyes narrowed speculatively as she gazed at the solid oak door. If Troughton was within, he would undoubtedly answer any summons and, more importantly, would tell her precisely what she wished to know. Supposing, though, he wasn't there, and Isabel Ashworth herself answered the door? What then? Might Miss Ashworth deem any enquiry into her nephew's whereabouts an impertinence? Furthermore, even supposing she did condescend to volunteer such information, could she be believed?

Emma began to gnaw at her bottom lip, wondering what she should do. How she wished that she possessed Benedict's God-given gift of knowing at once whether someone was telling the truth! Unfortunately she did not, and so could only rely on feminine intuition. And every instinct told her that Richard Ashworth was in danger.

After a further quiet moment's deliberation, she decided she must first discover if any of the servants were in the house, and this could best be achieved by making her way round to the kitchen entrance. If anyone happened to see her before she had reached her goal, she would merely say that she had called in order to collect a recipe from Mrs Wright. No one would think this in any way out of the ordinary, as she had done so on a score of occasions in the past. Furthermore, should any comment be made as to the lateness of the hour, she would merely say that she didn't suppose that Mrs Wright would have returned from Andover very early.

Having decided on this plan of action, Emma delayed no further, and headed across the drive to the path which eventually led to the courtyard at the rear of the building. She had walked almost half the length of the massive east wing, when she clearly detected the sound of a voice filtering through one of the open windows.

With one swift, side-stepping movement, she had her back pressed against the grey stone wall, and began to edge her way stealthily towards what she believed must be one of the library windows, while praying that her approaching footsteps on the gravel could not be detected from within the room. It appeared her prayers had been answered, for she distinctly heard Isabel Ashworth's voice again, this time clearly bemoaning the fact that they were having to wait.

'Why on earth could you not have arranged for them to come here earlier?' she demanded of someone obviously in the room with her. 'The servants might be back before they decide to show their faces.'

'For heaven's sake, woman! You don't suppose they would be willing to come here in broad daylight, not after their last escapade? Be thankful that they agreed to offer their services a second time!'

Emma had no difficulty in recognising that responding voice. Flint had tried to hold her in conversation too many times during the dinner she had eaten at the Hall on Wednesday evening for her not to be positive that it was he. Isabel began speaking again, and Emma listened intently, certain now that something was afoot.

'They were paid well enough. They've no cause to complain.'

A raucous shout of laughter followed. 'What's the use of money, if you don't live to spend it? They have no wish to end their days dangling from a rope. And neither have I.'

'You've no cause to complain, either, Flint.' Isabel's voice was harsh and scathing, singularly lacking its usually soft, ladylike tones. 'You've done well enough out of me over the years.'

'True enough.' There was the unmistakable sound of chinking glass, as though someone was making use of the contents of a decanter. 'But I'll tell you this—as soon as you've achieved your aim, and your cousin has the title, you and I are parting company. And do not think to stop me. Your secrets are safe enough with me, providing I too do not meet with a sudden end. You see, I have taken the precaution of leaving a letter with a certain Notary and Commissioner of Oaths in Salisbury who has been instructed to hand the document over to the authorities, if I should just happen to leave this world in suspicious circumstances.' A pause, then, 'I don't deny that I've done well out of our long and eventful association. I just hope Cedric's as grateful to you as I've always been.'

'Cedric's a fool! He'll never suspect. I can twist him round my little finger. And that nincompoop son of his will be easy enough to manage when the time comes for him to take his father's place as head of the family.'

Again there was the sound of masculine laughter. 'Well, I for one wouldn't care to be in Cedric's shoes if he doesn't prove so malleable as you suppose. Though why in the world you couldn't have given your nephew a chance, I don't know.'

'I've already explained that. Good God! Do you take me for a fool? I could see at once that the damned young upstart would prove a problem. If he'd betrayed the least sign that he might be susceptible to Clarissa's charms, I might have given him the benefit of the doubt.'

'Well, that's your own fault. You spoilt her. Had you spent time instilling some manners into the chit, she might have had more to commend her than mere looks. Not many men wish to take a sulky little shrew to wife. But I still say you'd have done better to have waited,' Flint continued, when he failed to elicit a response. 'You might have managed to win him round.'

Emma's breath caught in her throat, as she saw the shadow fall across the window, and heard Isabel's voice, clearer than before, announce, 'No, not he. He's too much his father's son. I've already told you that, on the night of the dinner-party, I overheard him telling someone that he wasn't happy about Clarissa and me residing here. He would have had us out at the earliest opportunity…and after all I've done.' There was an unmistakable bitter edge to the surprising shout of feminine laughter which followed. 'And if you imagine I'd allow that damned young puppy to take away what would have been mine if only…'

'Yes, you should have been a man,' was the amused response. 'There's no compassion, no gentleness in you. Though, I must say you're losing your touch. You managed to finish the serving-girl off with one blow, but young Ashworth's still very much alive.'

'But not for much longer if those rogues arrive and do their job.'

'They didn't fail the last time, when you wanted the doctor out of the way,' Flint wasn't slow to remind her. 'When I first approached them I warned them I might require their services at a moment's notice. It was pure chance that I discovered Sir Lionel was planning to cancel his evening with Dr Hammond. When I rode over to their lodgings in Salisbury later that Friday morning, they were more than willing to accompany me back to Ashworth Magna. And they did the job.'

'Well, see that they do a thorough job again! They can even use the same spot in the lane leading to Brent's place. If I'm ever asked, I'll merely say that, when he left here, my nephew intended to call on Sir Lionel.'

'Ye gods, you're a cold-hearted wench! Don't you ever suffer pangs of conscience?' Flint demanded.

Emma thought she detected what sounded suspiciously like a scoff before Isabel parried with, 'Do you?'

'I didn't like having a hand in Hammond's death.'

Appalled and sickened though she was at what she

was hearing, Emma was inclined to give Flint the benefit of the doubt, for she had detected an unmistakable hint of regret in his voice.

Isabel Ashworth, on the other hand, sounded callously matter-of-fact as she said, 'I knew he wasn't happy over the Pritchard girl's death. If I could have been certain that he intended keeping his suspicions to himself he'd be alive today. But I felt sure that, sooner or later, he would confide in Sir Lionel, so he had to be disposed of…and my nephew will suffer the same fate. Are you sure he's still unconscious?'

'Of course I'm sure. And even if he should come round, he ain't going anywhere. He's safely trussed up like a chicken. So stop worrying! As soon as our friends arrive we'll have him out of here.'

Emma had discovered all she needed to know. Richard was somewhere in the house, and it was up to her to find out where before the villains hired to dispose of him arrived at the Hall.

Stooping low, so as not to be seen passing the window, Emma held her breath as she tiptoed towards the corner of the east wing. Once safely in the courtyard at the back of the house, she took a moment to gaze across at the row of outbuildings, and was not unduly surprised to discover no grooms or servants about their work. Nor was she particularly daunted to find the door leading to the kitchen securely locked, for she knew that the catch on the larder window was loose, and could be opened from the outside with little difficulty.

How glad she was that she had been on friendly terms with the Ashworth Hall servants all these years, and had paid numerous visits to Mrs Wright's domain, she reflected, as she inserted a finger between window and frame and effortlessly raised the catch. The Ashworths' cook had not infrequently bemoaned the fact that certain young male servants had, over the years, used the larder window as a means by which to gain entry when they had arrived home late, after a night's carousing, to find themselves locked out. Emma recalled clearly Mrs Wright remarking that anyone of slender build would have little difficulty in using this means to break in. And thankfully she was correct!

Emma soon found herself standing in the kitchen. She did not suppose for a moment that anyone in the library would be able to hear, but she took great care not to bump into anything as she wasted no time in going across to the door leading to the back stairs.

Once again she thanked Providence for ensuring that she had enjoyed friendly relations with the Ashworths' cook, for Mrs Wright had on one occasion used the narrow back stairway to take Emma on a guided tour of the servants' quarters. She had obligingly pointed out the door leading to the long gallery, which Emma now had no hesitation in using.

Conscious of his ancestors peering down at her from the walls, she set about trying to locate Richard's whereabouts. After searching without success every room in the west wing, she retraced her steps along the gallery to the other wing, only to discover that here too each and every room was frustratingly empty. She was wondering whether it might be worthwhile making a search of the cellars, when something that she ought to have realised at once suddenly occurred to her, and she cursed herself silently for a fool. Tall and muscular, Richard was no lightweight. Isabel might be able to bludgeon someone with deadly accuracy, but she didn't possess the strength, even with the help of her villainous steward, to carry Richard any great distance. Therefore it was more than likely that they had left him in one of the downstairs rooms.

For the first time since entering the house she paused to consider her own predicament. Fear suddenly gripped her like a vice, holding her captive at the head of the main staircase. Isabel had the blood of two people on her hands, possibly more. She was now planning the destruction of another: her own nephew, no less! It was unlikely, therefore, that Isabel would hesitate in putting a period to the existence of someone whom she no doubt considered of no more worth than the servant-girl she had murdered only months before. Oh, no, Emma reiterated silently. If she was discovered, she could expect no mercy from either of those heartless blackguards in the library.

The sensible thing to do was to return to the village to summon help. The one flaw in this plan was, of course, that time was not on her side. The men hired to dispose of Richard might arrive at any moment. Dusk was fast approaching. Already the hall below was cast in shadow. Before too long it might prove difficult to search the ground floor without some means of artificial light. If she was to be of any help to Richard, she must act now.

Grasping the banister-rail, she took her first tentative step down the staircase, and felt the pistol in the pocket of her skirt brush against her leg. The comfort it brought was immense, giving her the courage to descend further. How glad she was that Samuel had insisted, much to dear Martha's intense disapproval, on teaching her how to handle firearms so that she would be in a position to protect herself in the unlikely event that there was ever any trouble at the inn.

For someone who deplored any form of violence, Emma had been astounded at her surprising skill at handling a pistol. But shooting bottles set on top of fence posts was one thing, she reminded herself; levelling a pistol at another human being was quite another. Would she have the courage to fire it? She wasn't certain and could only hope that she wouldn't be put to the test.

Several of the stairs creaked in protest, sounding like thunder to her ears, as she made the slow descent to the hall. To her intense relief no one came out of the library to investigate, so she did not delay in commencing her search.

Lady Luck, it seemed, had decided to favour her thus far, and generously continued to do so, for within a very short time Emma discovered her quarry, arms and feet bound, lying prone upon the sofa in the small salon into which she had been shown on the night of Clarissa's party.

Although it was by now quite dark, there was still sufficient light for Emma to see the crust of dried blood in Richard's blond hair. How long he had lain there unconscious she had no way of knowing, but blessedly he murmured as she removed the gag and began to free him from the constricting ropes.

Once this task was successfully completed, she did not hesitate to make use of the contents of the conveniently positioned brandy decanter nearby. Gently supporting his head, she placed the glass to lips that were alarmingly blue, and quickly tipped a small quantity of the liquor down his throat. He coughed in protest, but did not attempt to prevent her from repeating the process, and thankfully after a further moment his eyelids flickered open.

'Richard…Richard, it's Emma,' she whispered, as he gazed up at her in frowning silence, as though he were having difficulty in bringing her features into focus. 'Richard, can you hear me?'

'Emma?' He made a feeble attempt to raise one hand, then let it fall. 'My head…'

'Yes, my dear. You've sustained a severe blow. But there's nothing I can do for you now. I must get you out of here.'

Placing the glass to his lips again, Emma encouraged him to sample a little more of its contents, before coaxing him to sit up. It was quite obviously an effort, but eventually he did succeed in swinging his feet to the floor. The dazed look was beginning to leave his eyes, but she was not so foolish as to suppose that in his present state he could walk very far. The best she could hope to do was hide him somewhere, perhaps in one of the outhouses, and then go for help.

'Where the deuce am I?' he demanded, gazing about the shadowy room in obvious confusion.

'At Ashworth Hall. You rode over in the afternoon, remember?'

'Yes,' he said after a moment's frowning silence, 'I remember. My aunt wished to see me.'

'Yes, I know she did,' Emma muttered sardonically. 'It was she who administered that blow to your head. She wants you dead, Richard. I, on the other hand, intend that you shall remain very much alive.'

'And how, may I ask, do you propose to ensure that?'

The half-empty glass falling from her fingers, Emma swung round to discover the figure of Isabel Ashworth staring across at her from the open doorway.

Emma had never considered Isabel Ashworth a handsome woman; she was far too angular and sharp featured to be considered even remotely attractive. Yet now she appeared almost ugly, with her thin lips twisted by an unpleasant smirk, and with a sinister glint in her hard and pitiless dark eyes.

'I was right, Flint, I did hear something,' she flung over her shoulder, before moving to one side to allow her steward to pass into the room.

For a moment Emma focused her attention on the pistol in Flint's hand before offering her assistance to Richard who was attempting to rise to his feet. He swayed slightly as he clung to her for support.

'What is the meaning of this?' he demanded, proving to Emma that there was precious little amiss with his mental faculties. Whether he would prove of much help in the present situation was unlikely. He was undoubtedly still suffering badly from the blow to his head, but he certainly did not lack courage, as he proved when he suddenly thrust her behind him, shielding her with his own body.

The action caused him to sway yet again, and he took an unwary step forward. Before Emma could reach out a supporting hand, there was a deafening report, and the next moment Richard had slumped to his knees, grasping his left shoulder.

'You damned fool!' Isabel rounded on her henchman in a cold fury. 'I didn't want him shot.'

'Shot…battered to death, what's the odds? I thought he was going for the pistol,' he growled back at her, before turning his attention to Emma who had not been slow to act during the brief altercation.

Having extracted her own pistol, she held it hidden between the folds of her skirt, no longer troubled about making use of it, when she detected the telltale glint in Flint's dark eyes as he cast an insulting glance over her figure. His intent was patently obvious, as his next words proved.

'You can leave the wench to me. I don't intend to dispose of her quite yet. I'll take her to the lodge.'

'I do not think so,' Emma countered, raising her right hand. 'Take one step nearer, and I shall fire.'

The unexpected sight of the pistol clasped in her steady, slender fingers certainly gave Flint pause for thought, but Isabel merely sneered. 'Don't be a fool! I doubt she even knows how to fire the thing. Take it from her!'

'I would strongly advise you to disobey that order,' Emma cautioned, while deep down knowing that she was wasting her breath and that she would ever afterwards be forced to live with the knowledge that she had taken a human life.

As anticipated he chose not to heed the warning, and made to dash forward, leaving Emma no choice but to squeeze the trigger, and a moment later Flint lay on the ground, with a lethal piece of lead shot firmly embedded in his chest.

Hardly had the second deafening report died away than there came a thunderous hammering on the front door, quickly followed by the sound of breaking glass, and a beloved voice frantically shouting Emma's name. She was so overcome with relief that she discovered it was as much as she could do to answer his call, and a moment later Benedict came striding into the room.

In one sweeping glance, he took in the deplorable scene. His eyes momentarily focused on the smoking pistol still clasped in Emma's hand, before he rounded on the woman now cowering in the doorway.

It was obvious by her distraught expression that Isabel knew it would be useless to attempt to convince him or anyone else of her own innocence, and he did not hesitate to assure her of this fact. 'Sir Lionel will be here in a very short time, and then you, madam, shall be brought to book for your crimes.'

A spark of defiance returned to her eyes. 'At least when I go to the scaffold I shall have the satisfaction of knowing that *he* shall never reside under this roof.'

Emma, having dropped to her knees to examine Richard's wound, was appalled by Isabel Ashworth's expression of unholy satisfaction, and gained no little amount herself in announcing that the young Baron was not dead yet. 'And be assured, madam, I shall do everything within my power to ensure that he remains alive.'

A piercing scream rent the air as Isabel made to dash forward, but her frantic attempt to lay violent hands on Richard, or Emma, or perhaps both, was easily foiled by Benedict who grasped her arm and almost flung her back against the wall, his expression one of utter loathing.

'You have committed your last evil deed, madam.' He almost spat the words at her, and the answering shout of hysterical laughter clearly revealed the state of Isabel Ashworth's mind, before she slipped quietly from the room.

'Do you not think you should go after her, Ben?' Emma suggested, momentarily raising her eyes from the task of placing her handkerchief over the wound in Richard's shoulder in an attempt to stem the flow of blood, which had already alarmingly stained a large portion of his shirt.

Benedict, who had been watching Isabel's headlong flight up the stairs, came across to kneel beside Emma, and examined the wound for himself. 'If she attempts to escape, she'll not get far. My first priority is to get this young man to a doctor. If he continues losing blood at this rate, your desire to thwart that fiendish woman will come to naught.'

Agonisingly aware of this herself, Emma did not attempt to argue. She watched him leave the room, and was relieved when he returned only minutes later with his groom. Richard was then carried out to the carriage, and Emma quickly scrambled in beside him in order to hold both her own and Benedict's hand-kerchiefs over the wound, which she prayed would not prove fatal.

'John will take you back to the inn now, Emma.' Benedict cast one last anxious glance at the young lord's unconscious form. 'The sooner he's in the hands of a physician the better. I shall remain here until Sir Lionel arrives.'

He took a step back from the door, and was about to issue orders to his groom to return to the inn as swiftly as possible, when Emma uttered a strangled cry, and he swung round in the direction of her point-ing finger to see Isabel Ashworth, framed in flames and billowing smoke, standing at one of the upper floor windows in the west wing.

Cutting across Emma's demand to remain, Benedict successfully thwarted her attempt to alight by slamming the carriage door firmly shut. He remained only until his groom had given the horses the office to start, and then hurried back into the house.

By the time he had mounted the stairs the gallery passageway was thick with choking smoke. Isabel in her frenzied state had attempted to set light to each and every room in the west wing, undoubtedly in a determined last effort to ensure that her nephew would never reside in the house she had always considered her own. Her vindictiveness knew no bounds, it seemed, and Benedict very much feared that her last malicious act would turn out to be wholly successful.

Flames began to appear beneath several of the partially closed doors, and swiftly spread across the red carpet, halting his progress towards the room where he guessed Isabel was to be found. He called out frantically, and was answered by a cackle of demented laughter, before a firm grasp on his arm checked any further attempt to save her, and Harry's anxious voice begged him not to try.

As they reached the foot of the stairs, the whole of the gallery was ablaze, and even though Harry rode straight back to the village to get help, little could be salvaged. The fire continued throughout the night, and could be seen for miles around. By morning the house was a smouldering shell, its roof completely destroyed, its few remaining walls smoke-blackened and crumbling, a ruin beyond repair.

Chapter Twelve

During the following days Benedict was destined to see too little of Emma. Naturally he apprised her of the total destruction of the Hall, and of Isabel Ashworth perishing in the blaze, and she in turn managed to find time to relate the conversation she had overheard between Isabel and Lucius Flint. None the less Benedict very much doubted that Emma was granted much opportunity to dwell overlong on either the damning revelations or the ensuing tragedy, for her time was taken up in nursing Richard.

Although Dr Fielding successfully extracted the piece of lead shot from Richard's shoulder, the wound became inflamed. This, coupled with the considerable loss of blood, resulted in his patient becoming feverish, and requiring constant attention. For three days and nights the high temperature raged, and Richard's life hung in the balance, but thankfully midway through the fourth day Benedict received word that the fever had broken, and that Dr Fielding considered his patient no longer in danger. Richard's appetite gradually began to return, and by the end of the week he was betraying definite signs of regaining his strength.

Returning to the inn after a midmorning stroll about the village, Benedict came upon Emma emerging from the sickroom. He nodded in approval at the scant remains of breakfast on the tray she carried. Unfortunately her own appearance did not afford him any such satisfaction.

She was looking pale and tired, which was only to be expected after all the time she had spent taking care of Richard. Both he and Harry had spent time in the sickroom during those first few days, when Richard had been feverish and had needed constant attention. Martha too had been of immense help, but, with the inn to run, she could not be on hand twenty-four hours a day. Consequently the brunt of the nursing had fallen upon Emma.

'The young invalid is continuing to regain his appetite, I see. A very good sign, I think.' He chose not to add that this would result in her being able to spend more time with him.

'Oh yes. I was speaking to the doctor earlier and he sees no reason to continue his daily visits, though he thinks it will be a while yet before Richard is fully recovered.'

'By which time, if I know anything, the only condition plaguing our young friend will be rank boredom. Which I shall do my best to alleviate now by paying him a short visit.'

He paused with his hand on the door-handle as he bethought himself of something. 'Emma,' he called, arresting her progress towards the stairs. 'I came upon Sir Lionel during my walk. He intends to call here later and would appreciate a word with you in private. I'll let you know when he arrives.'

Receiving a nod in response, Benedict entered the bedchamber to discover Richard propped against a mound of pillows, looking remarkably well considering the ordeal he had been through. The bandage had now been removed from his head, but his left arm was still strapped tightly across his chest in an attempt to stop him from straining the injured shoulder and re-opening the wound.

He smiled to himself as he made use of the chair placed by the bed. 'You will be pleased to know that you are beginning to look quite disgustingly healthy.'

'And not before time!' Richard muttered, betraying clear signs of tedium already. 'The pain in my head has gone completely, but the shoulder is still a little sore.'

'More than just a little, I suspect, you lying young rogue! Don't attempt to do too much too soon.'

'Not much chance of that.' Richard grimaced. 'The doctor insists I remain in bed for another week, possibly two.' He gazed into the intelligent blue eyes which betrayed a trace of sympathy now. 'I say, Ben, I'm glad you've taken the trouble to pay me a visit. It grants me the opportunity to thank you for everything you've done. Sir Lionel explained yesterday, when he called to see me, just how much I owe to you.'

Benedict dismissed this with a wave of one shapely hand. 'He exaggerated, my dear boy. If you should be grateful to anyone, then it is Emma.'

'By Jove, yes! And don't I know it.' There was more than just a hint of affection in Richard's lazy smile. 'What a girl, eh? You're a damned lucky fellow, Ben.' He looked up at him a little self-consciously. 'Harry warned me on the day I arrived here not to poach on his uncle's territory.'

'Oh, he did, did he?' Benedict was much struck by this. 'I didn't realise my nephew possessed such powers of penetration.'

Richard chuckled at the dry tone, and then winced at the pain which shot through his shoulder. 'No, I could never repay what she's done for me during this past week. Not to mention putting herself at considerable risk to come searching for me at the Hall. I understand that it was she who shot Flint.'

Benedict regarded the younger man in silence for a moment, before nodding his head in confirmation. 'But you will oblige me by not remarking upon that fact, especially not in Emma's hearing, for unless I much mistake the matter, that is the one incident in the whole wretched business with which she will find it difficult to come to terms.'

'Understood,' Richard responded, his eyes glowing with respect. 'She's a dashed brave little soul, none the less! A pearl beyond price!'

'You think so, young man?' was Benedict's laconic response. 'My opinion of her behaviour differs somewhat from yours... A fact that it will afford me the utmost pleasure to make perfectly plain to her at the first available opportunity.'

Benedict then changed the subject by informing him of the precise condition of his ancestral home, lest Sir Lionel had omitted to do so. 'With half the village at the Andover Fair, we couldn't round up enough people even to attempt to contain the blaze. Believe me, no one regrets its destruction more than I,' he went on to confess. 'I would have given much to have been able to thwart Isabel Ashworth's determination that you would never reside in that house.'

'Don't give it another thought, my dear fellow,' Richard surprised Benedict by announcing cheerfully. 'Although she didn't know it, my aunt did me a good turn by destroying the Hall. I only ever set foot in the place three times, but I was certain that I would never feel comfortable there. Now I can build a new house overlooking the lake, which will be mine from the first.'

He shook his head in wonder. 'When I first arrived back in England, I wasn't at all sure that I would wish to remain. I thought I should find life devilish dull. How wrong can one be! It has been anything but!'

An hour later Benedict wandered through to the kitchen to discover both Emma and Martha seated at the table, effecting necessary repairs to various items of household linen. 'If you have no objection, Mrs Rudge, I shall deprive you of your helpmate for a short while. Sir Lionel arrived a few minutes ago, and is wishful to have a few words with her in the privacy of the parlour.'

Benedict clearly detected the suddenly assessing look in her dark eyes. It was much to Samuel and Martha's credit that neither of them had attempted to uncover precisely what had taken place at the Hall a week ago. Sir Lionel had not delayed in extracting a promise of strict silence from both Emma and Harry, and although there had been much talk and speculation amongst the villagers since the tragedy occurred, very few remained in possession of all the facts.

'Do by all means take her, my dear Mr Grantley. And perhaps after she has seen Sir Lionel, you might oblige me by persuading her to rest for a while?'

'Be assured I shall see that she does so.'

'Oh, you will, will you?' Emma muttered, as she accompanied him from the kitchen.

'Most definitely,' he answered, smiling at the disgruntled tone. 'It is high time I took you in hand again, my girl... And in more ways than one,' he added in a husky whisper, as he opened the door for her to pass through into the parlour, where Sir Lionel and Harry, seated at the table, were enjoying a glass of wine.

If Sir Lionel noticed Emma's heightened colour, he decided not to remark upon it, as he rose to his feet, and requested her and Benedict to join them in a glass of mine host's fine burgundy.

'I cannot thank you enough, all of you, for maintaining a strict silence over this dreadful business,' Sir Lionel began, after dispensing wine for the new arrivals. 'The day after the fire, Grantley paid me a visit and put me in possession of all the facts.' He shook his head wearily, clearly betraying that he had been under considerable strain himself during the past days. 'I must confess I found what he told me hard to believe. However, acting on information given to me by Miss Lynn, I have spared no effort in trying to discover the identity of the lawyer in whose hands Flint claimed to have placed a certain document. Eventually my search proved fruitful, and in the light of recent events the lawyer in question had little choice but to hand over the papers with which he had been entrusted. I have apprised myself of their contents, and can report that it confirms your suspicions, Grantley.'

Sighing, he rose to his feet once again and went to stand before the window. 'Incredible,' he murmured. 'One can be acquainted with people all one's life, and never really know them.'

Harry, noting the stooping set of the Baronet's shoulders, privately considered that poor Sir Lionel appeared to have aged ten years in the past few days. 'It's clear that Isabel Ashworth had planned to put a period to Richard's life, sir. But surely she didn't have a hand in Hammond's death?'

'I shall leave it to your uncle to explain. He, I'm sure, can do so much better than I. Needless to say, what he tells you is in the strictest confidence.'

'Understood, sir,' Harry responded, before turning to Benedict who, appearing calm and collected as always, reached for his wine.

'Before we embarked on this visit to Ashworth Magna, Nephew,' he began, after fortifying himself from the contents of his glass, 'I had already apprised you of the fact that Lavinia Hammond suspected that there was more to her husband's death than the mere fatal attack by footpads which at first it had appeared to be, and I swiftly came to the same conclusion. It was obvious to me that Hammond's death and that of the maid-servant, Sally Pritchard, were in some way connected. Hammond certainly didn't believe the maid had met her death from a mere fall down the stairs, and after discovering the extent of her injuries, I have to admit that neither did I. Emma has since discovered that it was indeed Isabel herself who murdered the maid, and with Flint's aid placed the body at the foot of the stairs to make it appear like an accident.'

Emma sampled the contents of her own glass. What

had been related thus far she had managed to piece together herself. Something, however, continued to puzzle her. 'What I fail to understand is why Isabel should have wished Sally Pritchard dead in the first place.'

'Because, my dear, the girl knew something that would have brought about not only Isabel's ruin, if it ever became common knowledge, but also that of Clarissa Ashworth. Remember what the servants at Ashworth Hall told you—Sally was boasting quite openly that she was soon to come into a great deal of money. I suspect she was demanding a sizeable sum in return for her silence, and Isabel decided that it would prove far less expensive to silence her permanently.'

'But what could a maid-servant who didn't even come from these parts possibly know to Isabel Ashworth's discredit?' Harry demanded, looking utterly bewildered.

'To appreciate that fully,' Benedict answered, 'one must go back more than half a century to the day Richard's paternal grandmother gave birth to twins. The first to be born was Isabel. It was felt by all those who watched her grow into adulthood that it was a great pity that she had not been born the boy, for she was held to have had far more spirit and determination than her twin brother. It was she who ran the estate after their father's death. And from what I have learned from Sir Lionel and others, she ran things extremely successfully.'

'Yes, she was certainly efficient. I'll grant the woman that much at least,' Sir Lionel confirmed grimly, returning at last to the table. 'Her brother Roderick was a likeable fellow, but there's no denying he was indolent, content to allow others do the work. He lacked his sister's head for business. Isabel had the brains, there is no question.'

'And the ambition,' Benedict continued. 'She came to look upon the place as her own: mistress of the house; master of the estate. So imagine her chagrin, after years of ruling the roost, when her brother returns from an impromptu visit to the capital with a pretty young bride on his arm. Isabel must have been devastated at being forced to relinquish her position to the frivolous pea-goose her slothful brother had married after a whirlwind courtship, and in her very unsettled state she behaved for once in her life with foolish abandon by seeking solace in the arms of a handsome, young ne'er-do-well by name of Jonathan Kemp, who paid a brief visit early one autumn many years ago to the house which Colonel Meecham and his good lady wife now own.'

Again Benedict paused in order to refresh himself from the contents of his glass. 'I do not suppose for a moment that it ever crossed Isabel's mind to form a permanent attachment with the handsome man who was some ten years her junior, and who was merely the younger son of an impoverished country gentleman. She certainly acquired the means by which she might have induced him to offer for her hand. Their short and passionate affair, you see, proved—er—fruitful.'

'Good gad!' Harry didn't attempt to hide his astonishment. 'Do you mean she bore him a child? That's the first I've heard of it.'

'Isabel took great pains to ensure that no one living

hereabouts should discover her secret,' Benedict assured him. 'As soon as she realised she was with child, she went away to live with a maiden aunt, a somewhat reclusive woman, by all accounts, who lived in the heart of rural Northamptonshire, with only two servants to bear her company—a woman in late middle-age and a young manservant by name of Flint. In the late spring of the following year, just a few short weeks after the death of her aunt, Isabel gave birth to a daughter, and swiftly afterwards returned to Ashworth Hall, leaving her child in the care of the woman who, since her aunt's demise, had become her own devoted servant, as too had Flint.'

Benedict noticed a look of dawning wonder replace puzzlement in a pair of soft grey eyes, and smiled to himself. Emma was certainly beginning to see a chink of light, even if poor Harry remained fumbling blindly about in the dark.

'Isabel's confinement took place just two or three weeks before her sister-in-law's,' he continued. 'As we all know Lady Ashworth contracted childbed fever shortly after giving birth to a baby daughter, and sadly died. The baby too, according to the aged doctor who attended the birth, was weak and sickly, and not expected to live.' He stared across the table at Sir Lionel. 'Perhaps, sir, you would care to continue with the story, as you yourself can recall the tragic events, and have also read Flint's written testimony, which I have not.'

'Very well,' Sir Lionel agreed a trifle grimly. 'According to Flint's account, he received an urgent summons from Isabel Ashworth to close the house in Northamptonshire and bring both child and maid-servant to Ashworth Hall, and to travel through the night if necessary. He arrived late the following evening and, as had been previously arranged, was met by Isabel herself and smuggled secretly into the house. In the nursery, he discovered the Ashworth baby dead in her crib.'

'You don't suppose that…?' Harry's words faded, but Sir Lionel guessed the question that the young man could not bring himself to ask.

'In the light of recent events one is certainly given to wonder whether Isabel did in fact murder her baby niece, I must agree,' the Baronet conceded. 'But, no, I do not think it. Dr Hammond's predecessor made it clear to me, as I was a close friend of the family, that he believed that within a few days the child would join her mother. Which, according to Flint's account, is precisely what happened. He was ordered to place the child in her mother's coffin.'

Benedict raised a sceptical brow. 'One would like to suppose that this was a charitable act on Isabel's part. But I'm inclined to think that she considered her sister-in-law's recently dug grave the safest place to hide the infant.'

'An exhumation would confirm the truth of Flint's story,' Emma suggested, but Benedict surprisingly shook his head.

'Neither Sir Lionel nor I am in favour of that. But we will discuss the matter further, presently. To continue—having successfully installed her own child in the house, she dismissed the nursemaid, replacing her with her own servant who, I am given to understand, has since died—through natural causes, one must assume, given that she was quite advanced in years when

she first came to Ashworth Hall. Isabel also arranged
for a new wet-nurse to nourish the infant. If members
of the household staff thought these arrangements
strange at the time, they certainly considered Isabel
had acted in the child's best interests when the baby,
against all the odds, survived. No one suspected the
truth. The doctor who had brought Lord Ashworth's
baby into the world was far from well himself, and
retired at this time. When Dr Hammond arrived here
shortly afterwards, he wrote in his diary that he could
not understand his predecessor's concerns, for Clarissa, as she had by this time been christened, was
perfectly healthy.'

'All the luck was certainly running Isabel Ashworth's way,' Harry muttered, disgruntled.

'It certainly was,' Benedict agreed. 'And continued
to do so for very many years. She resumed her former
position in the house, and had the satisfaction of
watching her own child raised as her brother's legitimate offspring. However, Lady Luck, as we all know,
is apt to be capricious, and eventually turned her back
on Isabel. Ill fortune then began to strike some dev-
astating blows. Her brother died and she discovered
that the heir to the Ashworth estate was not her weak-
willed cousin Cedric, but a nephew of whose existence
she had been in complete ignorance.

'Worse was to come. The young woman whom she
had engaged as parlour-maid was not slow to remark
upon the strong resemblance her young mistress bore
to a certain family she had known in Worcestershire
by the name of Kemp. This untimely reminder of her
ex-lover had been a further crushing blow. I wouldn't
be at all surprised to discover that Isabel made enqui-

ries, and discovered, as I did myself last week, that Jonathan Kemp married a wealthy farmer's daughter, and has two legitimate offspring. Undeniably, Clarissa bears a strong resemblance to her father, but the resemblance to her half-sister is most striking. I also discovered that a man by the name of Pritchard worked as a labourer on the farm, and shared a cottage with his younger daughter who, after his death, left the district and went to live with her married sister in Andover.'

Emma shook her head sadly. 'Sally's knowledge sealed her fate, just as Dr Hammond's suspicions sealed his. And Richard's desire to remove his aunt and cousin from under his roof very nearly sealed his. How many more would Isabel happily have sent to their graves in order to achieve her ambition to see her daughter as mistress of Ashworth Hall and her own place secure there for the rest of her life?'

'One can only wonder whether both Cedric and his wife might have met an untimely end,' Benedict responded in all seriousness.

Sir Lionel nodded his head, acknowledging the possibility that this might well have turned out to be the case. 'I for one cannot be sorry that Isabel did perish in the fire,' he admitted at length. 'She can harm no one else, and for the sake of the family it is as well that the full extent of her misdeeds will never become generally known.'

'Yes, that's all very well, sir,' Harry put in, after giving this a moment's consideration. 'I wouldn't like to think that Richard might suffer as a consequence of his aunt's actions by having the Ashworth name dragged through the mud. Isabel and her scheming henchman are both dead. But what of those two men hired to murder Dr Hammond, and dispose of Richard? I do not believe any strangers were seen lurking near Ashworth Hall on the night of the fire. Which isn't very surprising—the fire could be seen for miles around. They would have known something was wrong, and possibly decided not to venture near the place. Surely, though, fresh enquiries can be made to discover their identities?'

Sir Lionel betrayed clear signs of unease. 'Yes, my boy, they could of course,' he reluctantly agreed. 'In view of the fact that Flint made certain references to the hired assassins in the document he left with his lawyer, mentioning that they are, in fact, brothers and that he had learned of their existence and their unsavoury reputation from the landlord of a certain inn Flint frequented in Salisbury, fresh investigations could be undertaken to uncover their identities. But I have no intention of instigating a search. If those two villains were ever captured and put on trial, then I'm afraid the sorry truth about Isabel Ashworth and her nefarious deeds could not remain a secret. I'm not just thinking of the boy upstairs, I'm also trying to consider my ward, Clarissa. If it ever became common knowledge that she was Isabel's illegitimate daughter, her life would be as good as ruined. She would become a social outcast.'

Emma gazed sightlessly down at her lap, silently acknowledging the truth of what Sir Lionel had said. She had had firsthand experience of just what it was like suddenly to find oneself a social leper, ostracised from polite circles. True, she had been welcomed into the homes of people like Lavinia Hammond and Colonel Meecham in recent years. Sir Lionel, too, on the few occasions their paths had crossed, had always treated her with respect, even though she had never been invited to join social evenings at his home. It wasn't until Benedict's arrival that she had been granted entrée into the world of those more affluent members of the community.

For someone like Clarissa, who had been socially acceptable throughout her life, to find herself suddenly barred from the polite world would come as a crushing blow. The girl might be totally spoilt and utterly thoughtless, but she didn't deserve such a miserable fate, Emma decided. Why make the girl suffer through no fault of her own, when it could be so easily avoided?

'I agree with Sir Lionel,' she said softly, breaking the silence. 'I do not suppose for a moment that Clarissa was ever in the confidence of the woman whom she had always believed to be her aunt, so why should she be made to pay for Isabel's misdeeds?'

'Yes, you have something there, Emma,' Harry conceded.

Sir Lionel's smile of approval encompassed them both. 'I spoke briefly to Richard earlier, and can assure you that he is not wishful to take matters any further... So that just leaves you, Grantley.'

All eyes turned towards Benedict, but he left them waiting for his decision whilst he finished the wine in his glass. 'I did not come here to Ashworth Magna for the purpose of damaging reputations or ruining innocent lives, but to uncover the truth about Hammond's death, which I have done. So, I will agree to maintain a strict silence on one condition—Lavinia Hammond must learn the truth. I do not suppose for a moment that she will wish to take matters further in view of the repercussions. But I insist that she, having suffered such a tragic loss, is given the final say.'

It was several moments before Sir Lionel nodded his head in agreement, and then rose to his feet. 'Very well, Grantley. I shall go and see Lavinia now,' he announced, before turning eyes filled with admiration on one of those still seated at the table. 'I have not yet had the opportunity to thank you for what you did that night, Miss Lynn. You are a remarkably brave young woman.'

'I second that,' Harry announced, adding to the colour which had sprung into Emma's delicate cheeks. 'Richard will be forever in your debt. Why, I do believe he's half in love with you, Em! He can't stop talking about you. Which reminds me… I haven't seen him this morning. I'll go up for half an hour and bear him company.'

Benedict waited until Harry had followed Sir Lionel from the room before giving voice to his own opinion, denouncing her actions in a few well chosen, pithy phrases which had the colour flooding back into her cheeks with a vengeance.

'Featherbrained?' she echoed, more annoyed than upset by the blistering condemnation. 'Well, let me tell you, Benedict Grantley, that if you had been here, or at the very least had shared your suspicions with me, last week's whole sorry escapade might have been—'

Surprise checked her scolding tongue, as she found herself unexpectedly hauled off the chair and held captive in two strong arms on Benedict's lap. To have put up the least struggle would have been undignified, she swiftly decided, besides being a complete waste of effort. Furthermore, she was surprisingly not wholly averse to these unexpected displays of male dominance, though she felt obliged to remark that she hadn't taken into account that her future husband might turn out to possess a masterful disposition.

'I couldn't possibly marry a man of whom I was afraid,' she added for good measure.

'Delicious little liar,' he muttered thickly, as he ran a trail of feather-light kisses down the length of her slender neck to the base of her throat. 'You are not in the least afraid of me. You know full well I would never harm so much as a hair on that beautiful head of yours.'

He then proceeded to silence any further absurdities she might be inclined to utter by capturing her mouth and kissing her thoroughly. 'On the other hand, though,' he added, when at last he drew his lips from hers, 'I might be forced to take a firm stand if you continue flirting with young Ashworth.'

Emma might have supposed that he was faintly resentful over the time she had been obliged to spend nursing Richard during these past days, and possibly a little jealous too of the sisterly affection in which she held the younger man, had she not easily discerned a teasing glint in those striking blue orbs.

'I shall take leave to inform you sir,' she returned, with all the starchiness of a prim schoolmistress, 'that I have never flirted in my life. Furthermore, I wouldn't know how.'

'No?' His sceptical expression was most marked. 'Well, you've certainly been granted ample opportunity to put in some practice, my girl. According to my information, you've been enjoying several informal and jolly dinners together. Yet not once,' he did not hesitate to remind her, 'have you ever attempted to join me for meals in the parlour.'

'Oh, well,' she responded, little realising the effect her fingers were having on his libido, as she began to tease them through his thick crop of waving black hair. 'I knew instinctively that Richard posed no threat; whereas you, sir, were clearly a danger from the first.'

'Just as you are proving a severe trial to my good intentions now,' he rejoined.'

Unable to withstand the arousing touch of those tantalising fingers a moment longer, Benedict eased her off his lap, grasping her hands and holding them securely before they could wreak more havoc on his senses. 'I vowed from the first that I would treat you with no less respect than I would the daughter of a duke,' he freely admitted, as he too rose. 'But I must confess that you are placing me under considerable strain. So, I would suggest, for your sake as well as mine, that we are married as swiftly as possible. Otherwise, my girl, you will be enjoying the delights of the wedding night before the ceremony has taken place.'

The clearly inviting look she cast him through her long, curling lashes was proof enough that the prospect of doing just that did not disturb her to any great extent.

'Baggage!' He shook his head at her in mock reproach. 'It's as well for you that I know you're a complete innocent. I shall leave for the capital tomorrow, obtain a special licence, and then you will pay for your tantalising, you provoking little temptress.'

He felt obliged to silence her gurgle of mirth, but released her at once when he detected the click of the door, and turned to see his nephew standing on the threshold, the expression of mingled embarrassment and amusement on his young face clearly betraying the fact that he had witnessed the embrace.

'Sorry, bad timing. Only popped in to say Richard's asleep, so I'm off up the road to inflict myself on the Meechams for an hour or two.'

'No, don't rush off just yet,' Benedict enjoined, swiftly capturing his future wife's hand and retaining it in a gentle clasp. 'You may be the first to congratulate me, Nephew. Emma has done me the very great honour of agreeing to be my wife.'

With a whoop of joy, Harry came forward to shake his uncle's free hand warmly, and to place a smacking kiss upon Emma's cheek. 'What an aunt you're giving me, Ben! I could not be more delighted!'

Although secretly pleased by this reaction to his news, Benedict bent a sardonic glance upon his nephew. 'You do not appear unduly surprised by the news.'

'Good gad! You must take me for a complete simpleton. You can't go about behaving quite out of character, and expect me not to suspect that something's in the wind.' Harry turned to Emma, beaming at her with approval. 'You're a wonderful influence on him, m'dear. He was in the gravest danger of becoming set in his ways, and turning into a devilish dull dog. But there's no danger of that happening now, thank the Lord! When do you intend to tie the knot?'

'As soon as it can be arranged,' Benedict answered, more amused than annoyed by these slurs on his character. 'I'm off to London in the morning to arrange matters. Do you wish to accompany me?'

'No, I think I'll take a jaunt into Devon. Received a letter from a friend of mine, Freddy Farnham, whilst you were away. He's invited me to spend the rest of the summer with him at his parents' place. It'll be a dashed more agreeable than squiring Mama round Brighton. I discovered in a letter I had from Papa that she's in Bath at the moment, taking care of great-aunt Agatha who, apparently, hasn't been too well. I'll ride over to Salisbury in the morning and arrange the hire of a post-chaise, and will leave the following day.'

'So, you are abandoning me again, and so soon,' Emma remarked the instant Harry departed.

Benedict could not fail to hear the note of disappointment in her voice. 'Yes, but for the very last time, I promise you. There are matters I must attend to, not least of which is closing my town residence, and arranging for the servants to return to Fairview in order to have the house in perfect order for the arrival of its mistress.'

Mistress of Fairview…how perfect that sounded! Emma mused, happy to rest her head on the broad expanse of chest and feel those strong arms automatically wrap themselves about her. They would be parted for a few days only. Surely she could manage without him for the short time it might take for him to arrange everything for their wedding? Then they could enjoy the rest of their lives together, she told herself, sublimely ignoring the strange little shiver which unexpectedly rippled through her.

Chapter Thirteen

At about the same time as Benedict was on the point of paying a visit to a close friend in the capital, whose esteemed uncle was no less a personage than a Bishop, Harry was entering a fashionable dwelling in Bath.

Having decided to spend the summer with his friend, he had considered it only polite to pay his respects to his mother, since he had not been in contact with her since leaving London, and inform her in person that he had changed his plans and would not now be joining the family in Brighton. He knew his esteemed parent well enough to be sure that she would not kick up a fuss over so trivial a matter, and she justified this faith in her by receiving his decision calmly, merely saying that he would surely attain far more pleasure in the company of his friend than he would parading round the fashionable seaside resort.

'So, how did you enjoy your stay at Fairview?' she asked, after seating herself with her back to the window in the sunny front parlour. Bright morning sunlight was no longer flattering to a woman of her years, and she possessed sense enough to realise this. 'Not that I need to enquire,' she added. 'You always enjoy your uncle's company.'

'Yes, I do,' he freely admitted. 'We remained at Fairview a few days only, then we travelled into Wiltshire. Didn't Father let you know? I wrote to him.'

'No, he did not. Which is no great surprise, of course. You should know by now that your father allows the world to pass him by once he's safely back at his country estate. It would come as no great surprise to me either to discover that he still thinks I'm in London.'

Harry frankly laughed, for this was possibly all too true. Both he and his father much preferred life in the country, and were inclined to absorb themselves so fully in rural pursuits that the world tended to pass them by. 'I'm astonished that you've managed to persuade him to accompany you to Brighton.'

'Well, dear, I'm afraid for the next few years he must accustom himself to leaving his Berkshire acres. We've husbands to find for your four sisters. Caroline will be eighteen early next year,' she reminded him. 'I'm seriously considering the idea of bringing her to Bath in the autumn to prepare her for her come-out next spring. Aunt Agatha is more than willing to put us up here for the duration of our stay, so that will save me the trouble of renting a house.'

Suddenly recalling the reason behind his mother's visit to Bath, Harry belatedly enquired after the health of his great aunt. 'Not still keeping to her bed, I trust?'

'No. She's much improved. It was nothing more serious than a summer chill. She's resumed her daily visits to the Pump Room. She's there now, as it happens, taking the waters. I do not think there is the least necessity for me to remain here very much longer. I shall probably return to Berkshire at the end of the week in good time to prepare for the trip to Brighton.'

For a few moments Lady Fencham allowed her mind to dwell pleasurably on the planned sojourn by the sea. Then she suddenly bethought herself of something that now occurred to her as most odd. 'You've been in Wiltshire, you say? What on earth possessed you to go there?'

Harry was instantly on his guard. He had pledged his word not to divulge the reason behind the visit. None the less, it was fairly safe to assume that sooner or later his mother would discover precisely where they had stayed, so he saw little point in striving to conceal the fact now.

'Ben took it into his head to do a spot of sightseeing. We stayed at Ashworth Magna, as it happens. Put up at the inn there. Saw quite a bit of Mrs Hammond and Deborah.'

Lady Fencham did not attempt to hide her surprise. 'Good heavens! I didn't realise that Benedict was planning to stay there. It's a pretty enough place, I grant you, but you must have been dreadfully bored.'

'On the contrary. Spent quite a bit of time over at Sir Lionel Brent's place. I expect you know him quite well.' He then went on to disclose the fact that he had met and become friendly with the new Lord Ashworth, and also informed her of the destruction of Ashworth Hall, an account of which would almost certainly appear in the newspapers in the very near future.

'How dreadful! I sincerely hope nobody was hurt.'

'Miss Isabel Ashworth perished in the blaze. Did you know her?'

'Yes…well, vaguely. I met her on several occasions when I visited Lavinia. She seemed quite content to spend all her time at Ashworth Hall. What a strange creature she was! No one else was hurt, I trust? I seem to recall a niece living there.'

'Yes, Clarissa Ashworth. She's in Brighton, staying with relatives. Sir Lionel has gone there to break the news. Isabel was buried a few days after the—er—accident.' He refrained from disclosing that there had not been much left of the villainous woman to bury. 'In the circumstances, Sir Lionel thought it best to keep the funeral a very quiet affair.'

After nodding her head in approval, Lady Fencham changed the subject by enquiring the present whereabouts of her younger brother.

'Oh, he's taken himself off to the capital for a few days. Then he intends to return to Ashworth Magna.'

Once again his mother betrayed surprise. 'What on earth can possibly induce him to return there?'

'Believe me, Mama, there is a great inducement,' Harry informed her, certain that Benedict would not object to his sister knowing about his plans to marry, even if he had every intention of keeping the ceremony very private. 'You'll never believe it… Uncle Benedict's only gone and found himself a charmer at last!'

Lady Fencham visibly bristled with indignation. 'I shall take leave to inform you, my son, that I do not consider that a suitable topic to raise in polite company.'

Harry did not misunderstand, and frankly laughed. 'Not that sort of charmer, Mama,' he assured her.

'Against all the odds, Ben's finally fallen in love. When you meet Emma you'll understand why.'

Realising that her son was not trying to hoodwink her, Lady Fencham was momentarily lost for words, 'But—but who is this female, Harry? Who are her people?'

'Dash it all, Mama! I didn't go asking questions like that. I seem to recall someone telling me that both her parents are dead. Her name is Emma Lynn. She's a great gun. And she'll make Ben the perfect wife.'

These few snippets were insufficient to satisfy Lady Fencham's curiosity. 'But where did Benedict meet this young woman?'

'Oh, she resides at the inn at Ashworth Magna. She's the cook there. And a dashed good one too. Best food I've tasted in years!'

Never before had Lady Fencham been so thankful for her innate powers of self-control. Her son might suppose his tidings joyous; she most assuredly did not. Yet, no one observing her sitting calmly in the chair, hands clasped in her lap, would have supposed for a moment that she was striving to control both astonishment and outrage at this totally unexpected and appalling turn of events.

She was at a complete loss to understand what could possibly have come over the brother whose keen intelligence and impeccable manners she had always so admired. How could he even think of polluting the proud Grantley blood by marrying such a creature? Every fibre of her being recoiled at the mere thought of calling such a one 'sister'. No, it was not to be borne! Benedict might have lost all sense of pride and honour, but she most assuredly had not. She would put a stop to this nonsense before it went any further!

'Well, aren't you delighted by the news, Mama?' Harry prompted, after having had his attention momentarily diverted by a rather smart racing curricle bowling along the street.

'Believe me, my son, I am utterly overwhelmed,' she responded, focusing her attention on an imaginary crease in her skirt. 'Evidently much has happened during my short sojourn in Bath. I think it behoves me to hasten my departure, and return to the bosom of my family.'

It was early the following afternoon when Emma received an express from Benedict, informing her that his business in the capital had taken less time than expected, that he would be returning to Hampshire on the morrow, and would be with her again the day after. She read and reread the words written in that bold, flowing hand, cherishing each and every sweet endearment he had managed to insert in the brief missive.

'If you read that many more times the ink will fade,' Martha warned, entering the kitchen before Emma had a chance to return the note to the pocket of her apron.

Samuel, glancing up from the weekly list he always made of provisions needing to be purchased, chuckled at this. 'No need to ask who it's from, Martha.'

'No, indeed. Though why Mr Grantley didn't take his belongings with him when he left, I cannot imagine. It would have saved him the bother of returning here for them.'

Samuel's great shoulders shook again. 'He's coming

back for more than just his baggage if I know anything, m'dear.'

Emma gazed from one to the other. She would have
much preferred to wait until Benedict's return before
informing them officially, but as it was patently obvious by the twinkles in their eyes that they had already guessed, she saw little reason not to confirm
their suspicions.

'Yes, you're quite right, Samuel. Mr Grantley has
asked me to be his wife. I've been longing to share
my news with you both,' she went on to tell them,
after receiving hugs and heartfelt congratulations,
'only for some reason Ben wished to keep our betrothal secret for the time being, though he did inform
Harry before he left.'

'Well, I dare say dear Mr Grantley had his reasons
for wanting to keep his intentions secret. Not that we
needed to be told,' Martha openly admitted. 'We both
knew there was something in the wind. Sam, here, was
far quicker to realise it than I was.'

'Can't mistake the look in a man's eye, Martha,
when his intentions are serious, like.' Samuel raised
his head, when he detected a voice raised in the coffee
room. 'Now, who be that, I wonder?' He rose to his
feet. 'Someone else trying to ferret out what's happened to young Lord Ashworth, I expect. Well, they'll
learn nowt from me.'

Emma didn't suppose for a moment that whoever it
was would learn anything from Samuel, or from Martha either, come to that. Both were completely trust-
worthy, and not given to indulging in idle, malicious
gossip. She just wished she could have been perfectly

honest with them both and told them the complete truth.

When she had returned to the inn with Richard on that dreadful evening, there had been no time for detailed explanations. Obviously, the fact that Richard had been shot could not be concealed, and she had not hesitated to inform them of the perpetrator of the crime. After having had a brief consultation with Benedict the following morning, however, it had been decided that, if possible, the full facts should be concealed. So Emma had made it known that the fire which had resulted in Isabel's death had been started by accident, and that Flint, fearing that he would lose his own privileged position at the Hall, once the new master had taken up residence, had planned to murder Richard.

Now, of course, she had pledged her word never to reveal the whole truth to another living soul. Even Lavinia, who had called at the inn the previous day, had agreed wholeheartedly to Sir Lionel's proposal that the full facts should never become generally known.

'Nothing can bring my husband back, Emma,' she had said, when they had managed to attain a few minutes alone together. 'It grieves me to think that that evil woman has gone to her grave with her reputation intact, and I do consider it grossly unfair that the blame for the recent tragedy is being placed squarely at Flint's door, even though he deserves no pity, I know. None the less it would cause needless hardship to others if the truth ever came out. Why should Richard be made to pay for his aunt's crimes? You know what people are, Emma,' she had gone on to say. 'Malicious tongues would start to wag, suggesting that the Ashworth blood was tainted. Why should the poor boy be made to suffer more than he has already?'

Samuel's return brought an end to these melancholy reflections, and turned Emma's thoughts in a completely new direction when she learned the identity of the visitor now waiting to see her in the private parlour.

Delaying only for the time it took to remove her apron, check on the state of her hair, and shake out the folds of her serviceable, plain grey gown, she went into the parlour to discover the lady, fashionably attired in a dark blue carriage dress, staring out of the window. 'Good-day to you, ma'am. This is an unexpected pleasure,' she said, after closing the door and moving across to the table where she and Benedict had enjoyed a last breakfast together before he had left for London.

'Unexpected, I dare say,' was the cool response, before the visitor at last turned away from the window.

Emma wasn't perfectly certain, but she thought there might have been just an element of surprise in the eyes which began to look her over slowly from head to toe, taking in every detail of her appearance. She, in turn, subjected the unexpected caller to a swift scrutiny, deciding as she did so that Lady Fencham bore little resemblance to her attractive brother, and singularly lacked his abundance of charm.

'You are, I take it, Miss Lynn?'

Emma stared gravely back at her, experiencing now a feeling of disquiet. She knew that Lady Fencham had earned herself the reputation of being excessively high in the instep. None the less she would have ex-

pected her to display at least a semblance of warmth
towards the female who was soon to become her
brother's wife. That of course must be the reason behind this unexpected visit. Benedict must have written
to her, apprising her of his intentions.

'Yes, I am Emma Lynn,' she confirmed, dropping
a slight but graceful curtsy. 'I assume, ma'am, that you
have received a letter from your brother.'

'You assume wrongly, Miss Lynn. I have had no
contact with Grantley since he left the capital several
weeks ago.'

The tone remained clipped, and Emma was not in
the least surprised when the lady refused the belated
offer to take a seat, and partake of some refreshment.

'My errand will not take long. I am here on two
counts, Miss Lynn. Firstly, I wish to know whether
the disturbing tidings my son saw fit to impart yesterday, when he paid me a brief visit, are indeed true.
And if so, I want your assurance that the marriage will
never take place.'

Refusing to be cowed by the dictatorial manner,
Emma continued to stare levelly across at her auto-
cratic visitor. 'Although it has not been announced officially, Benedict and I are secretly betrothed, yes.'

In view of the fact that Lady Fencham had made it
abundantly clear that she opposed the match, Emma
did not expect to receive rapturous congratulations, but
she was slightly taken aback by the clear note of de-
rision in the shout of laughter which swiftly followed
her confirmation.

'Oh, yes, I am certain that he did wish to keep the
whole ludicrous business a secret. But for how much
longer do you suppose he'll be able to continue to

protect you from this censorious world of ours, Miss Lynn, once your origins become common knowledge? Which assuredly they will,' she warned. 'How long do you suppose it would be before the invitations which at first flood to your home in great numbers rapidly begin to dwindle, and those you continue to receive bear only your husband's name?'

The implacable gaze grew noticeably harder. 'Undoubtedly my brother would continue to do the honourable thing and stand by the female he had foolishly married. I do not doubt, either, that his friends, who bear him a sincere regard, would continue to make you wholly welcome in their homes. But the vast majority of the polite world would shun you both. Are you willing to condemn Benedict to a life where he is no longer considered acceptable company by the vast majority of his class? Are you prepared to see his social standing plummet, and his entry barred to the highest echelons, where he has freely entered throughout his life?'

The brutally challenging gleam in the hard-eyed stare was no less wounding than the cruelly taunting voice. Emma longed to scream at her to stop, to say that it was utter nonsense to suppose that Benedict's social standing would suffer as a direct result of marrying her. But the words would not form, simply because Lady Fencham, Emma very much feared, had spoken no less than the truth. She wouldn't mind so much for herself if the prediction turned out to be distressingly accurate, but she could not place Benedict in a position whereby he would be frequently called upon to protect her from cruel barbs.

She recalled with disturbing clarity his reaction to

Clarissa Ashworth's thoughtless remarks on the night of the party. He had been angry, bitterly so. How long would it be before he was obliged to protect her name by more than just words? Duelling might be unlawful; it was still practised none the less.

'Furthermore,' Lady Fencham continued, determined to thrust home the advantage the sad and tortured expression clearly betrayed she had won, 'Benedict is his brother's heir. That is unlikely to change. Therefore it is safe to assume that Benedict's son will eventually hold the title. What indignities the poor child will be made to suffer when he is reminded constantly that his mother at one time earned her living by working in a tavern!'

Unable to bear more, Emma took swift advantage of the slight pause. 'You have made your views perfectly clear, ma'am. There is no need for you to say anything further.' Her eyes betrayed clearly enough the all-consuming wretchedness writhing inside her, but her voice remained remarkably free of emotion as she added quietly, 'You may leave, now, safe in the knowledge that you have the assurance for which you came.'

Betraying clear signs of puzzlement, Lady Fencham looked as if she were about to say something else, then evidently thought better of it, and left without uttering anything further, not even a word of farewell.

Emma waited until she heard the faint click of the door as it was closed quietly, and then went across to take up her visitor's former stance by the window. She did not notice the perplexed glance Lady Fencham cast over her shoulder, before she climbed into her carriage. She hardly noticed the fine equipage pull away from the front of the inn. She was only painfully aware of the fact that her fairy-tale dreams of happiness were shattered, and that fate had dealt her the cruellest of blows from which she would find it hard ever to recover.

Chapter Fourteen

Lucy hovered in the coffee room, hands nervously twisting the dusting-rag as she cast a furtive glance towards the doorway leading to the road. He would walk in at any moment, and she mustn't forget what to say. Miss Emma had told her, before disappearing upstairs herself a minute or so ago, that it was very important to get it just right. Lucy frowned, as she turned those recently issued instructions over in her mind. But why was it so important not to keep Mr Grantley talking, and not delay in telling him Miss Emma was upstairs with Lord Ashworth? she wondered. And why was it also important that he go up alone and she remain downstairs?

Prepared though she was, the tall figure suddenly appearing in the doorway made her start, and she brushed against one of the tables, almost sending a chair toppling to the floor.

'Ah, Lucy! On excellent form, I perceive!' Benedict entered, smiling as he heard the familiar nervous giggle which always followed one of the buxom serving-maid's slight mishaps. How he had missed this place! So refreshingly peaceful after the capital's bustle!

He placed the bag he was carrying down on the floor, deciding as he did so that the inn seemed quieter than he remembered. 'Your master and mistress not about, Lucy?'

'No, sir. They be in Salisbury this afternoon, collecting urgently needed provisions.'

'Sounds as though you've been busy here since I've been away.' He bent a glance of mock severity upon her. 'I hope you haven't gone and let my room, because I tell you plainly that I have no intention of sharing a bed with my groom above the stables.'

'Oh, sir, you are a caution! As if we'd expect you to do such a thing! There's only Lord Ashworth staying with us at the moment.' Mentioning Lord Ashworth succeeded in jolting Lucy's memory. 'Oh, yes…and you can go straight up, sir…Miss Emma's there now…with Lord Ashworth.'

Benedict needed no further prompting, and was about to head off in the direction of the stairs, when the sound of a light footfall caught his attention and he turned to see Deborah enter the inn, holding a small bowl containing one of his favourite fruits.

'Good day, Mr Grantley.' She smiled shyly up at him. 'I heard that you would be returning today. Is Emma about?'

'According to what Lucy here has been telling me, she's upstairs with the invalid,' he responded, eyeing the contents of the bowl with relish.

'In that case, I'll just pop up with these strawberries. His lordship is quite partial to them.'

'He's by no means the only one,' Benedict informed

her, and was on the point of helping himself, when Lucy forestalled him.

'Oh, no, you mustn't do that!'

'I'm certain he won't miss just one, Lucy,' he protested.

'No, sir, I weren't meaning that.' She began to tug nervously at the dusting-rag once more. 'I mean, Miss Emma never mentioned nothing about Miss Deborah going up.'

'Do not concern yourself, Lucy. I shall be there to ensure that the proprieties are observed at all times,' Benedict assured her, before popping one of the strawberries into his mouth.

After leading the way up the stairs and along the passageway, he paused to tap lightly on Richard's bedchamber door. Then throwing it wide, he stood to one side to allow Deborah to precede him. When she made no attempt to do so and, furthermore, uttered an unexpected gasp of consternation, he peered above her head at the spectacle which was causing her such acute dismay.

For a few moments it was as much as he could do to stare in stunned disbelief at the sight of the woman he loved, the woman he had swiftly come to trust above any other, half lying on the bed, gown pulled down about her shoulders, breaking free from the passionate embrace. Then searing pain, the like of which he had never experienced before, tore through him, leaving him prey to virulent emotions, not least of which was ice-cold fury at the clear evidence of cruel and wanton betrayal.

'It would seem that our arrival is ill-timed, m'dear,' he drawled. 'Or perhaps the opposite is true.'

Deborah's only response was to utter a half-suppressed sob, before brushing past him, and spilling the contents of the bowl she carried in her headlong flight towards the stairs. Benedict felt no similar compulsion to flee. He remained in the doorway, watching Emma attempting to straighten her attire, while fighting to suppress a further surge of anger as it occurred to him that Richard had glimpsed far more of her charms than he had been privileged to see, and that he had been a crass fool to treat such a faithless little strumpet with the utmost respect.

Had he not been battling to maintain a grasp on his emotions, he might have taken a moment to consider why it was that Richard, far from appearing embarrassed at being caught in a compromising situation with another man's affianced bride, was looking utterly bewildered.

'My compliments, Ashworth,' he said, his voice remarkably controlled. 'You appear to have recovered your strength remarkably quickly. Undoubtedly you have been offered every inducement to do so.'

Richard did not attempt to respond to the sarcasm, but looked instead at Emma, who rose from the bed and went over to stand by the window. Benedict watched her too, but as she had never once attempted to glance in his direction, and was now standing with her back towards him, he did not know, as Richard did, that she was deathly pale, and fighting to hold back the tears.

'My compliments to you too, madam,' he added, his voice once again cutting through the air charged with tension. 'In one comprehensive lesson you have proved beyond doubt that I am not omniscient. My assessment of your character, I openly concede, was entirely flawed. Have the satisfaction of knowing that I would never have supposed for a moment that you were ambitious. The title Baroness is not to be sneered at, I grant you. Had you been just a little patient, and bided your time, you might one day have been called Countess.'

Richard, watching Benedict turn away, closing the door quietly behind him, without uttering anything further, could not but admire the man's admirable self-control. Had their positions been reversed, he would, at the very least, have done justice to his feelings by indulging in a virulent verbal attack. It was not beyond the realms of possibility that he might have resorted to physical violence. He could not say for certainty that the sight of a heavily bandaged shoulder would have restrained him had he caught the woman he loved being embraced by another man.

His earlier bewilderment had not been feigned. No one could have been more surprised than he when Emma had entered the room, had seated herself on his bed, and had calmly begun to draw down the bodice of her gown. Desire had quickly mounted when that sweet mouth had pressed itself down upon his. He was only human, after all. What red-blooded male would shun the advances of such a lovely young woman, totally unexpected though they had been?

He shook his head, marvelling at his own foolishness. He should have known, of course; should have realised at once that it was a complete sham. Emma was a well-bred young woman, with impeccable manners, not some flirtatious wanton. Why, since he had begun to regain his strength, she had never once attempted to venture into the room alone. She had always insisted on being accompanied by either Martha or Lucy, in an attempt, he supposed, not to compromise him, and to protect her own reputation, which up until this day had been flawless.

It was patently obvious to him now that she had planned the whole interlude. She had intended to give Benedict such a disgust of her that he would walk out of her life. The sound of footsteps swiftly passing the closed door suggested strongly that she had succeeded in her aim. But what on earth had prompted her to do such a thing?

'It isn't too late to go after him and explain, Emma,' he suggested. 'You'll catch him if you hurry.'

'No, I shan't do that,' she responded, her voice barely a whisper. 'We shall never see each other again.'

'Possibly not,' he agreed gently. 'But it is highly probable that I shall cross his path at some point in the future when I visit the capital. May I at least be permitted to know why I must bear the condemnation of a man for whom I have the utmost respect?'

It was a moment before Emma turned her head, and once again Richard found himself experiencing a deal of respect. She was undoubtedly labouring under the greatest strain to keep her emotions in check. Yet her eyes, when they looked down at him, were surprisingly free from the tears which would surely come before too long, and were shadowed only by a look of acute remorse.

After a further moment, she moved away from the window, and seated herself in the chair by the bed. 'I was foolish not to have considered that,' she admitted, her voice strengthened by self-reproach. 'I am so very sorry to have involved you in all of this, Richard. If I could have thought of some other way…'

Richard did not hesitate to reach for one of the slender hands, and retain it comfortingly in his own. 'Some other way of ending your association with Benedict,' he finished for her. 'Yes, I had realised that that was your intention. What I quite fail to understand though, Emma, is why you should wish to part from the man you so obviously adore.'

'For that very reason, Richard,' she answered, her voice once again barely audible.

He saw tears begin to moisten the long lashes, but amazingly they still did not fall. He waited a moment to allow her to regain her composure before prompting her further. 'I'm sorry, Emma. I am just a doltish male who cannot understand that reasoning. At some future time I might be justifiably called to account for my actions, so do you not think I deserve to know precisely why?'

Emma managed a wan smile at this. 'I do not suppose for a moment that that will ever happen. Ben is far too much of a gentleman to instigate a common brawl… But, yes, you do deserve an explanation,' she agreed. 'However, you must promise me, Richard, that you will never repeat what I am about to tell you to Benedict in the future.'

He did not hesitate to pledge his word, and then listened, experiencing sympathy and increasing annoyance, as she disclosed the reasons for her astonishing behaviour.

'Confound this country!' he cursed, when he had discovered all. 'Is a person's station in life the only thing that matters? I shall never understand you people!'

'You are one of us too,' she reminded him, moved by this show of support.

'Yes, perhaps,' he was reluctantly forced to concede. 'None the less, I was raised to consider a person's qualities more important than his social standing. And I'm certain Benedict is of a similar mind. He evidently did not care a jot that you were forced to make your own way in the world.'

'No, he did not,' she agreed. 'But one day he might have reconsidered, have experienced regrets that he had married me.' Tears began to moisten her lashes yet again, and yet iron resolve still held them in check. 'My one regret is that I was forced to use you so shamefully.'

Richard dismissed this with a wave of his hand, before a rueful smile tugged at his lips. 'And my only regret is that dear little Deborah should have witnessed what for me was, I freely admit, not an unpleasant experience.'

An expression of total astonishment, quickly followed by one of acute dismay, was proof enough that Emma had been ignorant of this fact up until a moment ago. She was on her feet and leaving the room before Richard could guess her intention.

In the passageway she encountered Lucy, busily picking up strawberries from the carpet, further proof had Emma needed any that her friend had indeed been there.

Deborah had paid numerous visits to the inn during the past two weeks, never failing to bring with her some little treat to tempt the invalid's palate. Emma had very much enjoyed witnessing an ever-increasing bond of friendship developing between Deborah and Richard, and could not bear the thought that she may have been instrumental in preventing their evident regard for each other from developing into something more meaningful.

'I do not suppose Deborah is still here, is she, Lucy?'

'No, Miss Em.' Lucy was agog with curiosity, and it plainly showed. 'She went running back out not long after she'd arrived. Looked as if she were crying to me. And that ain't all,' she added, eyes widening. 'Mr Grantley's gone too. Paid his shot, and left without uttering above half a dozen words. Mistress came back in time to see him drive off in the carriage. Wants to know what's been going on, so she does.'

'Yes, I can well imagine. But I cannot see her now, Lucy. Tell her I'll talk to her when I return.'

Not delaying even for the time it would take to collect a shawl, Emma raced out of the inn, in much the same way as Deborah had done a short time before. Not surprisingly she arrived at the Hammonds' home, a few minutes later, breathless but determined to see her friend, and was admitted to the house by Mrs Hammond herself, who was not slow to divulge the information that her daughter had locked herself in her room, refusing to see anyone.

Emma did not allow this to deter her. Hurriedly mounting the stairs, she scratched lightly on Deborah's bedchamber door, and was not unduly surprised to receive no response.

'Deborah, it is Emma. Please let me in. I must speak with you. It is important. Things are not what they seem,' she assured her, and a few moments later she heard the key, blessedly, turn in the lock.

Having to explain her actions a second time was no less heart-rending. Emma felt emotionally drained, but at least gained some satisfaction from seeing the happiness return to her friend's eyes, even though she knew it would be a very long time before she would experience that feeling again herself.

Refusing both Deborah's and her mother's invitation to remain to partake of some refreshment, Emma returned to the inn, and went directly up to her room to stare sightlessly out of the window. She was not unduly surprised to hear the click of the door a few minutes later. There was no need to turn round to see who had entered, for she knew full well who it must be, and ran straight into those loving arms which had offered such comfort when she had been a child.

Martha did not attempt to stem the flow of tears, which at last began to flow and continued to flow. After learning all, she continued to cradle Emma in her arms. The tears gradually subsided, but the pain, Martha knew, was no less intense.

'The first time that ever I set eyes on the man, I feared something like this might happen,' she murmured, stroking the chestnut locks. 'You loved him too well, my darling girl…you loved him too well.'

Chapter Fifteen

Unlike her husband, who would have been more than content to remain in the country all year round, enjoying the peace and quiet and the occasional visit from a genial neighbour, Lady Fencham much preferred the hectic social whirl. Three weeks of bucolic tranquillity had been quite sufficient to revitalise her, after the rigours of the London Season and her short sojourn in Bath, and she was more than ready to embark on the next major event in the social calendar.

It was mutually agreed that she should travel on ahead to Brighton to set the house in that fashionable seaside resort to order. It was an arrangement which suited both husband and wife admirably, for it granted his lordship the chance to remain in the country for a short while longer, and her ladyship the opportunity to make a short detour in order to pay a brief call on her favourite brother, and put her mind at rest by discovering for certain that he had indeed overcome the madness which had possessed him to contemplate marriage with someone far beneath his station.

On the day of her departure, Lady Fencham went

outside to the carriage to discover the mid-July morning was both dry and bright, and yet not so warm as to make the journey ahead of her uncomfortable. With only her personal maid to bear her company, she was granted ample opportunity to indulge in lengthy periods of quiet reflection and, as had happened all too frequently during her short stay at her country home, her mind began to dwell on that brief visit which she had made to Ashworth Magna.

Being an innately honest person, Lady Fencham would have been the first to admit, if ever called upon to do so, that Miss Emma Lynn had turned out to be something of an enigma. In truth she had been expecting to discover some vulgar, scheming hussy who had entrapped poor Benedict in her toils by her dazzling beauty; instead, she had come face to face with a demure young woman whose gentility had been clearly evident in both speech and manners. There was no denying that, dressed appropriately, Miss Lynn would have been lovely enough to grace any ballroom. It was indeed a pity that her humble origins made her an unsuitable candidate, for in every other respect Lady Fencham very much suspected that she would have made Benedict an ideal mate.

Lady Fencham was not frequently plagued by pangs of conscience. None the less, she found herself experiencing a slight twinge of regret now as her coachman turned into the impressive gateway leading to her brother's country home. If the lack of any official announcement in the newspapers was anything to go by, then Miss Emma Lynn was undeniably a young woman of her word who had released Benedict from any obligation he might have felt to wed her, leaving him free to look about for a more suitable bride.

A surge of hope quickly silenced the voice of conscience which suggested that she might have been grossly at fault to interfere in her brother's personal concerns. Why, he might even be persuaded to join her and her husband in Brighton for the summer, she mused, where he would undoubtedly meet dozens of young women infinitely more suitable to be his wife!

With this very satisfying prospect in the forefront of her mind, Lady Fencham stepped lightly down from the carriage, and quickly mounted the steps leading to the house which she considered to be one of the most charming country residences she had ever been privileged to visit.

Purchased by her brother some ten years before, the mansion, built in a mellow yellow stone, was set in several acres of delightfully rolling park land. Modest in size compared to many of the more famous country residences, Fairview was none the less a perfect example of a building erected in the Classical style. Benedict had gone to considerable expense to redecorate the whole of the interior, and the house now seemed to reflect its owner's personality—quietly elegant and altogether aesthetically pleasing.

Fingle, opening the door in response to the summons, did not attempt to hide his dismay at this unexpected visit. Nor was he slow to impart, as he moved to one side, allowing her ladyship to step into the hall, that this was not the best of times to pay an impromptu call, as his master had given strict instructions not to admit anyone to the house.

Lady Fencham dismissed this with an imperious

wave of one gloved hand. 'Don't be ridiculous, Fingle! Of course he will see his own sister.'

The middle-aged butler was decidedly sceptical, and made no attempt to hide the fact. 'My lady, he has seen no one since his return from Wiltshire. He—he rarely leaves the house.'

Lady Fencham had learned of Benedict's return to Fairview in a letter she had received from a close friend conveniently living in the area. She had not, however, heard from any one of her reliable sources, whereby she managed to keep track of his comings and goings, that her very eligible younger brother was behaving in any way out of the ordinary.

She experienced a moment's alarm. 'You are not trying to tell me, I trust, that your master is ill? If so, why was I not informed at once?'

'I wouldn't go as far as to say that he is ill, my lady,' Fingle responded, swiftly allaying her fears. 'But I would be forced to admit that the master hasn't been—er—quite himself of late.'

'What do you mean by "not quite himself"?' Lady Fencham had not been slow to note that the loyal retainer seemed quite unable to meet her gaze. A hideous suspicion filtered through her mind. 'I hope you are not suggesting that my brother is foxed?'

It was indeed an effort, but Fingle managed to suppress a smile. Lady Fencham was nothing if not brutally direct. 'I wouldn't go so far as to suggest that, my lady. He has, however, been incarcerated in the library with the brandy decanter for well over an hour. Which would lead me to suspect that he's no longer perfectly sober.'

'I simply do not believe it!' she announced, loyal

to the last. 'I have never seen my brother in a state of inebriation in my life.'

Well, you will now, Fingle mused, as he watched her set off across the hall in the direction of the library.

He made no further attempt to dissuade her, simply because things could not continue as they were. Not a day had gone by when his master had not had recourse to the brandy decanter in an attempt to lessen the pain. A woman was at the root of all the trouble, of course. Every servant in the house was very well aware of that fact. Even had the head groom not disclosed that the master had at long last been struck by Cupid's dart, the instructions they had received from their master to have Fairview in perfect order by his return would have been sufficient to convince the entire household that they would soon be welcoming a mistress to the house.

Fingle shook his head, at a loss to comprehend what might have occurred. His master was far too discerning a gentleman to be beguiled by just a pretty face. Consequently Fingle had come to the conclusion that the young woman who had, against all the odds, succeeded in capturing Mr Grantley's heart must be a rare specimen indeed, and he had been very much looking forward to welcoming her to her new home. Yet the master had returned alone, and in a mood of black despair from which he had not recovered. Only in the mornings did he ever attempt to leave the house in order to ride, as though the devil himself were at his heels, across the estate. If he did not end by breaking his neck, then it would not be for the want of trying.

No, he reiterated, as he watched the unexpected visitor sweep majestically into the room, things simply could not continue in this way. Her ladyship might not have been his first choice to deal with a delicate situation such as this, but if she could manage to restore at least a semblance of the master's former good sense, he for one would not be sorry that she had unexpectedly turned up on the doorstep, even if it meant losing his position for deliberately disobeying strict instructions. But then, he reminded himself, it certainly wouldn't be the only order he'd quite failed to carry out since the master's return to Fairview.

For a few moments Lady Fencham remained on the threshold, appalled at the sight which met her eyes. Even from this distance she could see that Fingle had not exaggerated. Sprawled in one of the chairs by the hearth, her brother bore little resemblance to the impeccably attired gentleman whose faultless appearance had been much admired, and aped, by the majority of his peers during the past decade.

He had dispensed with his coat, which now lay strewn across the floor at his feet. His waistcoat was unbuttoned, revealing a shirt that was both creased and stained, and his cravat was limp and so abysmally arranged that it resembled nothing so much as a well-used dusting-rag. Unless she much mistook the matter, his face had not felt the touch of a razor for some considerable time, and there was a telltale glint in his half-closed eyes which betrayed clearly enough the quantity of liquor already consumed that day.

'Yes, you may refill the decanter, Fingle,' Benedict murmured, without bothering to turn his head, but the derisive snort which swiftly followed his instructions eventually induced him to glance in the direction of the door. He was then forced to blink several times in an attempt to clear his vision.

'Good gad! Is that you, Aggie?' He made not the least attempt to rise. 'What the deuce brings you here?'

'I did not come, I assure you, expecting to discover my brother in an advanced state of intoxication!' Her sharply spoken response made him wince, but she steadfastly refused to spare him further discomfort, and closed the door none too gently before moving towards the hearth. 'You look little better than a vagrant! Whatever has come over you?'

'Well may you ask, dear sister.' Resting his head against the back of the chair, he gazed down into the contents of his glass, although, much to his sister's intense relief, he made no attempt to reduce the level further. 'I fell in love with a girl whom I foolishly imagined would make me the perfect wife.'

His unexpected shout of laughter distinctly lacked any semblance of humour. 'For the first time in my life my judgement has proved sadly flawed. I lost my heart to a faithless little strumpet!'

Lady Fencham was genuinely shocked. A female of loose morals was certainly not the impression she had taken away with her, after her short meeting with Miss Emma Lynn at the Ashworth Arms.

'If that is indeed the case, then it is most fortunate that you discovered her true character before you foolishly announced your engagement to the polite world.'

The glazed look rapidly faded from his eyes, and they were suddenly disconcertingly direct, as though he were seeing her clearly for the first time. 'You appear very well informed, Agnes. Did your son, perchance, make a slight detour during his journey to Devon?'

'Yes, as it happens, he did call on me when I was in Bath.' Dropping into the seat opposite, she made a great play of rearranging her skirts. 'Not that I didn't consider the whole idea of your marrying such a female utterly preposterous. I cannot imagine what must have come over you to contemplate such a thing. Really,' she scoffed, 'a girl of that class!'

'A girl of what class?' he enquired, one well-shaped brow arching quizzically. 'You appear to be labouring under a misapprehension, m'dear. Miss Lynn is the daughter of a gentleman. Furthermore, she is a cousin of my good friend Charles Lynn, no less.'

'Great heavens!' Lady Fencham's jaw dropped perceptively, clear evidence of her astonishment. 'I had no notion,' she freely admitted. 'Why on earth didn't the silly chit say something when I…?'

'When you…what, sister dear?' Benedict prompted when her voice trailed away.

No response was forthcoming.

The brandy's numbing effects had been miraculously decreasing with every passing second, and although Benedict would never have tried to pretend that he was now stone-cold sober, he was certainly as near to it as made no difference. 'Would I be correct in assuming that you took it into your head to pay Miss Lynn a visit?'

'Well, of course I did,' she admitted, knowing full well that it would be futile to attempt a denial. Her younger brother was far too perceptive. 'You did not suppose for a moment that I would sit back and do nothing when I discovered my brother was contem-

plating such a deplorable *mésalliance*? And it is no
earthly use your staring at me in that odiously hateful
way, Benedict!' she snapped, faintly defensive. 'I had
no notion the girl was so well connected. What on
earth possessed her to find employment in a common
inn, I should like to know?'

'We shall leave that for the moment.' His penetrating, hard-eyed gaze never wavering for an instant, he
reached out an arm to place his glass down on the
table by his elbow. 'What did you say to her, Agnes?'
he enquired, with deceptive mildness. 'What did you
say to my darling girl?'

'Darling girl?' she echoed in astonished disbelief.
'But—but you just said that she was a designing—'

'I know what I may have said, Agnes,' he interrupted, his voice all the more menacing because of its
softness. 'But I am beginning to suspect…oh, yes, I
am very much beginning to suspect that I have been
a damnable fool.' He leaned forward in his chair so
that she could not fail to see the determination in his
eyes, even had she failed to detect it in his voice. 'And
you are going to supply me with the proof I need, dear
sister, by disclosing precisely what passed between
you and Emma during your visit to the Ashworth
Arms… You are going to tell me e-v-e-r-y last detail.'

Lady Fencham's nature could never have been described as submissive. Yet, against all the odds, she
found herself automatically complying, the result of
which had Benedict out of his chair and towering
above her, and she herself almost cowering beneath
the crushing tirade which subsequently fell about her
ears.

'I—I shall not be spoken to in such a fashion, Benedict,' she managed faintly, after having been forced to listen to her character comprehensively pulled to shreds. 'I—I would never have believed you so unfeeling as to speak to your own sister in such a fashion. I had only your best interests at heart.'

'Fortunately for you I am well aware of it. That is the only thing to have spared you the thrashing your husband ought to have administered years ago!' Swinging away, he began to pace the room. 'Damn you for an interfering baggage, Aggie!'

It needed only that to repair her severely dented spirits. 'I refuse to remain here and be insulted a moment longer! Why, I can almost feel sorry for the poor girl. You will quite obviously make an odious brute of a husband. And you may tell Miss Lynn from me that I for one shall always be there if she should ever feel the need of my support. Or seek protection from you!' Gathering the shreds of her dignity about her, she rose to her feet. 'I wish I'd never come here!'

'Aggie,' he called after her, halting her stalking progress across to the door. 'I'm not in the least sorry you came.'

She swept majestically out of the room, but not before Benedict had detected the faint smile of satisfaction. His own swiftly faded, as he cursed himself silently for every kind of a fool. He ought to have realised at once that it had all been a complete sham, a ruse to prompt him to terminate the engagement. And like a simpleton he had walked straight into that well-baited trap!

Anger and elation, a potent mixture, had him once again pacing the room, his mind's eye clearly seeing now what ought to have been so blatantly obvious from the moment he had entered the inn—Lucy, conveniently awaiting his arrival in the coffee room, slightly confused and striving to repeat parrot-fashion what she had been instructed to say, and Richard quite obviously completely bewildered by what had taken place. Little wonder Emma had not dared to face him, he reminded himself. The devious little minx had feared that, had he chanced to look into her eyes, he just might have realised that it wasn't mortification she was experiencing, but searing heartache. Oh, yes, it was all so crystal clear now, he mused, marvelling at his own gullibility. Had he not allowed shattered feelings, and a severely bruised ego to cloud his judgement, he would have suspected the truth long since.

Finding himself now standing beside his oak desk, he noticed the mountain of correspondence neatly stacked in one corner, awaiting his attention. Locked in his own private misery, he had lost complete interest in the outside world. It had been as much as he could do to ride over occasionally to see his steward. Not surprisingly he experienced a twinge of conscience, quickly followed by a sense of shame, as he seated himself at the desk and began to read through letters from several of his neglected friends.

Eventually he came to one written in an elegantly sloping hand which he did not immediately recognise, and which informed him of the surprising news that Richard Ashworth, now convalescing at the Hammonds' home, had become engaged to the daughter of the house.

He read Lavinia's interesting missive, dated two weeks ago, a second time, paying particular attention to the very revealing postscript: *I understand from sev-*

eral sources that your sister paid a visit to the Ash-worth Arms recently, but as I have seen so little of Emma of late, the poor child having been unwell and keeping to her room for much of the time, I have been unable to discover what could possibly have induced Agnes to pay an impromptu visit. I sincerely trust nothing untoward has occurred. No doubt it might prove interesting to unearth the purpose of her visit, because she certainly did not come to see me.

Benedict smiled to himself. Lavinia knew all right. She would have guessed at once just what Agnes had been up to, and had done her level best to rouse his curiosity and spur him into action. He needed no further prompting.

Reaching out a hand, he gave the bell pull on the wall behind him a sharp tug, and a few moments later Fingle entered, his eyes brightening at sight of his master seated behind the desk, looking so businesslike.

'You require something, sir?'

'Yes. I've suddenly discovered I'm famished. Ask Cook to send up some food on a tray. Nothing fancy, you understand—a cold collation will serve.'

'Certainly, sir. Will there be anything else?'

'Yes.' Benedict frowned slightly as he clearly detected the sound of several bangs and grunts. 'What's that confounded din taking place in the hall?'

'It is the carrier, sir, this moment arrived with the *chaise-longue* you ordered for the boudoir during your brief trip to London a month ago. There are also several boxes. I believe they have been despatched from the same Bond Street modiste who sent those other parcels which arrived last week.' A muscle twitched at one corner of Fingle's mouth. 'Do you wish me to dispose of them in a similar fashion to their—er—predecessors, sir?'

A gleam of alarm flickered momentarily in violet eyes as memory stirred. 'Would I be correct in thinking that I issued instructions for their contents to be burned on the kitchen range?'

'You most certainly did, sir,' was the solemn response.

'Oh, Lord!'

The mournful groan produced a further twitching smile. 'Do not disturb yourself, sir. It was an order I quite happily ignored.'

The bark of laughter which followed the admission was music to the butler's ears. 'Devil take you, Fingle! Where did you place them?'

'Safely upstairs in one of the spare bedchambers, sir. Shall I now instruct one of the maids to consign them to their rightful place?'

Smiling fondly across at his loyal retainer, Benedict shook his head. 'You're an old rogue, Fingle. I swear you know me better than I know myself... Yes, see to it at once. Oh, and Fingle,' he added, checking the butler's immediate departure, 'send word to the stables to have the light travelling carriage ready at the door directly after breakfast in the morning. I shall be returning to Wiltshire.'

'Mr Grantley, sir, rest assured that that is an order I shall not fail to carry out!'

Having made excellent time, Benedict arrived at Ashworth Magna shortly before noon the following day. It had been his intention to go directly to the Ashworth Arms to see Emma. However, in view of the fact that Deborah and Richard had recently become betrothed, and that it would be unlikely that he would see them again for some considerable time, he decided to call at the Hammonds' house first in order to offer his congratulations.

After giving the highly polished brass door-knocker several short, sharp raps, and receiving no response to his summons, he walked round to the back of the house, where he well expected to find Lavinia, as she so often was, happily working in her garden. Instead he discovered Richard, quite alone, sitting beneath one of the trees that offered pleasant shade from the noon-day sun's strong rays.

Detecting the sound of the footfall Richard turned his head, his expression a strange mixture of ruefulness and delight. 'Ah, Grantley! You'll excuse me if I don't get up?'

Benedict focused his attention on the right foot resting on the stool. His brow rose. 'It would appear you have been in the wars again?'

'It's this dratted country of yours!' his lordship retorted, sounding thoroughly nettled. 'It's been one thing after another since I arrived here.' A further rueful grin flickered. 'Still, I've only myself to blame for this, I suppose. I was warned not to overtire myself by the old sawbones, but I didn't listen. Decided to take myself off for a ride the other morning, came over dizzy and ended up on the ground.' He shrugged. 'Could have been worse, I suppose. The ankle's only sprained. I'll be up and about again in a few days.'

He gestured towards the chair next to his own. 'Er—won't you sit down? Deborah and her mother shouldn't be too long. They're paying a call on a neighbour.'

Accepting the offer, Benedict regarded the younger man in silence for a moment. 'I understand congratulations are in order?'

Richard appeared startled, as though he'd been locked in a world of his own. 'Oh, you've obviously received Lavinia's letter, then. We're not announcing the betrothal officially until the autumn, when Lavinia intends to hold a party in London.'

Benedict slanted a mocking glance. 'A trifle sudden, wouldn't you say?'

'Not really.' Richard responded, after giving the matter a moment's consideration. 'How long does it take to fall in love? I wouldn't have supposed time had much to do with it.'

'True,' Benedict agreed. 'But you, my dear sir, appear to make a habit of doing so.'

Subjecting Benedict to a searching glance, Richard wasn't slow to detect the flicker of amusement in those striking eyes, and relaxed visibly. 'I know you don't mean that. You must have guessed the truth by now…else why are you here? You have paid a visit to your sister, I assume?'

'No, but she called to see me,' Benedict enlightened him, before he detected the faint squeal of delight, and turned to see Deborah hurrying across the grass towards him, and her mother following at a more sedate pace.

'Oh, sir. You have come at last!'

Rising to his feet, Benedict captured the outstretched little hands, holding them for a moment in his own. 'Yes, my dear. I wished to offer you my heartfelt congratulations in person.'

'But, surely…?' Crestfallen, Deborah stared up at him, for all the world like a child who had just been deprived of its favourite toy. 'Didn't you come to see Emma?'

'Of course he's come to see her,' Richard put in, before Lavinia joined them, and sent her daughter's hopes plummeting again, when she said, 'You are missing the point, my children. It's whether she will agree to see Benedict.' Lavinia turned to the gentleman in question, holding out her hand in greeting. 'How are you, sir? You evidently received my letter.'

He nodded as he released her hand. 'It was my sister's visit yesterday which made me realise the truth at last. Your letter, which I read shortly after she had left, merely confirmed my suspicions.'

'Oh, I could shake Agnes!' Lavinia sounded as though she truly meant it too. 'Why must she interfere?'

'I rather suspect she'll think twice before doing so again, at least in my affairs.' The crooked half-smile faded from his lips as he gazed at Lavinia rather thoughtfully. 'Why do you suppose Emma will refuse to see me?'

'Because she can be as stubborn as a mule when the mood takes her,' Deborah answered, sounding cross. 'She made us all promise never to tell you the truth about what happened that day. It was only after Richard and I decided that we should like to marry that I managed to persuade Mama to write to you.'

'And even then I felt obliged not to divulge too much,' Lavinia admitted. 'Yet we've all been so wor-

ried. Both Samuel and Martha are so very concerned
about her, and I felt certain that such an intelligent
man as yourself couldn't fail to realise at once that
something was very wrong.'

'You give me too much credit, Lavinia. My common sense deserted me completely during these past
weeks, otherwise I might have guessed the truth long
since.' His lips twitched very slightly. 'Though I must
add in my defence that our young friend here gave a
very convincing performance of the ardent lover.'

'Dash it all!' Richard protested. 'That isn't fair! She
took me completely by surprise. She'd always behaved
with the utmost propriety before.'

'Maybe so,' Deborah put in, whilst casting her betrothed a decidedly disapproving look. 'But you did
not appear to be making the least attempt to resist her
advances.'

Richard moved uncomfortably in his chair. 'Now,
Debbie, you and I had not come to an understanding
then… And Emma's a dashed pretty female…and I'm
only human… And I've never made any secret of the
fact that I'm very fond of her.'

Lavinia decided to come to her future son-in-law's
rescue, before he could dig himself into a deeper hole.
'Stop teasing him, Deborah,' she scolded, and then
turned to Benedict. 'Emma might agree to see you, sir.
But whether or not you will manage to convince her
that what Agnes told her was all nonsense is a different matter.'

Richard, however, did not agree. 'She's bound to
listen to reason eventually. She might be stubborn, but
she isn't stupid.' He gave a start as an idea suddenly

occurred to him. 'I have it! Why not abduct her? Throw her over your saddle, and ride off with her.'

Deborah clapped her hands in approval. 'How excessively romantic!'

'Excessively uncomfortable, I should say,' Benedict countered, thereby igniting a mild look of reproach in brown, pansy eyes.

'But, sir, Emma would be forced to listen to reason if you threatened not to return her to the inn until she'd heard what you had to say,' Deborah felt obliged to point out, and had the satisfaction of seeing a thoughtful expression flit over his ruggedly masculine features.

He regarded her in silence for a moment, then said, 'Do you suppose you could go to the inn now, Deborah, and manage to have a quiet word with Samuel and Martha without Emma knowing? Ask them to come here.'

Richard watched her disappear round the corner of the house, before returning his attention to Benedict. 'What do you intend to do?'

'With a slight variation to your original suggestion, I fully intend to take your advice, young man,' was the surprising response.

Chapter Sixteen

Taking down the large bowl from the shelf, Emma automatically began her daily bake of meat pies. The kitchen was oppressive, but she didn't allow this to trouble her to any great extent. But then, she reflected, nothing seemed to worry her these days. It was almost as if she were becoming daily more desensitised, hardly aware of the sights and sounds around her. Why, it was only a moment or two ago, she silently reminded herself, that she had realised that both Samuel and Martha had at some point left her to her own devices.

She shook her head, wondering at herself for being so unobservant. Things could not continue this way; that much was certain. She was determined to emerge from this almost zombie-like existence into which she had foolishly allowed herself to plummet in a vain attempt to lessen the pain. Needless to say it had not worked. The heartache never left her, and she had to face the fact that perhaps it never would. Striving to distance herself from those around her, however, was no answer. In fact, she was swiftly coming to the conclusion that the opposite action might turn out to be more beneficial. Keeping herself occupied, while at the same time not shunning the company of others, was perhaps the best way to prevent herself from relapsing into those frequent moods of utter despair.

She could not prevent a tiny sigh escaping. Unfortunately at this time of year trade was slack, so keeping busy was not going to be very easy. Most of those privileged enough to enjoy the London Season had already returned to their homes in the country, or were now enjoying a stay in one of the more popular coastal towns, and until the Little Season began in the autumn there would not be too many travellers putting up at the Ashworth Arms.

It was not all doom and gloom, she reminded herself, determined not to succumb to a further bout of despondency. There was a ray of hope beginning to glimmer on her life's horizon. Lavinia's invitation to live with her in Bath, repeated just the other day, was perhaps the best solution. Lavinia was determined not to remain in Ashworth Magna after Deborah was married, and was set on making a new life for herself in that once fashionable watering-place.

Yes, a new environment was what she desperately needed too. Emma was firmly convinced of that now, for there was one thing of which she was daily becoming more convinced—she could not possibly continue to live here at the inn. The place was just too full of bittersweet memories.

'Emma! Emma!' Martha's frantic shouts and sudden eruption into the kitchen put an end to the reverie. 'Samuel has put his back out again, badly this time, and we're completely out of liniment. Do be a dear and go to the apothecary in Salisbury. I shall finish the pies.'

Emma automatically took off her apron, and was in the process of hanging it on the hook on the back of the door, when something occurred to her. 'But should I not summon Dr Fielding first?'

'No need to trouble the good doctor, dear. There isn't much he can do. You know it's just the liniment that manages to ease Sam a little.'

Had Emma been more herself, she might have noticed that Martha appeared to be having the greatest difficulty in meeting her gaze. 'Where is Samuel now?'

'Er—with Farmer Potts. Do you not recall that, when he failed to find a suitable animal at the Andover Fair, he was seriously considering buying Potts's mare? He was taking another look at her earlier when it—er—happened. Mr Potts is bringing Sam back in the cart. So you just pop upstairs and fetch your bonnet.'

Emma didn't hesitate to do as bidden, and returned to the kitchen a few minutes later to find it deserted. This didn't occur to her as odd, for she naturally assumed that Martha was awaiting Sam's arrival at the front of the inn in order to assist him up to their bedchamber, and swiftly decided that her time would be better spent in helping Josh to harness Peg to the gig.

When the boy failed to appear in response to her calling, she walked across the yard and into the large barn where Peg was always stabled. She clearly heard the friendly gelding's soft whinny of welcome, and then detected a further sound from somewhere off to her left. Before she could turn to investigate, her arms were grasped from behind, and a sack was ruthlessly pulled over her head, dislodging her bonnet and sending it toppling to the floor.

Lethargy was definitely a thing of the past. Each of her senses was fully alert, frighteningly so, as she struggled in vain to prevent a gag from being slipped beneath the sack and fastened over her mouth, and her wrists from being secured behind her back. Only her legs remained unfettered, and she didn't hesitate to put one to good use by kicking out with one well-shod foot. The satisfaction she gained from the muffled oath which swiftly followed her successfully making contact with one muscular calf was unfortunately short-lived, for a moment later she found herself giving vent to a stifled squeal, as she received a humiliating slap on the seat of her skirt, the force of which sent her toppling forward on to a pile of hay, where her ankles were deftly secured before her feet could inflict further injury.

It might have been purely imagination, but Emma thought she could detect what sounded suspiciously like feminine chuckles, quickly suppressed, before she heard what was unmistakably a vehicle drawing to a halt in the cobbled yard. Fear gave way to puzzlement, and then indignation, as she was hauled back to her feet, thrown over one well-muscled shoulder and carried from the barn.

The faint glimmer of hope that it just might have been Mr Potts bringing Sam back in his wagon was quickly dashed when she was bundled on to a well-padded seat, left half-lying and propped in one corner. A whispered exchange quickly followed, the carriage rocked slightly as someone clambered inside, the door was slammed shut, and moments later the carriage rocked gently as it bowled at a cracking pace along the open road.

Although her abductor never attempted to speak, she felt the grasp of strong fingers on her shoulder, steadying her, whenever they reached a sharp bend in the road. Emma considered this evident regard for her safety a little incongruous in the circumstances. Her bewilderment rapidly increased. Why should the villain who had abducted her be concerned that she did not tumble off the seat on to the floor? And why in heaven's name had she been abducted in the first place?

No logical explanation immediately sprang to mind. She was certainly not wealthy, so financial gain could hardly be the motive. She did not believe she had any enemies, so a thirst for revenge was unlikely to be the reason. Only one thing was clear—whoever her silent travelling companion was, he had certainly not carried out his outrageous kidnapping single-handedly. There had definitely been two men in that barn, she felt certain of that, and possibly a female as well... But who?

Emma abandoned her puzzling reflections as the driver of the vehicle checked his speed. Had her captor reached his destination? she wondered, experiencing a resurgence of alarm when she detected the sound of the blinds being pulled down. A few moments later the vehicle turned and came to a stop, and her fears were quickly vanquished by the sounds of raised voices, the clatter of hooves and the jangle of harnesses. They had stopped merely to effect a change of horses. This was accomplished swiftly, and they were soon once again bowling along the open road.

Presumably her abductor had some distance to travel, and was intent on reaching his journey's end as quickly as possible. The speed at which they were moving suggested very strongly that a team of four horses was being used to pull the carriage, a carriage that was remarkably comfortable and well-sprung. No poor man could possibly afford such a turnout. Beneath the sack her brows met above the bridge of her nose. Now, who did she know wealthy enough to transport his captive in such fine style?

A possibility occurred to her so startling that she almost dismissed it as ludicrous, but it persisted, swiftly becoming a firm conviction. Of course, there was only one person it could possibly be!

Had the gag firmly tied about her mouth not prevented it, Emma would have happily released the swell of indignation bubbling up inside by uttering a stream of colourful invective. It was all so blatantly clear now—she had been betrayed by those she trusted. And, worse, unless she very much mistook the matter, those she held most dear had aided and abetted in this disgraceful escapade!

Swinging her legs to the floor, she managed to ease herself into a sitting position, and then commenced to hammer her heels on the floor of the carriage for all she was worth. Her exertions had the desired effect. The carriage began to slow down immediately, the blind was raised, the window was pulled down, and her suspicions were confirmed a moment later by that unmistakable, beloved voice.

'It is all right, John. You may continue. Our passenger is merely feeling a trifle—er—fractious.'

Benedict clearly detected the muffled squeal as he

closed the window, and resumed his seat, but was not above fuelling the furnace of her justifiable wrath by announcing, 'Now, if you promise to be a good girl, and behave yourself, I shall remove your bonds.' Reaching out one hand, he pulled off the sack covering her head to reveal a riot of deliciously tussled brown locks, and a pair of stormy grey eyes. His lips twitched. 'Even though I suspect I am being most imprudent, I shall remove the gag.'

His reservations were justified, but he made not the least attempt to stem the ensuing diatribe which left him in no doubt of her opinion of his manners and morals. 'You wretch! Untie me at once!' she finished, breathless, but not in the least mollified.

Again he obliged her, but found his hand being slapped away none too gently when he made to untie her ankles. 'Your annoyance is very understandable, my darling, so I shall overlook these needless displays of childish temper.' He reached for the journal on the seat beside him. 'We shall discuss the situation when you are a little more yourself.'

Incensed that he could calmly apprise himself of the latest news at such a time, Emma snatched the paper from out of his hand, and screwed it up into a ball before tossing it into a corner of the carriage. 'You will return me to Ashworth Magna at once, do you hear! Otherwise I shall not hesitate to jump out of this carriage!'

The threat did not succeed in wiping the infuriating smile from his lips, but Emma was left in no doubt that he was very much in earnest when he said, 'Endeavour to do anything so foolish, and you might find it impossible to sit with any degree of comfort for some considerable time.'

Indignation held her mute, but only for a moment. 'Ha! And this from the very man who swore he would never so much as harm a hair on my head!'

The infuriating smile widened. 'It isn't your head that need concern you, my darling. Quite another part of your anatomy, in fact.'

It was an effort, but she managed to suppress a tiny squeal of vexation. 'And I suppose it was you who struck me back in that barn,' she accused, memory returning.

Benedict didn't attempt to deny it. 'No more than you deserved after the little farce you enacted for my benefit the other week.'

It needed only that to quell the anger which had sustained her thus far, and bring about a swift return of searing heartache. She lowered her eyes, but was very conscious that his own never wavered from her face. 'Who told you?' she asked softly.

'My sister.' This succeeded in raising her eyes once more to his, and Benedict, silently cursing himself, had little difficulty in recognising more than just puzzlement in those lovely grey depths. How he had ever been so foolish as to doubt the strength of her regard for him he would never know.

'The instant Agnes revealed that she'd paid you a visit, I began to suspect the truth,' he freely admitted, before the line of his jaw noticeably hardened. 'She'll think twice before interfering in my affairs again, you can be sure.'

For her part Emma had little difficulty in detecting his lingering resentment. 'Lady Fencham was only thinking of you, Ben,' she assured him, thereby revealing that she bore his sister no ill will. 'And what she said to me was no less than the truth.'

'What she told you was utter twaddle,' he countered. 'And she knows it!'

Although he had sounded totally sincere, Emma wasn't wholly convinced. 'If you honestly believe that what your sister predicted would not happen if we…if we did ever marry, why then did you wish to keep our betrothal a secret, if it wasn't in an attempt to protect me?'

Benedict was silent for a moment, scrutinising every fine contour of her face. 'So, that's what you thought…you thought I was trying to protect you from scurrilous, wagging tongues.' He shook his head at her. 'My darling, you couldn't have been more wrong. I was trying to protect you, right enough,' he readily confirmed, 'but from only one person—Isabel Ashworth.'

He smiled at the frown of consternation which swiftly followed the admission. 'I strongly suspected Isabel was responsible for the deaths of both Dr Hammond and the servant girl quite some time before I paid that visit to Worcestershire. Such a hard and ruthless woman would not have thought twice about making you a further victim. I knew that she was suspicious about my presence in the locale. Consequently I was afraid that if she discovered that I was near to exposing her, she just might be vindictive enough to extract revenge by harming you, if she discovered just how much you had come to mean to me. And I couldn't risk that possibility, remote though it might have been.

'Then, after my return from Worcestershire, you were fully occupied nursing Richard. Besides,' he shrugged, 'it was hardly the most appropriate time to announce a betrothal to the world at large, given the recent tragic events at Ashworth Hall.' He paused to run impatient fingers through his hair. 'Perhaps I was wrong not to have confided in you completely. Had I done so it might have saved us both all this quite unnecessary heartache.'

Emma gnawed at her bottom lip in an attempt to stop its trembling. 'Have—have you been so very miserable?' she managed in a shaky voice.

'Utterly wretched,' he wasn't too proud to admit. 'I suppose you have the right to make your own life a barren waste, Emma, because you are afraid of what a few, and I repeat, a very few foolish people may choose to say about our union,' he continued gently. 'But do you have the right to make me suffer the same fate? I would willingly sacrifice the good opinion of the whole of the polite world if it meant I would be granted the chance of attaining a lifetime of happiness with you.'

Stifling a tiny cry, Emma buried her face in her hands. 'Oh, I wish I knew what to do!'

'You may not know, my darling girl. But I most certainly do know,' was Benedict's prompt response.

That night, as Emma lay protectively cradled in her husband's strong arms, she could not help but reflect on the happenings of the past hours which would inevitably change her life forever. But it was rather too late to do much about it now, for she had become in every sense Mrs Benedict Grantley.

Using his no little expertise, Benedict had initiated his bride into the gentle art of lovemaking so tenderly that the moment's pain Emma had suffered not so very long ago, when she had become wholly his, was over almost before she realised she had felt the least discomfort. It was an experience which left her, now, wondering how it was humanly possible for someone to rise from the depths of despair to the heady heights of sensual euphoria in the space of less than twenty-four hours, and which left her foolishly fearing to sleep, lest she wake to discover everything that had happened had all been some wonderful dream.

Seeking immediate reassurance, Emma nestled more comfortably in the crook of her husband's arm, and absently began to reacquaint herself with the triangle of soft, dark hair which she had unexpectedly discovered covering his chest. This wholly masculine attribute had been no less a startling discovery as the array of beautiful clothes which she had found awaiting her in the bedchamber of her wonderful new home; had come as no less a delightful discovery as finding both Samuel and Martha, together with Lavinia, Deborah and Richard, amongst the small congregation in the village church to witness the wedding ceremony.

She could not say in all honesty that it had come as any great surprise that her new husband had managed to arrange everything so swiftly and so perfectly in such a short space of time. She knew enough about him to be certain that he was an immensely capable man, remarkably astute and methodical. Yet, the truth of the matter was that she really did not know him very well at all, for she would never have supposed for a moment that such a level-headed, meticulous person would ever lend himself to such an outrageous start as abducting a young female. Not that she would ever dream of remonstrating again over the less than gentlemanly tactics he had adopted in order to attain his ends. She only hoped that she would never experience the least regret that she had not displayed more strength of character by demanding time in which to consider more fully before willingly acquiescing to his every wish.

'If you intend to sleep at all before morning, madam wife,' the deep voice of her husband unexpectedly warned, 'I would strongly advise you to stop that at once.'

Chuckling as his hand came down over hers, stilling the trail of her tantalising fingers, Emma raised her head from the comfort of his broad shoulder to cast a glance towards the window. 'By the look of the sky, I should say that it very soon shall be morning. I wonder what time it is?'

'I neither know nor care,' was the surprising response. 'The only time which is important to me now is the time I spend with my wife.'

In one swift movement Benedict flicked her over on to her back and was above her, caressing the delicate bones of her shoulder before running his fingers down the length of her arm, marvelling yet again at the perfection of skin that was as flawless as silk and as soft as the most expensive velvet. 'Why aren't you asleep? What have you been thinking about?'

'About you, and everything that has happened.' Raising her hand, she traced with one finger the outline of a jaw now slightly roughened by bristles. 'A part of me, I suppose, cannot believe that it has all really happened, and that I am in truth your wife.'

His body shook with gentle laughter, and a look appeared in his eyes which left her in no doubt that he would have no objection whatsoever in putting her mind quite pleasurably at rest over that. He might have begun to do so immediately had he, in turn, not detected the flicker of unease in her eyes which her openly inviting, provocative smile could not quite disguise.

'What is it, my lovely Emma? You've no regrets, I hope?'

She quite sensibly accepted then that she would never be wholly successful in hiding anything from him, and did not choose to begin their life together by foolishly making the attempt. 'Certainly not at this moment in time, no,' she freely admitted. 'I only hope that in the future I do not come to regret not displaying more strength of character by demanding more time to consider.'

'More time in which to worry unnecessarily, you mean,' he corrected with that rapier-like perception which was all too often ruthlessly accurate.

A sigh escaped him as he was forced to satisfy himself for the time being by placing just one kiss in the cleft between her breasts. 'Very well, madam wife, I shall tell you precisely what will occur as it continues to cause you no little concern… Firstly, we shall journey to Paris at the end of the week, where I know you shall swiftly become the toast of that romantic capital. Then early in the autumn we shall return in order to pay visits to certain members of my family, if by then they have not already taken the trouble to cross the

Channel in order to make your acquaintance. My brother Giles is very fond of that particular city and makes frequent visits. Needless to say both he and his very complaisant wife, Serena, will adore you, as will Agnes, who has informed me already that she fully intends to offer you every support, as she now considers me the biggest beast in nature, for reasons into which I shall not go at this juncture. She will, of course, become your devoted slave after you have given birth to our first son, which in all probability will occur towards the end of next year.'

He took a moment to ponder pleasurably over this startling prediction. 'To continue—we shall also make time to visit several of my closest friends, including your cousin, Charles, before we travel to London in order to celebrate the engagement of Richard and Deborah. By which time, if I know anything of my sister at all, Agnes will have already smoothed the way for your introduction into the polite world by assuring one and all that you are the sweetest creature who ever drew breath, if slightly eccentric, which quite naturally only adds to your abundance of charm. Consequently in the spring, when we return to the capital in order to hold a ball to celebrate our marriage, the whole of the polite world will be eager for an invitation in order to make the acquaintance of the lady who is destined to become one of Society's leading hostesses, owing to the excellence of the food served at her table.'

'Stop, stop!' she laughingly begged, half-amused, half-exasperated by this outrageous display of self-assurance. 'Very well, I shall tease neither you nor myself further by worrying unnecessarily,' she promised.

Which was possibly just as well, because everything her wonderfully astute husband had predicted turned out to be uncannily accurate.

* * * * *

Modern Romance™
...seduction and
passion guaranteed

Tender Romance™
...love affairs that
last a lifetime

Sensual Romance™
...sassy, sexy and
seductive

Blaze Romance™
...the temperature's
rising

Medical Romance™
...medical drama on
the pulse

Historical Romance™
...rich, vivid and
passionate

27 new titles every month.

With all kinds of Romance for
every kind of mood...

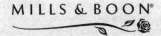

MILLS & BOON®

MB2

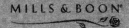

MILLS & BOON

Helen Brooks

Lynne Graham

Kim Lawrence

BUSINESS *Affairs*

Three brand-new stories about falling for the boss

Available from 17th January 2003

*Available at most branches of WH Smith,
Tesco, Martins, Borders, Eason, Sainsbury's
and all good paperback bookshops.*

0203/24/MB62

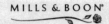

2 FREE

books and a surprise gift!

We would like to take this opportunity to thank you for reading this Mills & Boon® book by offering you the chance to take TWO more specially selected titles from the Historical Romance™ series absolutely FREE! We're also making this offer to introduce you to the benefits of the Reader Service™—

- ★ FREE home delivery
- ★ FREE gifts and competitions
- ★ FREE monthly Newsletter
- ★ Exclusive Reader Service discount
- ★ Books available before they're in the shops

Accepting these FREE books and gift places you under no obligation to buy, you may cancel at any time, even after receiving your free shipment. Simply complete your details below and return the entire page to the address below. *You don't even need a stamp!*

YES! Please send me 2 free Historical Romance books and a surprise gift. I understand that unless you hear from me, I will receive 4 superb new titles every month for just £3.49 each, postage and packing free. I am under no obligation to purchase any books and may cancel my subscription at any time. The free books and gift will be mine to keep in any case.

H3ZEA

Ms/Mrs/Miss/Mr ....Initials.................................
BLOCK CAPITALS PLEASE

Surname ....

Address ....

....

....Postcode.................................

Send this whole page to:
UK: FREEPOST CN81, Croydon, CR9 3WZ
EIRE: PO Box 4546, Kilcock, County Kildare (stamp required)

Offer valid in UK and Eire only and not available to current Reader Service subscribers to this series. We reserve the right to refuse an application and applicants must be aged 18 years or over. Only one application per household. Terms and prices subject to change without notice. Offer expires 30th April 2003. As a result of this application, you may receive offers from Harlequin Mills & Boon and other carefully selected companies. If you would prefer not to share in this opportunity please write to The Data Manager at the address above.

Mills & Boon® is a registered trademark owned by Harlequin Mills & Boon Limited.
Historical Romance™ is being used as a trademark.